LOVE *at first* KILL

OTHER TITLES BY MARY E. ROACH

We Are the Match

Young Adult

Better Left Buried

Seven for a Secret

LOVE *at first* KILL

MARY E. ROACH

Published by Montlake, Seattle

www.apub.com

EU product safety contact:
Amazon Media EU S. à r.l.
38, avenue John F. Kennedy, L-1855 Luxembourg
amazonpublishing-gpsr@amazon.com

ISBN-13: 9781662529443 (paperback)
ISBN-13: 9781662529450 (digital)

Cover design by Hang Le
Cover image: © RedlineVector, © Savvapanf Photo / Shutterstock

Printed in the United States of America

To Kim Roach, aunt extraordinaire,
who is such a force of good in my life and everywhere.
I hope you read this by the pool.

Chapter One

Murder was a meticulous business.

Meticulous, and each one was different.

They had to be, if you wanted to live long enough for the next job, and the next after that.

And Jack O'Sullivan very much intended to live.

He stretched out his legs beneath the café table and leaned back against the booth. It was upscale for a café, but he would have expected nothing less from a place Cale Jacobson frequented. Sunlight filtered in through the carefully cleaned glass of the window, spilling light across nearby tables.

This was the most expensive target he had ever acquired, and he had been paid more up front than the other three jobs this year combined. That fact should have made him nervous: The higher profile the target, the *richer* the target, the more that could go wrong. That, and this time Jack had been hired by a small collective. He was used to working with solo clients, people who wanted somebody gone because they had been hurt or wronged.

Trust a billionaire to go and hurt more than a dozen people, enough for them all to turn to something like *this*.

Cale Jacobson, of course, didn't think of himself as a regular billionaire (none of them did, though). Jack had listened to his conversations every time he'd frequented this café, and he had listened to his assistant every time *she* came in to pick up his order.

Jack had spent days learning the man's schedule. His haunts, his security detail, his moments alone. His schedule, both the regular—like this café in downtown Portland—and the varied, the business meetings that dragged the man all over the city. All over the country, too, but Portland was his home base—a compound outside the city, closer to the Canadian border, and a high-rise downtown where he spent most of his time.

Jack sipped his tea, an iced matcha with oat milk, a habit he had picked up because a former girlfriend of his had insisted that Big Dairy was destroying the planet. So were most companies, but that wasn't Jack's business.

A woman's voice interrupted his focus. "Can I get you anything else?" The barista had stopped near him, a pitcher of water in her hand.

It was his frequent downfall—he was often too focused on what he was doing to notice the others around him. One ex had told him it made him "hardly human," but Jack personally thought his profession, not his social skills (or absence of them), was a more likely measure of his humanity.

"I'm good, thanks," he said. Was this typical of baristas? His experience was that he was on his own once they'd handed off his coffee. "I appreciate it, though."

"Sure," she said, bumping him gently with her elbow. "I'm off in an hour."

It was a clear invitation, though one he had had to be told about more than once when he was a younger man (more evidence from his ex that he was destined to be alone, because who *couldn't* read a social cue that obvious?).

And the barista was a good-looking woman. Tasha, her name tag read. He cataloged all that clinically: tall, curvy, dark-brown skin and long lashes, tightly coiled curls and a winning smile. If he were not on a job, he'd take her up on that invitation.

"Sorry," he said. "I'm working. But if I get off early . . ."

He let the invitation hang there.

Tasha shrugged one shoulder. "Sure," she repeated. "I'm here Monday through Friday."

She moved on, hips swinging, and he watched her go, but only for a moment.

When he was on a job, it consumed him. Nothing and no one else existed. It was just him and a target, zeroing in on the end of the job with ruthless efficiency.

And now:

Across the street, Cale stepped out of the private entrance to his office building, one guard holding the door for him. He was a thin white man, late thirties, heir to an empire. Dirty-blond hair, neatly pressed designer suit, recently shined shoes.

That was another step in the routine when Cale was in Portland: Most days, his assistant brought his shoes to be shined at a local place near the river, but every Thursday he went himself. Maybe he liked sitting up there, a king above men in every way it was possible to be. Maybe he just liked a routine.

Either way, it was another opportunity.

Cale crossed the street at the crosswalk, his pace brisk. He had investors to meet with, beaches to frequent, nineteen-dollar sandwiches to buy from this café, a private jet to take. He walked like he owned the world.

A laugh jarred Jack out of his focus.

Not Tasha the barista this time.

No.

Across the aisle, seated on a wooden stool, sat a woman with olive-toned skin and curly auburn hair. She was wearing a viciously red dress, and she had one hand pressed to her mouth as if covering a laugh.

And she was looking directly at *him*.

She leaned her elbows on the round, smooth wooden table in front of her and folded her hands. He noticed, vaguely, that the knuckles on her right hand were scabbed, the knuckles on her left only slightly less bruised.

"You have *no* game," she told him.

A smile tugged at the corner of Jack's mouth despite himself. "You don't think so?" he asked her.

The woman was shorter than him by a good six inches, short and curvy, with sharp hazel eyes that crackled with life.

"I know so," she said, wrinkling her nose at him. "That was . . . pathetic."

Jack lowered his mask only to sip his matcha, immediately sliding it back into place as he did. He had his back to the nearest camera, so he did not have to worry about his face being visible. Not that they would recognize him if they *did* see him. The mask was a habit—good for avoiding infection while traveling as much as he did, and equally good for avoiding detection and making eyewitness descriptions that much more difficult.

But this woman was looking directly at him, eyes traveling up and down his face *and* his body with an eagerness—and a sharp, nervous energy—that unnerved him. She would be able to pick him out of a lineup. She would be able to give a sketch artist a detailed description.

"I'm not here to flirt," he told her, turning his shoulders slightly away from her.

Collaboration was the death knell of a job like his. Besides, he *liked* his work, liked it better than he ever liked people—well, all but one. It made killing them a great deal easier, too.

"That's clear," she said. "I'm Ava, by the way."

"Ava." He said the word slowly, thoughtfully. "I'm here to work, Ava."

"Well, it's a good thing you're not here to flirt," Ava said before sipping her smoothie (something pink and probably sweet, not in a to-go cup like his) and continuing to giggle at him. "Since you suck at it."

"Thanks," Jack said flatly. He was wearing a suit and tie, not a hoodie, though he generally felt safer in one. It covered more of him than a suit and tie did, but a suit and tie was the uniform that blended best *here*.

The bell on the café door rang as Cale stepped through. He didn't seem to notice the woman who was staring at the menu, considering, or the man waiting for the barista, either. He certainly didn't ask whether they were in line. Instead, he stepped up to the cash register and called for the barista with an impatient wave of his hand.

When Jack's eyes flicked to Ava, her entire demeanor had changed. Her dark hazel eyes, which had been fierce but warm just moments ago, were crackling dangerously now. Her shoulders were tensed, her jaw set.

It was a clear sign, a social cue that was *not* hard for him to recognize. One that said *Danger. Danger. Danger.*

Cale was ordering. A green juice and a turkey club sandwich, his usual.

He was telling Tasha about his recent bike tour, something that had taken him deep into a desert somewhere in Nevada. There was merit to suffering, he was telling Tasha, who smiled politely. Suffering stripped away everything, and you found clarity in its simplicity.

"What do you do?" Ava asked him suddenly. "For work?"

Jack startled, looked at her again. Her skin tone was darker than the ruddy Irish complexion he'd inherited from parents he couldn't remember. She was Italian, probably, maybe Greek, if he had to guess, but she looked pale in this moment. Almost as if she was about to be sick.

Or as if she was steeling herself for something that terrified her.

"Investment manager," he said. His laptop was open in front of him, his lie easy.

At the counter, Cale was still telling Tasha about himself while she politely listened.

When he finished paying, he dropped a handful of spare change into the tip jar. He was still talking about suffering, and how good it was, and how more people would have clarity and strength of purpose if they would do something as ascetic as a bike ride in Arizona.

He'd probably write that in a book someday, and a publisher would snap it up, and people would quote that shit on social media. It was meaningless. Cale had never suffered—and he wouldn't, not even when Jack killed him.

It would be a gunshot, because Jack always did it the same way: a single shot. Quick, clean, as easy as falling asleep. There were a few ways to do it, but this was simple, the gun easy to build, easy to dispose of, and easy to make untraceable.

"That sounds like a bullshit job," Ava said. "Made up by little sad men in suits who *optimize* and *circle back* and think that their emails matter in the grand scheme of the universe."

"What do you do?" Jack asked, his eyes remaining on Cale, who leaned against the counter, scrolling on his phone.

"I'm a librarian," Ava said. "Or I was. But my point is that I had a real job."

He didn't ask how she lost that job, or what she thought defined a real job, because this was a distraction. And distractions could mean death—or worse, prison.

A few minutes passed.

Jack watched Cale's subtle movements. He was unaware of the world around him—or maybe he just thought it centered on *him.*

"You're focused," Ava said. Her gaze flickered between Jack and Cale as if she was calculating something in her head.

He took her in more carefully now. He had watched the other patrons casually, of course. What they ate, who they watched, who they waited for, the fleeting emotions that crossed their faces when no one else saw.

This woman, she had been here almost as long as he had, nearly an hour.

Like him, she had only ordered a drink.

Her curves generously filled her little red dress, curves that he could explore, that he *would* explore if he were not working. Red lips, too, violently bright, but that was the only makeup she was wearing, and beneath the saucy grin she had given him, she looked weary in a way he understood.

Are you okay? he would be asking her in a different life, a different version of himself, one where he was not waiting to kill the man who was now telling Tasha another story about bike trips and how important they were for wellness.

"Hello? Earth to Professor Macintosh?"

He blinked at her, head tilted. "Professor . . . Macintosh?"

"You *talk* like my most boring professor." Ava shrugged, the sleeve of her red dress slipping to one side and revealing a glimpse of bare shoulder. "And you didn't tell me your name."

He met her gaze. "I'm AJ," he said.

"That's not on your cup," she said, squinting.

He glanced down at the to-go cup that had *Brad* scrawled in loopy handwriting on one side. Well, *shit.* "Shit, maybe I grabbed the wrong drink," Jack said. "They called a matcha, and I didn't look at the name."

Ava didn't look like she quite believed his cover, but she didn't push it. "Well, nice to meet you, AJ." She leaned across the aisle between them and extended her hand. "Let me guess. You're the dude with the brand-new Volvo out back. You look like you'd drive one."

He took the offered hand, noting no fingernail polish, no rings. Smooth skin, except for the battered knuckles.

"Guilty as charged," he said, holding on to her hand a moment longer than he had any right to.

Ava's eyes followed Jack's gaze, and she snatched her hand back and shoved it into her lap.

His mind was still trying to wrap his head around this picture—beautiful girl, cheap dress, expensive lipstick, overpriced café, bloody knuckles.

None of the puzzle pieces fit.

"Here you are, Mr. Jacobson," Tasha called from the counter. Her eyes flickered to the tip jar and then back to him.

Of course she knew who he was.

Maybe that was why Cale did this himself instead of sending one of his assistants. Maybe he liked the sense of importance, the recognition.

He worked in insurance—he was not exactly in a useful or well-loved industry.

But he *did* have money.

Across the aisle from Jack, Ava was twisting her hands in her lap, one finger picking absentmindedly at the scab on the knuckle of her right hand.

Christ.

"Ava." He said her name firmly, and her gaze snapped to him.

The smile on her face was plastered now, stilted and strange. "Yes?" Even the lightness in her voice sounded forced.

"Are you okay?"

Jack should not have asked. He should have turned away from her, back to his paper, attention focused on the man he would kill in one day's time.

"No," she breathed, and then caught herself, her fingers closing over the edge of the table, the battered knuckles turning white. "Yes. Of course I am. Are *you*?"

"Well, Ava." He lifted his newspaper again, reopening to the article he had been reading. "It was a pleasure."

"A pleasure," she returned, her words hollow.

She was a puzzle that would nag him for much longer than just this strange morning of reconnaissance, but he had other cares today. And Ava of the bloody knuckles and the haunted eyes and the sharp tongue would have to wait.

Cale took his juice and club sandwich and exited the café, the door slamming shut behind him.

Like clockwork.

Tomorrow was Friday, and Cale would be here earlier, around seven in the morning. Jack would be here, too, and when Cale left with his juice, Jack would kill him.

It hit him, a pang out of nowhere, that he hoped Ava wasn't here to see it.

Jack leaned back in the booth, letting his head thump against the soft cushion. A moment later, he froze.

Ava had disappeared.

For one disorienting moment, he thought he had imagined her. If Jay could see him now—well, he would know just how bad Jack had gotten in his absence. Jack was lost here, more lost than he had ever been. And he had *always* been lost.

But a breath later, a flash of red caught Jack's eye. Ava was outside the café, and when Cale stepped into the crosswalk, she fell into step behind him.

Christ.

Jack jumped to his feet, leaving his newspaper in unfolded disgrace beside his half-finished matcha, and then he snatched her own abandoned smoothie and followed her through the door.

It was raining lightly now, though Ava's back was already soaked through with sweat, the damp red fabric clinging to her skin.

Fuck.

Fuck.

How had he missed this, sitting three feet away from her?

She was going to ruin everything.

He caught up to her with long strides, but she was already reaching into her purse, and fool, *fool* that he was, he should have known that her strange bloody knuckles were not the only weapon this girl had. He should have known the nervousness was not about *him*. He should have known.

"Ava," Jack shouted.

She jerked around like a marionette whose strings had been pulled, and Cale turned, too, squinting back at the sound of the shouting.

Fuck fuck *fuck*.

He never got this close to his hits before the moment he killed them. Never let them see his face or gave them the opportunity to ask a single question about who he was.

And now Ava had fucked it all up.

Ava stared back at him, her face a raw mixture of fury and something more, something as vast and overwhelming and wretched as the sea in a storm, something he would drown in if he stood too close.

Her hand was frozen in her purse. "What the fuck?" she snarled.

"You forgot your smoothie." Jack held it out with his most charming smile. "I thought you might want it."

Ava opened her mouth to speak, but Cale interrupted them both.

"You," he said, his voice cracking with something resembling terror as he stared at Ava. "*You.* Security!" He was pointing at them both, and for one sinking moment Jack thought that his cover was blown, that everything was blown.

And then Ava stopped, as if deciding, before she dropped her purse and tackled Cale to the ground.

Chapter Two

Ava had been following this stupid rich fucker for months, and she had made sure he knew it, too.

Of course, it had gotten her fired. And a restraining order. And worst of all, a call from Ellie.

But none of that mattered now, because she was *here*, because this infuriatingly good-looking man from the café might have tipped Cale off before she could shoot him in the back like he deserved. Still, she could at least beat the absolute shit out of him.

Cale hit the damp pavement with a thump and a scream, and Ava landed on top of him. Everything else faded away: the other man's shout, the sound of rain on pavement, the cars screeching around them, the distant noise of doors opening and his security team shouting.

Her fist connected with Cale's short, squat nose. Once. Twice. His jaw. His eye. His jaw again. His nose a second time.

And then two strong, calloused hands hauled her abruptly off.

Cale was holding his nose and moaning, blood trickling down the side of his jaw.

He was, unfortunately, alive.

"You fucker," Ava heard herself screaming. "*You motherfucker.*"

The arms that held her firmly were well muscled and immovable, wrapped around her from behind as they lifted her off her feet.

"Easy." That steady, controlled voice murmured against her ear.

Not security, like she had originally thought.

She twisted around, attempting to swing at him, but he caught her arm.

It was the stupid man from the stupid café, holding her firmly against him. She flailed in his arms—and she may not have been subtle about her attack on Cale, but she made up for it now as she slipped one hand in his suit pocket. Grabbing for a wallet or keys but settling for a small notebook and pen there.

"Let me go," Ava snarled, continuing to flail. He didn't seem to notice he'd been pickpocketed. "Or I'll—"

What was she going to do? Take the knife out of her purse and stab him? The purse was discarded on the ground several feet away, and Cale's security guards were running from the building, big men who could stop Ava as easily as the one holding her right now.

To her surprise, the man dropped her. "Get the fuck out of here," he said softly.

She put both hands on his chest and shoved as hard as she could.

He raised an eyebrow at her, unmoved.

One of Cale's security guards was helping him up, and another had his gun drawn, pointed at Ava.

She snatched her purse and ran.

<>

Her sandals—why had she worn *sandals*? to a *murder*?—slapped the pavement as she ran, weaving around dumpsters and down the alley that led away from the scene of her attempted crime.

It wasn't that she had thought she had a *good* plan, not really, but how had it gone so spectacularly wrong? She had been flirting her way into information about Cale for weeks. She'd talked to assistants and former assistants. She'd called the woman who did his laundry. She'd even found his personal chef, for fuck's sake.

Ava rounded the corner, pausing for breath in the small parking lot for café patrons.

Of course, she had also been commenting on each social media post his business made, following him on every platform, and sending him furious letters about his complicity in—

That was too much to think about right now.

Her heart was pounding, her breath impossibly short.

She could do this. She could take a minute and right her breathing and she could get away before Cale's security found her, and—

Sirens sounded in the distance.

Ava reached into her purse and grabbed a Dove chocolate. Dark, always. She popped the chocolate into her mouth and tossed the wrapper in the direction of the dumpster. These chocolates calmed her, always had.

There was a handful of cars in the parking lot, but she recognized the sleek black Volvo that the man from the coffee shop—AJ?—had driven.

Impulsively, she pulled her keys from her pocket and scratched a long line into the car door. If she had more time, she would have drawn a whole dick.

Because he deserved it for thwarting her in her most crucial moment.

Ava should have planned better: a car, a bike, hell, one of those stupid e-scooters that littered the sidewalks and made the city unnavigable would have been better than getting there on foot.

She ran again, weaving through alleys until she reached downtown proper, where she flagged the next taxi she saw. Once she was inside, it felt like the first time she'd truly caught her breath all day.

Or maybe it had been longer than that. She popped another chocolate into her mouth and leaned back against the dingy seat.

The hostel was at the edge of the city, a dozen small bedrooms that had seen better days. Hers, at least, was a single, directly across from the shared women's bathroom, and she managed to enter without having to talk to anyone. Most people who stayed in places like this didn't want to talk. That much Ava was banking on.

She dead bolted the door, letting out a sigh of relief. She would shower, rest, gather her thoughts, and make a new plan, one that couldn't be thwarted by handsome men with perfect hands.

Another chocolate, a sip of water, and Ava opened the notebook she'd lifted from the hot, annoying café man, Brad or AJ or whatever he was actually called.

And then she stopped, her blood running cold.

Inside the notebook were meticulously written notes . . . on Cale Jacobson's schedule.

For the next day, Friday. There was a note that said *7:00 a.m. PST* (who needed the time zone? Weren't they all in the same one, since they were *here*?) and beneath it *green juice, two baristas working, smaller security team.*

And beside it, a single red *X.*

Chapter Three

Jack surveyed his rental car—a black Volvo he'd paid for in cash—with a deep sigh.

How had he been so stupid? How had he missed so much?

"Hey!" Cale shouted behind him, still surrounded by his security guards. "Stop that man. Stop him! I need to thank him."

Jack winced but turned, adjusting his mask slightly. A nervous habit, fiddling with the one thing that so often protected him from surveillance cameras.

"Why'd you leave?" Cale was huffing down the alley behind him, out of breath.

"Sir, we should really—" One of his security guards, a large man with gray speckled in his dark-brown hair and a handgun strapped to his waist, reached out to pull Cale back.

Cale waved him off. "I want to meet the hero who saved me," he said. "A real man of the people."

Jack wasn't sure either of them knew what a real man of the people was, but it certainly wasn't *him*. It was hard to look at Cale without imagining the moment when he finished his job. One shot.

Always one.

Some clients requested custom messaging—these customers certainly had—but Jack had always refused that. The less personal a job was to *him*, the better.

"I'm AJ." Jack nodded to him. "And I didn't save you. Your guards had that under control. I just saw an upset woman and thought I could help."

"What's your last name?" The security guard had no pretense of politeness, and Jack respected him for it. Politeness was a luxury in that line of work.

Cale held out his hand. "Maybe I should make *you* my head of security," he joked, missing the look on his guard's face when he did. "AJ, huh? You wouldn't believe how many people want to hurt me or my family."

Jack could actually put an exact number to that. Seventeen. Well, seventeen who had pooled their money to take out a hit on him, though Jack was sure countless more *would* have if they could afford someone like him.

"Damn, that sounds awful. Sorry you're going through that," Jack said woodenly. "I'm glad you have a good team with you."

It grated at him like an itch he couldn't scratch, to have this man standing in front of him and to *know*, to know in his bones that the hit would be impossible to get away with from here—maybe even impossible to carry out at all. But he had the man *in front of him.*

Cale laughed, oblivious to the threat his life had been under from Ava—and, more importantly, was under from Jack. Jack's palms itched to wrap around the pale, pretentious throat.

"Are you from around here? Staying close by? I'll have my team send a thank-you from me."

Jack shook his head. "I don't need your thanks," he said. "Really, it's all right."

He had a *job.*

He'd been so *close.*

One day away from finishing it.

And that woman in the red dress had ruined it all.

"It's no trouble." Cale still had that jovial smile, bouncing back quickly from the multiple blows to his face—though his eye was still swollen, and one of his many guards was attempting to hold an ice pack to it. "My family likes to know who our friends are."

Jack shrugged. "I would have done the same for anyone," he said. "It's all right. Really."

"Sir, we have to get you out of here," Cale's head of security repeated, his icy gaze taking in every inch of Jack. "We'll coordinate with local law enforcement to find the woman. Do you know where we should start?"

"I don't," Jack answered. "Never met her before today."

At this, Cale shivered. For all his smiling, the thought of this woman seemed to bring him discomfort. "Ava Cavalcante," he said. "She blames me for—oh, you know. The usual." He waved his hand, dismissing whatever concerns Ava had with one flick of his wrist. "It doesn't matter what. There are many bitter people in the world. But she's left me dozens of threats. Sent letters. Called my assistants. She even mailed me a—what was it called? A glitter bomb?"

Jack suppressed a smirk. "A *glitter* bomb?"

"That was her first threat," Cale confided. One of the guards was trying to usher him away now, but Cale was still talking, still grinning at Jack as if they were old friends.

It was amazing, his lack of a sense of personal safety. Or maybe he relied so wholly on these guards that he didn't need to think about that particular part himself.

"Then, of course, I got a restraining order and the police charged her with stalking and harassment," Cale continued.

It was a goddamn miracle nobody had popped this man yet. Jack put one hand in the pocket of his slacks and tilted his head, considering the other man.

"For glitter?" Jack said finally, when it was clear that Cale required his participation in the story.

"It was a *threat*," Cale said. "Anyway, as soon as she was released, she went straight back to harassing me." He leaned past one particularly burly guard and patted Jack's shoulder.

Jack refrained from drawing his weapon and completing the job, but just barely. He kept pristine physical and emotional boundaries. He kept meticulous care of his clothing and belongings. He did not want those boundaries crossed by anyone, but certainly not by a mark he intended to kill.

"I think your security team wants you inside," Jack said mildly. "Good luck, man. I hope you don't run into her again."

"Please come in," the first security guard said, his gaze steely where it landed on Jack. "I insist." His hand rested lightly on his sidearm, a threat if you were paying attention. An assertion of control if nothing else.

Jack's stomach sank. He could, of course, force the matter—insist that he wanted to leave, or even fight his way out, if it came to that. But that would raise every alarm, and any slim chance he had of still completing this hit relied on Cale Jacobson's team *not* being on the alert. This security guard in particular was clearly well trained, analytical enough to see beyond a surface-level threat.

Jack was going to *kill* Ava for this.

"Sure," he said resignedly. "But like I said, I'm not sure there's anything I can do to be helpful."

"I don't need your help," Cale insisted loudly. "I want to *thank* you!" He was clutching his bleeding nose and leaning on one of his security guards now.

Jack should have abandoned this job before he'd ever agreed to it—he'd known it was risky, even if he hadn't anticipated having a face-to-face with the mark *and* his entire security team before he carried it out. But Jack had bills to pay, a promise to keep. And the money for this had been too good to pass up. "It really is all right," Jack said, but they were already leading him inside.

"I'm Cale, by the way," Cale told him as one of the guards opened the door for both of them. "Cale Jacobson. I own"—he gestured again, a motion that could have encompassed everything from the building they were entering to the security team to Jack himself—"all this."

"He knows who you are," the security guard said evenly, his gaze scanning Jack up and down again. "Mind if we pat you down? Obviously we have some pretty high-profile people in this building."

"That won't be necessary," Cale said. "Give it up, Davis."

"Devin," the security guard said. "And sir, I really think—"

"Davis or Devin or Derek"—Cale gave another dismissive wave—"can you call for medical, please? And get my brother down here. He's going to want to know all about this. But avoid Clara? She'll just bitch me out."

Devin nodded tightly, his jaw set in a way that Jack recognized.

The entrance opened into a long hallway leading to a private elevator, where Jack reluctantly stepped inside. They reached the top floor, where a team of EMS were already waiting for him. In a world where everyone else waited for the care they needed, Cale Jacobson's bloody nose was treated immediately.

If Jack had the time and energy to be angry about it, he would have been. But as it was, he was in deep, deep shit. "I have another appointment soon," he said to Cale. "I don't mean to be rude—"

"We won't keep you," Cale promised in that booming voice that Jack could imagine commanding boardrooms. Cale looked at Jack again as the EMS team started asking him questions, with that gaze that never really seemed to *see* Jack, or anyone around him. "Just join us briefly? My brother will be up momentarily."

The EMS team and Cale split off into a nearby office, and the security team flanked Jack, faces immovable. They clearly had orders from Devin, not Cale, and Jack was sticking around. They led him into another large corner office with wraparound windows that showed off downtown Portland, and gestured to a chair that probably cost more than most people made in a month.

"Mr. Jacobson will be back momentarily," one of the remaining security guards told him.

Jack settled into the chair uneasily. He needed out of here, and fast. If his client knew he was this close, this visible to the Jacobson family, they'd pull the plug on this, and rightfully so—and probably turn him in to the cops, which was something most people who hired someone like Jack thought about at least once.

The door opened a moment later, a tall, willowy woman entering. She had showy blond hair, perfectly manicured nails in a subtle, soft mauve, and her immaculately tailored suit said *money*.

Jack stood. Of all the fucking people he could have encountered today, direct contact with a *second* Jacobson was quite possibly the worst. It was *not* in Jack's best interest to be seen by Cale's entire family—because when this was over, when Cale was dead, every second of his final days would be picked apart to find a suspect. It was better, always, to be invisible from beginning to end of the job.

"I'm Clara." She extended her hand to shake his. "I heard what you did for my brother, and I'm incredibly grateful. We're offering a significant financial reward for anyone who assists in the capture of this woman who has been stalking our family, but after what you did today—well, of course we would like to offer you something in thanks, too." Jack's job was so beyond fucked at this point that he briefly considered asking for enough money to leave the country and live comfortably somewhere with no extradition treaty—but a breath after that thought, the one promise he still clung to caught up with him. He had bills to pay, expensive ones. Someone here in the States who counted on him.

"I'm grateful," Jack answered carefully. He took Clara's offered hand and shook.

Her handshake was firm, her look piercing.

"I like to think anyone would have done what I did today," Jack continued. "I didn't know who Cale was until his security team rushed out."

She released his hand and stepped back, that analytical gaze sweeping him up and down. "Of course," she said. "Of course. A generous sentiment, Mr. . . . they told me AJ, but no last name."

"Reed," Jack supplied.

"Mr. Reed," Clara said. "I would like to leave you with my card—my direct number, where my assistant will be able to help you if you can think of anything we can do to thank you. And if you would like—"

The door opened before she could finish, a man who looked like a carbon copy of Cale Jacobson stepping through.

For *fuck's* sake.

There were only three Jacobson siblings, and now Jack had met them all. He had his mask up, sure, and he could change the rest—his clothes, his hair, his car, even his eye color with the right pair of contact lenses—but there was nothing that could change the fact that they had all seen him now, talked to him.

"Didn't Cale tell them all *not* to tell you?" the man asked.

"Carson," Clara said icily. "Good to see you, too."

Jack glanced back and forth between them. There was no friction between the siblings, at least not publicly—not since Carson's failed bid a few years back to gain more control of the company, a rift they appeared to have resolved.

Clara nodded crisply to Jack and handed him her card. "Reach out if there's anything we can do," she said.

That cold gaze swept her brother next, and then she was gone.

Carson—who had the same soft jawline as his brother, the same mousy brown hair, the same blue eyes—rolled his eyes openly. "*That's* why you never tell the eldest daughter when there's been an emergency," he said, and laughed as if he and Jack were just bar buddies in on the same joke. "Anyway, you're the man of the hour, aren't you? The hero the whole building's talking about? I'm Carson, Cale's brother. Very grateful and all that."

"AJ," Jack told him. "Pleasure."

After today he was disposing of every ID that said AJ or Aaron James on it. Every fake bank statement and any last shred of paperwork. AJ Reed needed to be gone, the next name and identity assumed.

"We don't want to keep you, of course," Carson said. "We're all here prepping for some shareholder meetings and other boring shit, so when Cale got himself involved in another kerfuffle, I wanted to meet the guy who saved him."

Carson met Jack's eyes, the expression colder than Jack had anticipated. Just like his sister.

Jack heard the undercurrents—he had never been good at parsing that kind of communication, but this steely note beneath Carson's words was too clear to miss. There was trouble in the Jacobson Health paradise, something that ran deeper than one rogue woman with a red dress and bloody knuckles and a grudge.

"I appreciate that you wanted to thank me," Jack said. "But I have a meeting I'm already late for, so if there's nothing else—"

Carson stepped back, opened the door. "Of course," he said. "Did my guys get your number? They might have follow-up questions. The police are already talking to my brother, and if we can pass your number to them for whatever they need—"

He said it questioningly, but not like *no* was a real option.

Jack forced back his sigh and supplied an old phone number before he finally made his escape, passing a few security guards in the hallway who, thankfully, made no further move to stop him.

Sirens outside were wailing, a team of police cars outside the Jacobson Health building, and Jack set a quick pace to his car. Damn Ava to hell for all this—and damn her recklessness, too.

He bent down when he reached his car. She'd eaten a damn chocolate and left the wrapper on the ground next to his car while she'd keyed his rental. This woman either had no idea the kind of trouble she could be in for this, or she had nothing left to lose.

By the expression on her face when she'd left the café, Jack guessed it was the latter.

But it also meant she would be easier to find—and he needed, more than anything, to find her.

He didn't realize until he was inside the car what she had stolen from him. She was an amateur, a hothead. She was out for personal revenge, not the kind of meticulous shit he had come to be known for in the niche industry he inhabited. She—

Had stolen his fucking notebook.

He cursed roundly before he shifted his car into drive, pounding his fist against the steering wheel. She had smashed everything. She had teased him in that café and broken his focus. And she had stolen the notebook where he had recorded, in shorthand, everything about Cale Jacobson's daily schedule.

He had even written the best time to find him:

Tomorrow. Friday. Seven a.m.

Before Cale even got to order his daily green juice.

Jack had decided before to spare Tasha the bullshit of having to take one more order from her most pretentious and least-likely-to-tip guest. It was stupid to decide that for personal reasons, and it was foolish to write it in a notebook.

Still, he had always thought of it as more secure than tracking all the information on a device that could be hacked or stolen, data too easy to steal no matter how good the VPN or cloud encryption.

But now it was gone.

He could not come back to this place, either, and it had been the optimal place to finish the job.

There was *nothing* meticulous about this now. He was going to fucking kill Ava.

Chapter Four

There was nothing for it but to eat *one* more Dove chocolate (this one extolled the merits of *laughing with your friends*) and shower off the stench of failure. First, Ava tucked the notebook into her jacket pocket and then crossed the hallway to the women's bathroom, double- and then triple-checking that the hostel bedroom was locked securely behind her.

Her shoulders tightened at the thought of the look on Cale's face when he'd realized who she was. The fear in his eyes as she landed one punch and then another and another.

It hadn't been enough to kill him.

More's the fucking pity.

He deserved it.

But of course he had money and—fuck's sake, *health insurance*, not that he needed it, because he had the kind of money health issues *couldn't* bankrupt. He was going to be all right.

She, on the other hand?

The police were probably coming for her ass. And if they didn't, Cale's security team of large, evil former Navy SEAL chuckleheads would be on their way to finish her off.

Ava turned the shower to the hottest setting as she tried to work out her next move.

She couldn't just show up in front of his office again, not after she'd alerted his entire team. She couldn't even rely on him returning to that juice spot he loved.

Fuck him for that, too. Fuck anyone who could afford to drop that much money every morning on some overpriced juice.

Ava pulled the bar of soap from her toiletries bag and began scrubbing, fighting back the tears that were finally catching up with her. Why had he stopped her? And why hadn't she just pulled her stupid knife out and stuck it between Cale's ribs like she had planned all along?

She was a fucking failure. At this, at everything else.

She had planned, and waited, and—

And when it came down to it, she hadn't been able to do it. She'd been able to punch him, at least. But sweat had been running down her back and soaking her red dress. Her heart had been pounding. She could barely catch her breath.

She could barely catch her breath *now*, and she was alone, safe in her hostel. Nobody knew she was here. Nobody knew where she was, period, because she didn't have anybody left. Nobody she'd spoken to in months—not since that final, disappointed call from Ari's mom, Ellie.

The soap slipped from Ava's hands, clattering to the ground. "I'm sorry," she said aloud to nobody in particular.

When she exited the shower, wrapping herself in her towel, she let out a string of colorful curses. She hadn't brought her clean clothes—they were across the hallway. She snatched up her things, shoving her sweat-stained red dress into her toiletries bag and wrapping the towel around her as tightly as she could.

Ava fumbled with her room key at the door for a moment before the lock clicked and the door creaked open.

When she stepped inside, eyes adjusting to the dimness of her room—there was only one lamp, a soft light close to the bed—she startled, dropping her towel and toiletries with a small scream.

There was a man sitting on her bed, his posture relaxed, his knees spread in a stance that said *commanding*. That said *at ease*.

It was the man from the café, the one with the big hands and corded forearms and sharp jawline. The one who had dragged her off Cale and held her firmly against his chest.

In one hand was his stolen notebook, open to the page with the red *X*.

And in the other was a gun.

Chapter Five

Jack had it all worked out. He'd found her easily: traced a trail of Dove chocolate wrappers, asked a bus driver if he'd seen an anxious redhead, and gotten off in the hostel district, where he'd worn an easy smile and asked whether anyone had seen his sister, said that he was supposed to pick her up here and she'd maybe mixed up the numbers in the street address, and had they seen her?

People had pointed him in the right direction—and even if they hadn't, a little more digging and she would've turned up. As it was, the hostel manager had only shrugged when he asked whether she was staying here.

So he'd gone around back, pried open a window when he'd seen his notebook sticking out of a jacket pocket, and been waiting for her ever since.

And now here she was, naked and dripping wet, her scream still echoing in the small room.

Good.

Not because he was leering at her; he wasn't. She was a good-looking woman, of course. But he was on a *job*. The important thing was that it made her vulnerable, and that would make it easier to convince her that she needed him.

"You work for me now," he said quietly.

The initial shock was fading from her face, and Ava didn't seem bothered—by her lack of clothing, by his gun, by any of it. Instead, the fear was evaporating into pure confusion.

And then she looked *angry*.

"And who the fuck are *you*?" she asked.

"My name is Jack," he said. "And you interrupted me on a job. In fact, you've ruined it in just about every way somebody can ruin a job. So now you're going to make it right."

"Or?" Ava didn't even blink at the new name. He'd introduced himself as AJ, not Jack.

He lifted the gun. Clicked the safety off.

And aimed it straight for her head.

And then Ava Cavalcante did the unthinkable.

She stared down the barrel of his gun.

And she laughed.

They stared at each other for the longest of moments.

The smile on Ava's face was grim, hard. "You're just some dickhead from the café who ruined *my* plans," she said. "You think a gun is going to stop me? A billionaire couldn't stop me."

"I stopped you already," Jack said. "And I'm the one with the gun, so I'm the one in charge here."

His voice was smooth, commanding. Controlled.

All the things he had trained himself to be, because loss of that control was unthinkable.

And here was Ava Cavalcante, laughing in the face of it all.

"And you want me to, what?" she snapped. "You want me to do something for you, or you'll, what—kill me? Turn me in? My life is already over, motherfucker. There isn't anything that can be taken from me."

He heard it in her voice—the loss echoing through it all. He knew that kind of loss, the kind that ate you alive.

Still, Jack knew well enough that there was always something more to lose. Even at rock fucking bottom. "You'll get something you want," he said tightly. "Something you didn't have the guts to do today. But I saw in your eyes that you wanted to, Ava Cavalcante."

She flinched, and he knew his knowledge of her name, her full name, unnerved her. Despite the way she was playing it cool—or at least unbroken—she was running scared.

"I had something important planned," Jack continued when Ava said nothing.

She was still dripping wet, fully naked. Her curves were generous, her breasts full, the look in her eye as deadly as it was alluring. But it was the way she stood tall, staring down the gun, that made his own breath catch unevenly.

"Do you hate him, too?" she asked.

Because it was that simple for her.

"I don't hate anyone that I kill," Jack said.

At this revelation, her eyes widened.

It wouldn't matter that she knew any of this, of course. If she survived this somehow, which was doubtful based on her impulsive behavior today, who would she tell? She was already discredited, a mad woman with a grudge. Regardless of the truth, Cale had seen to that. So who would believe her when she was arrested and told stories about a contract killer? She'd have a description, certainly. A first name. But nothing beyond that, and he'd be in the wind.

"Were you hired?" Ava asked.

He could see the next question forming on her lips: *Who?*

Were they friends of hers, people she knew?

The likelihood was the simplest answer: that everyone except billionaires hated billionaires. There was always a *reason* to hate them.

"Yes, I was hired," he told Ava now. "And no, you don't get to know who hired me. As I'm sure you saw from my notebook, my completion date was supposed to be tomorrow."

"Completion," Ava said, her lip twisting in scorn. "That makes it sound a little like you've scheduled an . . . an orgasm. Not an execution."

Jack choked.

"What?" she asked. "You make it all sound so . . . professional. But you're not a professional. You've been staring at my tits and telling me that we're going to work together whether I like it or not. Not much of a professional if you can't even finish your own damn jobs, are you?"

He was speechless for the second time in as many minutes. This woman was nothing like anyone he had met before—not in his old life with Jay, and not in the new one he had built brick by bloody brick.

"Are you going to get on with it?" She sighed and walked past him. Just—walked past. Not even sparing a glance at his gun.

"Ava."

Jack said her name sternly.

She froze for a shadow of a moment, stopped in her tracks by the growl of his voice when she did not seem to be fazed by his Glock.

Then she kept going, bent over to rummage through her bag for clothes to wear.

It was a shame, because the view he had of her ample ass was . . . well, continuing to prove distracting.

"Well?" She peered at him over her shoulder.

His own face burned hot for a moment. "He's seen my face," Jack managed. "I can't get close to him again until it's time to take the shot, and his security is going to be high for at least the next several days, if not the next several weeks. Especially if they don't catch *you*."

"So why don't you turn me in, then?" Ava pulled on a thin black tank top, but no bra, her nipples pushing against the sheer fabric.

"Because I think you can help me," Jack told her. "And because this delay has cost me money and the happiness of my customers. The way I see it, you owe me a debt."

"I have plenty of that," she said easily. "You'll have to get in line."

She did, too.

He'd done some research while he waited for her to finish showering. The woman took long showers.

Ava Cavalcante had credit card debt, medical debt, and a defaulted mortgage, a house that had already been repossessed. That was as far as he'd gotten. He'd heard her coming across the hall just as he was scrolling through a copy of the restraining order Cale Jacobson had taken out on her.

If he had to guess, she blamed Cale for the medical debt, maybe. He owned a majority share in his family's health insurance company, one famous for two things: record-breaking profits for shareholders and efficiently denying customer claims.

"Well, this debt takes precedence," Jack told her. His phone buzzed, pulling his attention.

The only people who had direct access to this line were his clients—that was his habit on each job he carried out.

Don't play with us, the first text said.

Another buzz.

We heard there was an unsuccessful completion attempt.

A third buzz.

We expect to get what we paid you for. No delays.

Jack's hand clenched tighter around his burner phone, knuckles whitening. *Of course* the client was pissed. And of course Ava's attempt on Cale's life had made the news.

"Am I keeping you?" Ava said, moving toward the door. "Don't let me be a nuisance. You were just going—"

He stood, blocking her path, and she crashed into him.

For the second time that day, he caught her against his chest with one arm.

"How did you find out his schedule?" Jack asked. He was close enough to her now that he could feel her breath, hot against his neck. "That takes social engineering that most people would have no idea how to do. How did you find him? Did somebody *send* you?"

She was a puzzle, a goddamn enigma, and an infuriating one at that.

"How did *you*?" Ava retorted, putting two hands on his chest and shoving.

He didn't move. She was petite, despite her curves, not even big enough to jostle him.

"Fuck you." Ava smacked his arm and stepped back. She returned to the side of her room that contained her bag and pulled on a pair of joggers, her dark-brown eyes darting toward the window.

Jack sighed. "You'll come with me to my place," he said. "You'll tell me everything you know about Cale, and every contact you spoke to, and every possible piece of information you've gained. And if I need you to, you'll use your existing contacts to find more information. Do you understand me?"

"And what if I don't?" Ava asked, shoving her phone into her pocket.

It was probably a phone registered to her, too, one still on some plan in her name, pinging off every cell tower in the area. Their first step was to get rid of that phone. Their second step was to get the hell out of here before the police or Cale's security squad arrived in full force. Their *third* step was Ava doing something useful.

"Ava," Jack ground out. "Do you not understand how serious this is?"

"If I don't, what's the punishment? Are you going to spank me?" Ava tilted her head at him. She was smirking, as if the threat Jack presented was nothing but a fun, sexy little challenge.

It was a tempting offer.

She must have seen that thought in the hungry look on his face, because she took another small step back toward the window.

"I think you know as well as I do that your *only* option is to help me," Jack said. "Because you're right. I could just turn you in to the police. Or I could make sure nobody ever hears from you again."

He didn't want to kill her, not least because it would add a layer of mess he didn't need in an already-messy affair.

"I think you're scared," Ava shot back. And then she moved, faster than he thought was possible. The second time he'd underestimated this spitfire today.

And the last.

She knocked the gun from his hand with a well-placed kick and launched herself at his throat, her arm wrapping around it as the weight of her momentum knocked him backward.

Maybe that shove earlier, the one that hadn't so much as moved him, was to catch him off guard. *Maybe* she had been playing a longer game than he'd realized.

Those were the thoughts in Jack O'Sullivan's head as this little hellcat of a woman knocked him on his ass.

Glass shattered before he was back on his feet, Ava Cavalcante's heavy bag breaking the hostel window, and then she was through it, bits of glass clinging to her as she ran for her life.

Chapter Six

Ava Cavalcante had learned three things today: (1) she was too chickenshit to stab somebody, (2) escaping out a broken window looked easier in the movies, and (3) hit men were apparently pretentious assholes and not cool, suave James Bond types who could sweep her off her feet.

Though this Jack, or AJ, or whoever the fuck he really was, certainly had the looks the movies had promised her.

And that look in his eye, the hunger when he stared at her naked body. That was the kind of hunger that, in another lifetime, would be enough to engulf her.

But Ava had the upper hand now, and she knew better than to eat any more damn chocolates and leave the wrappers (really, this was what she got for littering in the first place, even by accident. Even on a stressful day).

The back of the hostel was a thick tangle of trees planted too close together. Ava ducked and wove between the trees, brushing glass from her shoulders as she did. There was a bit of glass in her hair, too. She could feel it, lodged there, ready to fall into her ear. Would the shards work their way into her ear and make her go completely deaf? How did you clean this much glass off yourself *without* bleeding in a bunch of places?

No more going through glass to escape hot hit men, that was the main takeaway here.

She rounded the corner toward the alley that ran alongside the hostel, craning her neck for signs of his stupid Volvo.

Sirens wailed in the distance as her feet pounded the hard pavement of the alley, crunching gravel and trash beneath her as she ran. For a city that seemed to pride itself on its eco-friendly status, there sure was a lot of shit in the alleys of Portland.

The sirens drew nearer, and Ava realized with a surge of horror that they were very likely coming for *her*. Had Jack decided to call the police, then? And if they picked her up and she told them a contract killer was also on Cale Jacobson's tail, who would believe her over him, when he was the good-looking, even-keeled businessman who had stopped her from doing the unthinkable just this morning?

Tires squealed, and a black sedan pulled up in front of her, at the intersection where the alley ran into the road.

Jack had one hand on the top of the steering wheel, the other resting calmly on one muscular thigh. What was wrong with ten and two? Did he do this all the time, or was he just trying to show off his stupid muscles in his stupid forearms?

Fucking hit men.

"I hate you," Ava told him, but she tugged on the door to the passenger side of the car.

It was locked.

Jack rolled down the window, his movements slow and calm as if he had all the time in the world.

"You'd be safer in the back," Jack told her. "We could toss a blanket on you, and traffic cams won't pick you up. They're *all* looking for you, you know. You even made the news."

"Go fuck yourself," Ava said, but, infuriatingly, he was right.

So she hopped in the back of his car, like a lunatic, and let him throw a blanket over the top of her before they drove away. If she'd paid attention at the true crime book club she'd facilitated in her library days, she would probably know better. Then again, if she'd paid attention at true crime book club, she might've had a better plan for killing Cale Jacobson to begin with.

"By the way," Jack said as he seamlessly pulled into traffic. "You dropped your wallet. So I gathered that, along with all the clothes you left strewn across the floor with your DNA all over them, and some of Cale's, too."

"Fuck you," Ava said again, but her words were muffled beneath the fleece blanket he'd thrown over her.

"You're welcome," Jack said.

Ava popped her head up when the car lurched to a stop. "Don't they teach you how to drive in hit man school?" she said.

"Hit man school? What do you think exists out there in professional development for hit men?" Jack asked, his tone threaded with disbelief.

She wanted to climb up there and wrap her hands around his throat and scream *Take me seriously, you prick* into his face. But so far, physically accosting this man had not gained her much, and Ava might learn slowly, but she *did* learn.

"I don't know," she snapped. "I kind of didn't think hit men even *existed*."

"Go back under your blanket," Jack said.

It was a shame he kept his car so neat. She desperately needed something to throw at him.

But she did as she was told. Only because the wail of sirens was still perilously loud.

"That might be the first time you've ever done as you're told," Jack complained. "If I call you a good girl—"

"I'll strangle you," Ava told him.

"His security team was pulling up just as I left the hostel," Jack told her. "Do you know how they found you?"

She could tell by the acceleration and the change in noise that they were on the highway now, and relief pumped through her, a welcome change from the adrenaline that felt as if it had been flooding her system for hours now. Who cared how Cale Jacobson's team had found her?

"Oooh," Ava said. "What would they have thought if they had seen *you* again? Once is a happy accident, but twice is no coincidence. They might start to think we're working together."

"We *are* working together," Jack said evenly. "But you're right. It would be a death knell for this project if they see us together. And I have too much riding on this one for you to fuck it up again."

"Technically, if they had seen *you*, it would have been your fuckup, not mine," Ava said. "And besides, I don't know you. I don't give a shit about your little paid operation. So it can't be a fuckup if your project didn't matter to me to begin with, can it?"

She could hear Jack's frustrated sigh through the thick shield of her blanket.

"There's water in the seat pocket," he said after a moment of quiet. "Drink some and try to get some sleep. We'll be about half an hour yet."

"I don't need a nap," Ava insisted.

But she did take the water bottle, fuming the entire time. Apparently attempted murder and making deals with contract killers made her both sleepy and dehydrated, but she hated that he'd been right about it all the same. Also, if he was going to stock anything, he should have had the decency to have a Diet Coke, not some Costco-brand plastic water bottle.

Ava woke with a start when the car door slammed. Jack had shut his door, and now he opened her door next and then offered a hand to help her up. Her neck was cramped from how she had fallen asleep, and it cracked loudly when she tilted her head.

Fear caught up with her a moment later, the tightness in her chest growing until Ava couldn't quite catch her breath.

She was with a *hit man*. She had gotten into his car on purpose, for fuck's sake, and let her guard down enough to fall asleep.

Jack helped her up, his hands surprisingly gentle on hers.

He stopped there in the driveway, arms folded over his chest, considering her more carefully than she had been looked at since—

Well.

Ava couldn't think about any of that, about how Ari had looked at her or how gentle Ari's hands had always been with her. Not if Ava wanted to keep it together long enough to finish this.

"All right, Ava," Jack said, one hand dropping to rest on his Glock. "It's time to get to work."

Chapter Seven

The house was removed from the road, set back into the trees so far it was barely visible to anyone driving by. The listing had advertised privacy, and it had more than delivered.

The house was *also* owned by a host who had happily accepted cash. It was the perfect location, as far as Jack was concerned. And more than that, it was far enough from the city that when there was inevitable uproar and a manhunt for him, the police would run circles trying to find enough security cameras out this way to properly track him.

By the time investigators had found this place at all, it would be clean and ready for the next guest, with no trace he had ever existed at all.

Ava wrinkled her nose as he helped her out of his car. "Why did you take me all the way out here, again?" she asked. "The hostel was *so* much closer to Cale."

"You were about to get *caught*," Jack told her, pinching his fingers on the bridge of his nose. There was no way to stave off the headache that was Ava, though. Especially since she never stopped *talking*.

"Do they teach you that in James Bond school?" she asked. "Which hostels to stay in, and how far from the crime scene you're supposed to be?"

Jack lifted her bags and headed for the house, ignoring her. It was a beautiful three-bedroom log cabin, with a pool and hot tub out back, enclosed to keep guests in and wilderness out. The driveway was long, lined with trees, the nearest neighbor mostly obscured.

The fewer eyewitnesses, the better.

"I won't take the rental car when I complete the job," he told her when she caught up with him, still pestering him with questions. Truthfully, his path to killing Cale Jacobson had grown a lot murkier, and he didn't *have* answers to her questions.

He unlocked the door with the keypad and let Ava go in first. The house was open concept: vaulted ceilings above the entryway, hardwood floors through the living room, and an expansive kitchen that contained a large refrigerator, a double oven, and pristine marble countertops.

"I'm going swimming," Ava said the moment she saw the back steps leading down to the pool and hot tub. "And I don't have a swimsuit, but you've already seen me naked, so."

"You need to focus," Jack told her sternly.

"You don't decide what I need," Ava told him, pulling her tank top over her head. "And don't sneak any peeks at me while I'm swimming."

"Ava."

"Jack."

"I kill people for a living. I am going to kill you if you don't do this for me. How much clearer do I need to be?" Jack had never met anyone with such an impaired sense of personal safety—her meter for acceptable risk was as broken as his.

"So you've said." Ava was shrugging off her shorts now.

A moment later she was naked. Again.

In other circumstances he would be delighted at the chance to see an ass like that twice in as many hours. But this infuriating woman wouldn't see the danger standing right in front of her.

Jack reached out, hand closing over her wrist.

Hauled her back to him.

Ava was not hard to pull, and she didn't offer any resistance, either. Instead, she crashed against his chest, eyes widening, breath quickening as she stared up at him.

For a moment, just a moment, he thought she was about to acquiesce, agree to work with him.

And then something sharp pinched against his stomach. A knife. A small one.

How could he have missed that?

Ava grinned up at him, her brown eyes crackling with fury as much as mirth. “Checkmate, motherfucker,” she said.

“Easy,” Jack told her slowly. He could still strip the knife, break her wrist, but in that split second, if she had the guts to cut him, it would be game over. For good.

And he had someone still counting on him, someone he would let down if he were dead on the floor of this rental.

“You said you’d kill me. What do I have to lose?” Ava leaned closer, naked breasts pushing against his chest as the tip of her knife dug in farther. She tilted her head up, lips nearly brushing his jaw as she spoke. “You think you’re better than me. Smarter, scarier, stronger. But underestimate me again, *Jack*, and see what fucking happens.”

“O’Sullivan,” he said stupidly.

“What?” Ava hesitated, startled.

“That’s my name,” Jack said. “My real name. Jack O’Sullivan. And I don’t think I’m—”

But he *had* thought he was smarter and stronger and scarier, hadn’t he?

“I was going to kill Cale Jacobson with this knife,” Ava said icily, letting the tip of the blade drift lazily down, just centimeters from touching his skin. A little lower, and she’d have that knife at his balls.

Think, O’Sullivan.

“Did you really think,” Ava murmured, the words warm against his throat, “that I wouldn’t try to kill you, too?”

He sucked in a breath. “Ava,” he said.

“Saying my name like that won’t get me to change my mind,” she said, and then, just as suddenly as she’d leveled her knife at his gut, she stepped back, hands raised, the small weapon still held in her right hand.

Jack moved instinctually before rational thought caught up with him, pinning her against the wall behind them, his fingers wrapped around her wrist. She opened her hand, laughing, and let the knife clatter to the ground.

"I didn't kill you, Jack O'Sullivan," Ava said. She was still laughing, but the sound was a jagged, harsh thing, sharper than the knife she'd dropped. "But if we do this, you're going to stop discounting what I'm capable of, and we do this as equals. Is that clear?"

It was achingly clear.

Mess or not, Ava Cavalcante was capable of surprising him. And like it or not, she both had information he needed and too much information *about* him.

He kicked her knife, sending it spinning across the floor away from them, and then stepped back, raising his own hands in a gesture of—peace, maybe. Maybe even defeat.

"Equals," he said. "All right. So, we—"

"No," Ava said cheerfully. "*I* have had a hard day, so I'm going to do some self-care in the pool while you figure out dinner. After we eat, I can tell you everything your silly little notebook was missing. And, damn, for a trained hit man or whatever you call yourself, there's a lot you don't know about Cale Jacobson."

"Contract killer," Jack said automatically.

"Hmm," Ava said. "More gender inclusive that way, I guess. 'I support women's wrongs' and all that."

He had no idea what she was talking about, but that seemed like a reality he had better start getting used to sooner rather than later. His expertise was narrow: reconnaissance, bullets, neatly wrapped endings. Hers was broader, apparently, encompassing library science, well-placed punches, and whatever "women's wrongs" were. He probably supported them, too, though.

She turned and walked away from him, hips swaying infuriatingly. She picked up the knife as she went, too, and when he next saw her through the window, she was sitting in the hot tub, head tipped back and eyes shut, knife on the edge of the pool beside her.

Murder was a meticulous business.

And Ava Cavalcante, naked in his hot tub with a knife at her side, was anything but.

Chapter Eight

Ava's heart was thumping painfully in her chest. Jack must have felt it when she was pressed against him a few minutes ago, and even the warmth and comfort of the hot tub—and it was a *nice* hot tub—did nothing to calm the racing of her heart.

She'd managed to catch Jack off guard when she'd pushed her knife against his belly. So she'd bought herself time, at least.

Fuck.

What was she supposed to do *now*?

Everything was happening faster than she could catch her breath.

But then it had felt that way ever since—

"Ava?"

Jack was leaning against the doorframe, one hand resting on the handle of the sliding glass door. His posture was casual, but the look in his dark eyes was so intense she nearly had to look away.

"What do you want?" She was not going to pretend to be casual. Not when she had just agreed to work with a *hit man*. For fuck's sake. Some things should not be normalized, actually. She lifted the knife at the edge of the hot tub and looked back at him, a challenge on her face.

And in her hand. That too.

"I was wondering if we could talk." Jack's voice was soft.

This was a far cry from the man who had dragged her off Cale's prone body earlier that day or snapped orders at her as if he just expected her to listen to them. He sounded hesitant now. Uncertain.

"As long as you don't have any more lectures ready about how I work for you and have to love, honor, and obey you or whatever." Ava shrugged, turning the knife over in her hand carefully as Jack stared at her, mouth slightly open as if he couldn't quite believe her.

In fairness to him, she couldn't, either.

She had been a librarian before all this. But the craft nights, the meditative work of reshelving stray books, the soft-spoken conversations in the romance section, the preschool story times with stuffed bears and eager parents and distracted three-year-olds—all of it felt like a lifetime ago now. Because that was before.

Before she'd lost everything to Cale Jacobson and his evil fucking company.

If Ari could see her now, would she even recognize Ava? Stark naked in a hot tub, twirling a knife and staring down a hit man as they planned a murder together?

Scratch that. The *Ava* of a few years ago wouldn't have been able to recognize the person in the hot tub today, either.

"No more lectures," Jack interrupted the racing chaos of Ava's thoughts. "I thought I could go first. To build trust between us. I share what I've learned, and then you tell me any intel you've picked up along your way."

"Awfully convenient." Ava stood, water running in rivers down her shoulders. She shook her head, sending water droplets flying. To her satisfaction, Jack was standing close enough to receive a shower across his neatly pressed shirt.

He grimaced a little, shaking slightly as if he could rid himself of the mess Ava brought with her.

"What do you mean *convenient*?"

"I already know everything you know," Ava said. She hadn't *really* had time to peruse his little murder manual, of course. But it was better if Jack thought she had more leverage than she actually did. "I had your stupid little book, remember?"

"My *stupid little book*?" A flicker of anger crossed Jack's face, but it passed, his look stony and impenetrable again. "You keep calling it that. You mean my case notes?"

"Case notes are something social workers and grad students have," Ava said. "*You* have a murder manual. Or a stupid little book. Whichever you prefer."

"A murder ma—no, I do not," Jack said. "That's not what we're calling it. And did you actually read all of this? I caught up with you pretty quickly. And you were in the shower a *long* time."

Of course she hadn't read the whole thing, or even much, but it was insulting that *he* didn't think she had, either.

Ava resisted the urge to splash more water at the hit man standing in front of her. "I read most of it," she told him primly. "And I know your hit was planned for tomorrow, which is no longer an option, so you need a new opportunity. Which I can get for you."

Which she could *maybe* get for him. If nothing else went terribly wrong, and that was a big *if*.

Jack arched an eyebrow at her. "Can I get you a towel? Some clothes? We can talk about this over drinks, and I'll tell you everything I have. Promise."

"You have to be the first man who wanted me to put my clothes back *on* after they came off," Ava grumbled, stepping past him. As she did, her foot slipped on the deck, slick from the water she'd splashed out, and—

A firm hand closed around her bicep, his other arm hooking around her waist. He'd dropped his book—the murder manual itself—catching her, and now their faces were inches away again, his dark eyes piercing hers like he could see all the way through her.

"Don't," Ava said softly.

Jack released her like she was a live wire, snatching his murder manual from the ground as he did. "I wouldn't have," he said tightly. "Now, can you please let me get you a towel and some clothes so we can make a plan?"

"You're bossy."

"I'm in charge. There's a difference."

Ava gaped at him. "Who died and made you king?" she demanded, even as the low growl of his voice chased a shiver down her spine. "This is a partnership."

When he didn't look like he knew what to make of that, she snapped her fingers in his face.

Because Ava had always been a brat, but these days she was a brat with an impossible mission and very little remaining self-preservation.

"Does that usually work for you?" she asked, her laugh hard and sharp from disuse. "You drop your voice into the lower register, tell people you're in charge, and they all just bend over for you?"

Jack shrugged one infuriatingly broad shoulder. "Yes," he said. "More or less. Generally, people are pretty obedient. They like being told what to do, and they like it even more when you sound like you know what you're doing. But I didn't tell you to bend over."

"I meant 'bend over' metaphorically," Ava snapped, waving her hand at him in frustration. He shouldn't be able to make her blush. Especially at a time like this.

"How do you bend over metaphorically?" Jack asked. He looked genuinely baffled. "I've only had people bend over physically, and I don't really see how that's relevant to the objective—"

"I meant submission," Ava cut him off, her face flooding with heat at the word. It always had made her blush, even in the good days when she'd had Ari around to tease her gently about it.

Jack looked more confused. "You're blushing," he said.

She stomped past him into the house, a trail of water dripping behind her as she did.

When she looked over her shoulder, Jack was following with a towel, wiping up the water as he went, a small frown etched on his face.

Ava grabbed a cutoff tee and pulled it on, not bothering with a bra. She pulled shorts on next, glowering. "All right," she said. "Happy now?"

Jack raised an eyebrow, his eyes sweeping low, just for a moment, where her nipples stood erect against her T-shirt. "Not remotely," he said. "Cale Jacobson is still breathing, my clients are displeased, and *you* aren't taking this seriously."

"Go fuck yourself," Ava told him pleasantly. She dropped onto the gray sectional that wrapped around the living room, letting out a sigh as she did. The furniture was *soft*, and she sank into it.

Jack came to stand in front of her, towel still in his hand. He surveyed her cooly but completely, his gaze sweeping her from head to toe as if cataloging every bit of her. "You haven't eaten," he said finally.

Ava stared at him, taken aback. She had eaten a few Dove chocolates. She'd forgotten breakfast, but he didn't know that. He couldn't. "I'm fine," she said.

He hummed thoughtfully in response. "I'll make you some grilled cheese," he said. "They have a Blackstone I can use. And I'll put a salad together, too."

"Why?" Ava asked, glaring up at him. She couldn't be bothered to stand up, though. The sectional was deliriously comfortable, and it had been a long, long day. "Are you going to poison me? Get rid of me via grilled cheese?"

It hadn't seemed like an outlandish theory to Ava, who was still reasonably sure Jack was less interested in partnering with her than he was in neutralizing any threat she posed, but Jack grinned, surprising her at just how it brightened everything about him. His eyes sparked fiercely, the corners of them crinkling into laugh lines.

"There are easier ways to kill somebody, Sunshine," he told her. "Besides, poisons are messy work in their own way, and some toxins are as easy to trace as bullets."

"That's the least comforting thing you could have said," Ava shot back, but she closed her eyes. Not least because looking directly at the grin on Jack O'Sullivan's face was like looking directly into the sun. "If there was an award for 'Least Likely to Successfully Comfort Someone in Distress,' that would have been next to your face in the yearbook."

"I actually got 'Most Likely to Start a Podcast,'" Jack told her. "It was pretty embarrassing."

"That can't be real," she said, leaning back against one of the pillows. It was so damn comfortable.

He hummed again, the sound soft at the edge of her consciousness.

The next thing Ava knew, she was waking up on the sectional, tucked beneath a knit throw blanket. It was dark outside, but the lamp next to the couch was on, and a plate with grilled cheese and salad waited for her, a bowl of soup beside it.

Ava rubbed at her eyes, her vision clearing a little.

Jack sat opposite her, a needle and thread in his hand. He was steadily working on something, though he looked up when she started stirring.

"Are you—are you fucking crocheting?" Ava searched for the right word, coming up short. In her library days, she'd helped out at a craft club run by an elderly woman named Betty who had liked everyone there *except* Ava. Fuck Betty for that, honestly.

"It's cross-stitch," Jack said.

"You sound as judgmental as Betty," Ava told him. "Nobody knows the difference between all the needle arts."

Jack's eyebrows furrowed. "Most people do know the difference, I think," he said. "Knitting and crocheting are done with yarn. Cross-stitch is done with a smaller needle and thread. They're very different art forms."

"Okay, Betty." Ava sat up, stretching her arms above her head, groaning miserably as she did so. *Everything* hurt. "So. We're killing good old Leafy at the end of the month. That's the plan. I know you've been all horny about planning, so now you have one."

"Leafy? *Horny?*" Jack paused his cross-stitch—it looked like the beginning of a motivational quote—and leaned forward, resting his elbows on his knees. "You're saying we do this three weeks from now. I can work with that timeline. But—did you call him Leafy? And who's horny?"

Ava rubbed her eyes so hard she saw stars flicker at the edge of her vision. "You know, like a leafy green? Since his name is Cale? Like—like kale, the plant? Man, you're no fun. And I only meant horny, like, you know, excited—"

Jack held up a hand for silence, and despite herself Ava found that the relentless stream of words stilled at the gesture. "Different spelling," he said. "So? End of the month, then? When and where, and what is the source of your intel?"

"Intel?" Ava snorted, swinging her legs over the side of the couch. She felt wobbly and headachy and sore all over. When she met Jack's eyes, hers darted away again at the steady intensity there. Instead, she took a bite of the grilled cheese.

A moan escaped her mouth.

"Oh."

"*That* sounded horny," Jack mused dryly, resuming his cross-stitch or whatever the fuck he did.

She glared at him, but she was too busy devouring the grilled cheese to say anything. Because, holy fuck, holy *fuck*. It was smoky and warm, and she could taste provolone, maybe, and it was buttery and she was so hungry, *so* hungry—how had she ever just forgotten to eat? It was gone in a few minutes, and she devoured the salad next.

"What's this dressing?" she asked through a mouthful of greens (no kale in sight).

"I made it," he said. "It's a honey mustard vinaigrette."

"You *made* it?"

Jack O'Sullivan refused categorization at every turn—homemade salad dressing, grilled cheese out of a wet dream, a gun to her temple. Cross-stitch on the couch. Covering her with a blanket while she slept. A look in his eyes that said he would kill her and do it easily.

"Mmm," he said. "I'd still like to hear about your intel."

"*Intel* is such a dramatic word," Ava told him. "What are we, SEAL Team Six?"

"No," he said evenly. "They follow orders significantly better than you do."

"How many Navy SEALs have you ordered around?"

"One." Jack held up a single index finger. "Now can we focus?"

"No, because are you saying you've topped a Navy SEAL?" Ava stood, crossed the dimly lit living room, and then flipped on the overhead light, wincing at the sudden brightness. Jack's *look* sent her stomach flipping. "Fine, okay. Damn, didn't know attempted murder left you feeling hungover. Anyway—Cale has a gala at the end of this month. A fundraiser for a nonprofit of his. One of those foundations that sends money around in a circle and never really does anything, but they sure get a bunch of tax breaks?"

"I'm familiar with the type," Jack said.

He stood and followed her to the kitchen, where he leaned casually against the kitchen island, those corded forearms of his visible. He had changed clothes, she realized now—instead of business professional and a suit that made her mouth water, he was wearing dark navy blue jeans, a black bomber jacket that was rolled up to his elbows, and a black tank top underneath that clung to the hard muscles of his stomach.

"Ava?"

"Hmm?"

"You're staring again."

Ava froze, her hand still on the refrigerator door as if the two were fused together, her mouth slightly open. "I'm not," she said.

"And I need you to focus on our plan."

That lower register again. His voice deepening, hollowing her out when he spoke.

What was wrong with her, that she could feel—well, like *this*—when talking to a murderer? But then again, she was a murderer now, too. Or trying her best to become one.

And was he *smirking* at her?

"What about the plan?" she asked, yanking the fridge door open with more force than was strictly necessary. It was meticulously organized, because of course it was. She snatched a bowl of strawberries, a pitcher of juice, and—was that whipped cream? Then she moved the half gallon of skim milk over, just a little, so it was blocking the view to the carrots.

That would really get under his skin.

She busied herself making a bowl of strawberries and cream, and poured herself juice while he watched her closely.

"You're bold, but you're terrified," Jack said finally. His voice was soft, dangerous, and it had an edge in it that was driving her mad. "You're determined, but you have no idea how to do this. You're angry—and you're hurt."

"Are you a therapist, too? A shrink who does murders on the side?" Ava shoveled strawberries into her mouth, buried in whipped cream. "Anyway, you should focus on your own looming problems. Like the fact that I messed up your rigid fridge organization. You'll never find the carrots now."

But the lightness in her voice was forced, and he must know it, must know that his words had cut her. Were *still* cutting her.

Jack sighed and came around the kitchen island. He rustled in the fridge for a moment, replacing the things she'd moved. Then he shut the door and joined her there, leaning on the island again. Right next to her.

"Move," Ava said.

He didn't. Just arched an eyebrow at her. "Tell me more about this gala."

"All his rich friends will be there," Ava said. "They'll eat food, celebrate how much money they have, and get sloppy drunk. Probably do a lot of fancy drugs that poor people would go to jail for."

"Right," Jack said. "And how do *we* get in?"

"The party will be at his compound," Ava told him. "The one near the mountains and the border. I flirted with one of his executive assistants and I stole her phone, added myself to her calendar so I can see it from *my* phone, and then slipped it back into her purse."

Jack blinked. "That's—that's surprisingly good," he said.

"I'm a librarian," Ava said. "Well, I was."

"And that helped you steal a phone how?"

"It didn't," Ava told him through a mouthful of strawberries. "I'm just saying you shouldn't be surprised that I'm smart. Do you know how hard it is to get a job in a library? In this job market?"

He nodded carefully, and then his lips twitched a little. He reached forward, his movement slow, and swiped his thumb on the edge of her jaw. It came away covered in whipped cream.

Ava swallowed hard. "Oh," she said. "Thanks?"

He nodded at her. "So do you know how people will be getting to his gala?"

"I mean, they're rich," Ava said. "Some will arrive in helicopters, and some in fancy cars. Don't you have a Prius? They'll spot us immediately."

"A Volvo. How will staff arrive?"

"Good question," Ava said. "And no idea. I'd been planning to kill him in front of his little juice shop, same as you. The gala was a backup plan to my backup plan."

Jack nodded again. "Can you make contact with his assistant again?" he asked.

"I met her at a club," Ava said, taking another sip of juice. If she had to tell Jack *which* club, she might sink into the floor with embarrassment. "I don't have another suitably slutty dress, but if we go dress shopping—"

"We aren't going dress shopping."

"*You* aren't going dress shopping," Ava said. "Because you are living a life without whimsy. *I* am going dress shopping."

"Do slutty dresses have a lot of whimsy?" Jack asked, folding his arms and leaning his hip against the counter again. It was unfair he was this relaxed, and also hot, especially when Ava was over here vibrating out of her skin.

"I can't believe you just asked me that," she said. "That's incredibly rude."

"Is it?" he asked. "All right, *I* am going to this club. Show me a picture of Cale's assistant, and tell me the name of the club, and I'll be on my way."

Well, *fuck*.

"If I shared all of my—what did you call it? Intel? Then you could just kill me," Ava said. "That's the oldest trick in the book."

"I'm sure there are older tricks," Jack said. "And I need you, remember? Because he's seen my face. So we need to do this together."

That sounded like something a hit man would say if he was using you for nefarious plans, but what was Ava going to do? He might be her only way to reach Cale Jacobson after she'd so royally fucked today up.

"Right," she said. "So you can frame me for the murder when all this is done. Also, in case you forgot, they have seen *my* face and happen to know I have an anti-Jacobson vendetta."

"Framing you was not my plan, no," Jack said. "I have a different fall guy in mind. And I certainly don't need you to complete the job. In fact, it would be smoothest if you didn't come with me at all for that part. But I *do* need your intel, and possibly your connections."

"Who's your fall guy, then?" Ava set her bowl and spoon into the sink.

"You know that dishes wouldn't stack up if you just washed them as soon as you finished eating," Jack said. "Otherwise you end up with a pile."

"Not if you wash them," Ava said. "And I *was* going to wash them."

Ari had often had the same gripe—why put something down when you could put it *away*? And Ava had never had a good answer, just a tendency to put an object on a surface and then immediately stop seeing it there until she tripped over it or knocked it onto the floor.

"When?" Jack asked. "What moment makes more sense than right now?"

"I'm busy planning a murder," Ava said. "That's a silly question."

Jack shrugged and turned the water on, pushing his sleeves up higher before he started the dishes. "What's the name of the club? I'd like to go as soon as possible."

"Let's go tomorrow night instead." Ava ignored his question. "She's there every Saturday, but she works late on Fridays."

"Can you duplicate the calendar for me?" Jack asked as he finished up the dishes. "I'd like a copy. I'll chase down some information on how party staff will arrive, because I think our best bet would be to enter as waitstaff. I could pass for security usually, but I've had face-to-face with his head of security, and the man strikes me as sharp."

"Fine." Ava pulled out her phone. There was a new crack spiraling across the screen, but that was a problem for later. Or never, if they caught her and sent her to prison. Did you get to keep your iPhone in prison? That seemed like something they didn't let you have. "And tomorrow, okay? I'll take you to the club, and point out the girl, and we can—I don't know, talk to her together?"

Jack wiped his hands carefully on the kitchen towel, his dark eyes trained on her. "Sure," he said. "We'll lie low until then. Neither of us leaves this house, understood? Not even for the hot tub."

"I can't do that," Ava said. "Have you *seen* the pool?"

Jack set a hand on her shoulder, the weight heavy and commanding, and then he steered her toward the front door. The living room remained dark, the driveway, too. Out here, there were fewer streetlights, but in the distance, she could see it:

Red and blue lights flashing. Searchlights pointing.

The police were nearby, and they were looking for her.

"He's a billionaire, Sunshine," Jack said. "The police are going to be all over this one. So nobody leaves the house. You attacked a very, very rich man, and even being outside the city limits won't keep us safe—the whole area will be crawling with cops until they find *something* to work with. Do you understand me?"

"Sir, yes, sir," Ava said, mocking a salute. "Did I do it right? Just like your Navy SEAL?"

The hand on her shoulder squeezed, ever so slightly. "Good," he said. "I'm glad we understand each other."

The words were a rumble in his throat.

"Good," she repeated, her voice wavering. "Then we have ourselves a plan."

Chapter Nine

Jack still didn't know what to make of this woman. He'd been studying her—her mannerisms, her habits, the way her eyes flicked away from him when he had looked at her too long. Her past.

Credit card debt, medical debt. House foreclosed on. And one, only one, run-in with the law: the glitter bomb, which had resulted in an immediate restraining order.

Now she was scarfing down his remaining strawberries—he made a mental note to order more groceries, especially since so far Ava seemed to have a chaotic tendency to skip meals and just eat whatever she could find in his fridge. She also had a habit of glaring at him, leaving dishes in the sink even though there was ample time to wash them, and stripping her clothes off at inappropriate moments. And, of course, lying to him.

About the dress shopping, and her plans, and the club itself. Her eyes betrayed her, darting toward the door when she said they wouldn't go anywhere until tomorrow.

"Get some rest," Jack said. "I'll call in a grocery order in the morning."

"Oh." She patted the corner of her mouth, missing the whipped cream on her nose entirely. "You mean you don't use the app? Are you seventy-two?"

"Thirty-one, actually. I call and ask them to enter my items for me," Jack told her. "And then I use a prepaid Visa, because those are untraceable. They don't allow those on the app, but they will take them on the in-store kiosk."

"Is this Hit Man 101?" Ava asked him. "And don't worry about getting any food for me. I'm good."

He cocked his head, surveying her carefully.

Ava was curvy—full at the hips, and breasts, too, though he was trying, *trying* not to openly stare at the way they stretched and filled her small cutoff tee, which advertised a 5K she'd presumably run when she lived back in Iowa. Still, there was a gaunt look to her face, like she'd recently lost a lot of weight, all at once, as if something had uprooted the person she had been and left a more skeletal shadow in her place.

Like so many people, she spilled details about herself, her past, all of it like water—a 5K you ran, the sticker on your water bottle, the chocolate wrapper in your purse, all details someone could use to identify, triangulate. Locate. Details available to anyone. A record of living, worn and shed like a second skin.

"You don't want breakfast tomorrow?" Jack asked her. Lying to him or not, she needed to eat.

"I usually just have coffee," Ava told him cheerfully. "Eating? In the morning? Couldn't be me."

"Hmm," he said. He was ordering her breakfast regardless, but now didn't seem like the time to pick a power struggle. Maybe she liked waffles. Or cinnamon rolls. She seemed like she would, and he suspected she would accept a breakfast if it was placed in front of her, even if she wouldn't bother fixing one for herself. "All right. You can take the primary suite tonight. There's a whirlpool tub."

Jack was still fairly certain this woman would attempt to sneak right out of the house as soon as she thought he was sleeping and chase down whatever lead she'd been certain she'd find at the club. Not that it would be that hard to figure out which club she'd sneaked off to—now that he knew one of Cale Jacobson's employees gave away secrets at a club, he could find the rest himself.

And Ava had been right—he didn't need her now, but he *did* need to keep her away from the authorities, who were so desperate to catch her. It would be far, far too easy for her to negotiate a plea deal in exchange for turning in someone who had been hired to complete a hit on a powerful businessman.

"Are you saying I need a bath?" Ava interrupted Jack's thoughts. "I had a shower today. And hot tub time. Which counts as a second bath, honestly. I bet the heat and chlorine kill all the germs."

Jack bit back another sigh. Ava was the only person he had ever met who took the offer of the nicest bedroom in the house as an insult. Or a suggestion to bathe. Though now that he knew she was feral enough to view a soak in the hot tub as equivalent to a proper bath, he might *need* to suggest that.

"I thought it might help you relax," he told her wearily. "You've had a long day."

Of course, it was also a strategic move. It put him between her and the main entrance, which meant he would hear if anyone entered the house, long before they reached her room, and he would *also* hear her, whenever she inevitably sneaked out tonight.

"Well, aren't you a gentleman when you're not murdering people?" Ava deposited her second set of dirty dishes into the sink and left them there.

It wasn't even that Jack minded doing the dishes—he didn't particularly; like cross-stitch, he found washing the dishes to be precise and meditative. It was just that setting dishes down "for later" was so desperately inefficient.

Ava's eyes found him, glinting as she watched his internal struggle.

She was goading him with a dirty bowl and spoon and the tiniest speck of whipped cream still on her nose, and worse: It was working.

"You're chill about contract murder but not dirty dishes," she said, snorting with laughter.

He washed the dish. Because what was there to say to that? Yes. Yes, he was.

"So I'll go dress shopping tomorrow morning," Ava said as he finished his task.

He followed it with his routine: drying hands, neatly replacing the towel so that it was dead center on the rack and not a centimeter off, and applying hand lotion thoroughly.

Ava watched him with interest. "And you'll stay here when I do that?" she asked. "And . . . plot? I'm not really sure what contract killers do. Y'all don't really have a lot of 'come along with me' videos on social media. Or maybe I'm just not on that side of TikTok."

"Can confirm that we do not make lifestyle content," Jack said. "Good night, Ava."

"Does 'good night, Ava' mean it's past my bedtime and you're sending me off to bed?" Ava walked past him.

Jack's hand shot out before his mind caught up with him, snagging her arm, trailing the soft expanse of skin beneath his thumb. Then he wiped the whipped cream from her nose and drew in a breath to steady himself. "Do you need a bedtime?" he asked. "Why do you keep asking if I'm ordering you around, Sunshine? If that's what you want, you'll have to ask nicely."

"Fuck you," she whispered.

Jack let her go, and she disappeared down the hall, one last glance over her shoulder at him as she went.

It was only after he heard her lock click into place that he realized the gun at his waistband was gone.

<>

Jack had more weapons, of course. Three handguns, all untraceable, pieces he'd assembled himself. Plus a truly impractical number of knives, a small syringe, and a long-range rifle, though that last one stayed at his little off-grid property out in Montana.

Still, that wasn't the point, and it did nothing to stave off the anger that was rolling through him like a wave. Ava Isabella Cavalcante had stolen his gun, and he had been too distracted by her proximity to notice, let alone stop her.

She had, however, left her phone out on the counter. Maybe a trap laid for him, maybe just carelessness because she was exhausted, untrained, and skipped meals.

That last part was baffling to Jack, for whom hunger cues were regular, and meals—healthy, filling, nourishing ones—were a thing of routine. As long as he and Ava were a working team, he was going to make sure she damn well ate. Even if he *did* end up framing her at the end of this, like she'd so angrily insinuated he would.

Because what good would Ava be for him if she was wasting away and so hungry she was jittery? It was impossible to retrieve useful information from someone who was too hungry to think.

Jack took her phone to his room, where he connected it to his laptop, opened it quickly—her password was her name, for fuck's sake. He didn't even have to mess with the phone's encryption, which would have taken him significantly longer. He just hazarded a few guesses, not enough to get him locked out more permanently, and . . . yeah, she needed to work on her password security.

Once he had cloned the schedule from her calendar app (Cale's schedule was largely something he had already documented, but there were a few additional appointments, one to a high-end salon and one to a very exclusive massage parlor, that could prove useful), he pulled up her history on Maps.

Sure enough, her past was cataloged there for anyone to see. Just like the 5K T-shirt and the chocolate wrappers, her app history was a trail to follow, and Jack was a determined man.

There was a corner grocery store, Taco Bell (listed under "visited often," so at least she had meals occasionally), a hardware store, and Cale's favorite juice place where they'd first met. That, and a club called Dynamo, just slightly northwest of Old Town, where most of the clubs in the area had sprung up along the Willamette.

He searched her contacts next. Only one number was saved, so at least she had (presumably) purchased a new phone for her little endeavor. He copied the number into his phone and then shared Ava's contact with his own phone, just in case, and adjusted her location settings so that her location was shared directly with him. Finally, he called the one number Ava had saved in her phone.

It rang a few times, and then a bright, cheery woman's voice said, *Hey, this is Ari. Sorry I missed you! Call me back, or send me a text, since this is the twenty-first century and let's be honest, nobody wants to talk on the phone. Love you! Unless you're a telemarketer, in which case, please take me off your list. Okay, that's it for real. Text me.*

The dial tone beeped, and Jack hung up, then deleted the call from the log. Whoever Ari was, she mattered to Ava. Enough that she was the only number saved in Ava's phone.

There were a few other apps—Snapchat, TikTok, and some mobile game Jack didn't recognize. Her notes app was full of half-written lists, one labeled "things that piss me off" with bullet points that included ads on the side of buses, one that just said *Wordle (men)*, and people who didn't know how to zipper merge on the highway, plus *BETTY* in all caps at the bottom of the list.

Jack checked Snapchat last. Ava had a few streaks with various people, one who was nicknamed "daddy domme" but whose handle was @x.msrae.x. He opened the most recent Snapchat. Pictured was a white woman in a sleek black dress and vicious red stilettos. She was smirking at the camera, and the photo was captioned with an invitation:

Dynamo again? Loved you in that little red dress, baby girl.

Sure thing, Jack typed in response. Tonight? He added a string of emojis, a little face with hearts that seemed like something Ava might use, and that one heart with the hands that a man he used to meet, and fuck, always sent. And a sparkle for good measure. That seemed like something someone referred to as *baby girl* might use.

Then he replaced her phone on the kitchen counter, returned to his room, turned out the lights, and waited.

To Ava's credit, she lasted nearly a full hour before she left her room.

If Jack had guessed, he would have calculated a much quicker escape attempt, especially given the impulsivity she'd displayed in the past half a day he had been observing her. She *shouldn't* have the patience to wait him out. She certainly didn't have the patience to wait until he was asleep.

Then again, he wouldn't have guessed Ava would have the wherewithal to steal his gun to begin with. She baffled him, and that made her dangerous.

Most people came with predictive text—he recognized patterns everywhere, saw them repeat over and over again across people all over the country, and could usually reasonably guess someone's next action or words before, maybe, they did themselves. It made him good at what he did.

Until Ava.

Now Ava's door quietly unlocked. Jack memorized the sound of her as she moved through the house—the soft footfall as she made her way down the hallway slowly, the catch of her breath as she paused outside his room, the sigh of relief as she found her phone still on the kitchen counter.

It occurred to Jack only after she had passed that she was armed, that she could have shot him through the door, that she had maybe even been considering *that* when she hesitated outside his room. That she had never actually been frozen in fear.

The front door eased open—she was making every effort to be quiet, and while he had considered he should and could stop her, he would probably gain more useful intel if he followed her, unseen. She would lead him to more unaware than she would be willing to if she knew he was following her.

Jack waited another moment before strapping a handgun to his waist and pulling on a jacket that was large enough to conceal it. If there was a metal detector at Dynamo—or wherever she was really going—he would have to stow the handgun near the building or find a rear entrance to sneak through. But in his experience it was always better to be prepared—and it was always better, when leaving a rental house, to assume you might not return to it.

Ava had probably ordered an Uber, or was planning to, so—

The sound of a car leaving the driveway stopped him in his tracks. He ran to the door, which was hanging open. Clearly Ava hadn't planned to return, either, because she had left the door open and—

She was stealing his fucking car.

<>

He had his keys. *He had his keys.*

That was the fucking thing. How did a librarian with a very limited legal record, who was nearly underwater in debt and legal trouble, have the skills to hot-wire a car in a few minutes?

Jack swore under his breath and waited for the taillights to disappear down the long, dark driveway before he went to the locked garage the property owner kept adjacent to the house. The owner had assured him he'd have complete privacy here, that this part was just for storage, which—in Jack's experience, at least—meant there was likely to be an extra vehicle, or sometimes necessary tools.

He jimmied the lock and was rewarded by a motorcycle, an older model that looked like it hadn't been driven in years. Well, Jack O'Sullivan was going to lose his perfect star rating as a model guest on the app. Jack had booked the rental under Steve Johnson—and Steve Johnson was going to need a new profile. Maybe he'd be Bill next time, or Joe, or something equally forgettable.

The motorcycle was parked next to a workbench, so Jack rummaged through the drawers until he found the key.

It took a few tries, but Jack managed to get the bike started, snagged a dusty helmet that was hanging on the wall, and followed Ava into the damp spring night.

He didn't see his rental car again until he found it, parked haphazardly in a fire lane in front of Dynamo, already booted and ready to be towed. A few disgruntled bouncers were lingering in front of it, talking to the man who drove the tow truck.

Jack sighed as he parked the motorcycle in an open spot and pocketed the key. Now he was stuck out here with two vehicles, and if he wanted that rental car back—and the hefty deposit he had placed on it in order to pay in cash—he would have to talk to the bouncers and the tow truck driver. Three—no, four—more people who would remember a name, a face, a conversation in passing.

And when it came to witnesses, descriptions, and the stories people would tell the police after all this was done, this was the kind of thing that could get someone like him killed or, worse, caught.

"Hey," Jack said resignedly, pulling his hood a little lower and putting his N95 on. "This is my car."

One of the bouncers, a tall man with light-brown skin and reddish hair, looked Jack up and down. "*This* car? We saw some lady park it here and sprint inside. We had to drag her back to show her ID."

"Yeah, she's with me," Jack said. "I have the key right here. Can I just go park the car?"

"If you pay me to take the boot off." The tow truck driver had pale skin and was wearing a faded red shirt with the picture of some kid on it, dates beneath the image, the numbers cracked and worn from many wears and many washes. His hands were dirty, the nails chipped.

"How much?" Jack asked.

The driver told him a number that made Jack wince, but he dug for cash and handed it over.

"That your wife?" the first bouncer asked. "Because if mine parked like that, it'd mean she was asking me to take her to one of those back rooms."

One of the other bouncers shoved him and laughed. "Come on now," he said. "Rita would take *you* to one of those back rooms just for suggesting that."

Jack ignored them—he had guessed that Dynamo offered a spicier option then some clubs, based on the leather he'd seen in Ava's Snapchat, so the man's banter provided him with no new information. Instead, he looked at the tow truck driver expectantly, waiting for him to move. The man huffed and complied, and Jack took the opportunity to get out of there quickly. The steering column was damaged, wires visible, but it was, thankfully, still drivable.

He parked it—legally—a few blocks away and returned to the club. The bouncer gave him another once-over and asked for ID, which Jack supplied—an old ID, not good enough for short-term rentals or law enforcement, but good enough for something like this.

"Rory O'Callaghan?" The man looked at him a second time, eyes narrowing. "Take your mask down for me, man."

The fake ID was a decent one. Jack had no worries about that. But being noticed, being seen, all of that was dangerous. And thanks to Ava's careless parking job, Jack was now firmly on the bouncer's radar.

The club's sign was blinking neon purple, pink and blue, **DYNAMO** in bold letters stretched over the entryway.

When Jack entered, it was to a mess of sweaty, dancing bodies in front of him, a bar to the left, and strobing lights above.

Jay would have needed his eye patch for something like this, or the strobe of the lights would have caused a seizure. He'd hated the eye patch at first and hated the incessant stream of pirate-related jokes he'd been subjected to by strangers with too much goddamn audacity, but in the end they had found one he'd liked. Jack had helped him pick it out.

Now Jack pressed the thought down firmly. Jay was usually buried deep, all those memories tamped down so firmly that nothing could touch that part of Jack. Nothing could shake him. Not even Ava Cavalcante and the way she charmed and aroused and *surprised* him.

Jack pushed through the throng of bodies on the dance floor toward a hallway leading off at the back right corner, past the stage where a few people of various genders were working a collection of poles. He dodged a woman who had bent over to throw up and stopped in front of a bouncer who was blocking the way to the hallway. He was another tall, broad man, though this one looked sharper than the ones who had been joking about wives and back rooms.

"Can I help you, man?" the bouncer asked him.

"I'm here to see someone," Jack said. "To meet with Ms. Rae."

He was familiar enough with the kink world, though not usually in a club setting—he had been to the dungeons, the play parties, but avoided the larger clubs, even before his line of work had demanded anonymity. Even when he'd had the safety of Jay at his side.

"You been here before?"

"No," Jack said.

"So this is a consult?"

"Yes."

"You know anybody here?"

Jack hesitated and then pinched the bridge of his nose. "Actually," he said, giving the detail slowly, as if reluctant. "My wife comes here to meet her domme. She's here with Ms. Rae now."

His reluctance held an element of the genuine: The ruse that Ava was his wife was becoming a recurring cover story, and not one Jack particularly liked.

The bouncer grinned at this. "Oh, the spitfire?" he asked. "She tried to steal my security badge."

He patted his pockets and then frowned.

"I'm guessing she succeeded," Jack said dryly. "Listen, I'd really like to go and get her out of your hair. And I also wouldn't tell anyone that she managed to lift your ID and have unfettered access to the most sensitive rooms in this club."

The grin turned to a scowl. "Fuck you, man," he said. "She always meets in the room down at the end with Ms. Rae. Get her out of here and get me back my badge."

Ava's chaotic tendency to lift other people's things and walk away with them had served Jack. For once. Though she still had his fucking *gun*.

The hallway narrowed, doors on either side firmly shut. An exit sign glowed dimly at the far end, very little sound coming from any of the rooms—most likely they were soundproofed, or at least close to it.

A door opened, a man in skintight leather pants and a leather harness on his chest emerging. His eyes trailed up and down Jack's body lazily, and he laughed when Jack held his gaze.

"Okay, *daddy*," he said. "I see you. You came here with somebody?"

"Yes," Jack told him. Another day, this might be an invitation he'd take the man up on. Another version of his life, maybe.

But right now he had a job to do, and if Ava left him in the dust, this entire thing would get a lot more complicated.

"Have you seen my wife?" Jack asked. "Short. Mean. Auburn hair. Likes to steal shit."

"I'm Gray," the man said. "He/they."

"Rory," Jack told him. "He/him."

"Yeah, I've seen your wife," Gray said. "She's in the room at the end of the hall with Ms. Rae. Probably getting topped and bratting the whole time, though you seem like you could manage that just fine yourself."

"Thanks." Jack shouldered past him toward a red door at the end of the hallway. He could feel Gray's eyes on him as he went, burning into his back.

Chapter Ten

Ava had stolen only one other car in her entire life, so yeah, you could say she was proud of hot-wiring Jack's rental car, even if it did mean he'd be coming after her with a vengeance now. Between keying it earlier today and stealing it tonight, she was off to a much stronger start on her car-related crimes.

This was the kind of thing she would have said while lying in bed next to Ari, and Ari would have looked at her over the top of whatever nonfiction she was reading (probably something about the animal kingdom, usually birds of prey) and shake her head fondly, roll her eyes affectionately.

And then the theft-related impulses would have stayed there, in their bed. Without Ari, all Ava's worst impulses became reality.

Like stealing a car. Like hunting a billionaire for sport.

Okay, Ari might have actually been partially on board with something like that. Her only concern would have been about Ava's safety—*If you can tell me how you'd do it safely, honey, I'm all in.*

Of course, Ava usually hadn't thought that far.

Now Ava was strapped to a play bench in the specialty wing of Dynamo, a club that featured some private back rooms with a variety of toys and furniture that could make any night more interesting. She wasn't here for pleasure tonight—well, not *just* for pleasure. If pleasure was part of it, that was a happy accident, if you will.

Ms. Rae was late.

Ava had targeted her in particular, not just because she was a female domme closish in age to Ava, but because Ms. Rae also happened to be Beatrice Rogers, executive assistant to the billionaire Ava was trying to kill.

Get tied up, learn about wax play and impact and sub space, and gather details about Cale Jacobson's schedule at the same time. Two birds, one stone, one dead billionaire, as the old saying went.

Ava had thought it would be sexy and fun to get onto the bench first, still dressed in her little red dress—in retrospect not her best move—and she had slid her ankles into the smooth leather cuffs. Outside of the handful of sessions she'd had with Ms. Rae and the experimenting she and Ari had done long ago, Ava was mostly a newbie to kink. But she enjoyed it. *And* she enjoyed winning.

Which tonight meant escaping the hit man (!) that she'd ended up with, stealing his stupid car, too, and taking his gun.

Ah, shit.

His gun.

That was in her purse, which was sitting on the chair across the room. If he got to her before Ms. Rae—

The door opened.

"Well, aren't you darling tonight, Mel?" Ms. Rae's voice purred behind her.

Ava turned her head. *Mel* was her much sexier alter ego, someone who met up with dommes at fancy clubs.

Ms. Rae was in a skintight black dress that hugged every curve on her body, her tits spilling out the top.

Ava shivered. Ms. Rae had the same energy Jack did—centered, commanding. A little bit mean, but in a fun way.

Which was a horrifying thing to think about a contract killer, but here they were.

"How are you, love?" Ava asked.

Ms. Rae shut the door and trailed a hand down Ava's back. "A man came looking for you tonight," she said. "We should get you up and talk about what you want to do tonight. I have a new flogger I could introduce you to, or the hot pink wax-play candles are back in stock."

Ava shivered again. Jack, here already? She had less time than she thought. And Ms. Rae's flogger sounded deliriously good, but tonight Ava needed information, especially since her window to get that information and get out of here was closing more rapidly than she'd planned. Specific information about Cale's party at the end of the month, something she technically knew about but maybe had overstated the depth of her knowledge on. To a killer. Who, now that she'd stolen his car, probably wanted to kill her even more than before.

"No floggers tonight," Ava said. She caught her breath. "Who was the man who came looking for me?"

"I'm not sure." Ms. Rae slid Ava's ankles out of the cuffs and helped her up. "Listen, he looked like he was bad news. I don't know if they let him in or not, but if you're mixed up with something dangerous, don't bring it this way."

Ms. Rae worked for a billionaire every day who did worse than anything Ava had done or planned to do, but Ava snapped her teeth shut and kept the thought to herself.

"Of course," she muttered. "It's hardly my fault if a creep came to the club looking for me."

"I think it was multiple creeps, actually," Ms. Rae said. "And you're right. I'm sorry. I didn't mean to victim-blame."

Ava froze. *Multiple?* Jack wasn't the type to work with someone, a fact he had made very clear from the beginning of their reluctant partnership, so this meant—

"Mel." Ms. Rae sat down on the bench and looked at Ava searchingly. "I'm sure I don't know your real name. I don't know much about your life, except for what you've told me about the library. But I have seen the people who came looking for you, and they're not good news. So whatever you're mixed up in—get out. You seem like a nice girl."

Ava shifted from one foot to the other. "I'm glad you think I'm a good girl."

"I said *nice*." Ms. Rae arched an eyebrow at her. "Now, are we playing, or are you getting out of here before they find you?"

"Let's play," Ava said. "Or talk. Or—I don't know."

This was the part she was *not* good at, no matter what she had told Jack. The social engineering. Lying, playing, getting information. She actually kind of *liked* Ms. Rae, despite the fact that she worked so closely with a billionaire. People had to work, after all. And if Ms. Rae was paid enough at either of her jobs, she probably wouldn't be working two jobs to begin with.

"What do you want to talk about?"

"You," Ava blurted.

She had gotten lucky with cloning Ms. Rae's phone. She had lucked into all of it, really, and now she was wildly out of her depth.

"Me?" Ms. Rae sat back, her look shifting to guarded.

"I know you probably don't share much about yourself to be safe," Ava continued frantically. "But I—"

"You're right," Ms. Rae said. "Mel, I care very much about my clients, and providing good service, but it's important to remember that this is a professional relationship. Maybe tonight isn't a good idea, after all. We can set up another night, and I'll refund you for now. How does that sound?"

Ava sighed, shoulders curling forward. "I heard there's going to be a kink party," she said. "A big one."

It was a shot in the dark. A wild one.

"This rich guy hosts it every year," Ava continued. "Out at a mansion in the mountains. That's what my friend Kord told me. He said it's a big gala, but a bunch of them—lots of rich people—have a play party, too."

Ms. Rae tilted her head, her dark hair brushing over her bare shoulder. "Are you asking if you can have an invite?"

"Yes," Ava said boldly. "It's that health-care CEO who hosts it. That's what my friend said."

Ms. Rae's eyes narrowed. "Hmm," she said. "You're talking about Cale Jacobson's gala."

Ava's heartbeat thundered in her throat. A shot in the dark, and it had *worked*? "Yeah," she said eagerly. "That's the name he said."

"His parties are known to be wild, but I haven't heard anything about a play party happening at the gala," Ms. Rae said. "And even if I had, I'm sure a party like that would be hard to score an invite to."

"But not impossible," Ava said. "You *said* that young women in the scene, both tops and bottoms, are always in demand. That the scene isn't always safe, so there's less of us, so—"

"You've been paying attention." Ms. Rae's eyes had that sparkle again, the little glint that said she thought Ava *was* a good girl, all evidence to the contrary be damned.

"I always listen to you."

Except when Ava was bratting. But that was purposeful, playful, prenegotiated not-listening, not *really* not-listening.

"Good," Ms. Rae said. "Well, I'll Snap you if I hear anything about the party, but I stand by what I said. I think it would be best if we met up a different time."

She ran her hands down her thighs and then stood, nodding at Ava.

It felt like rejection, though it shouldn't. Of course, nobody should play if they weren't into it. Of *course*. But Ava's heart stuttered in her chest.

She wouldn't see Ms. Rae again, she knew that. She would plan with Jack, if he didn't kill her as soon as he saw her again, and she would find a different way into Cale's party, and then she would kill Cale or die trying.

But either way, this connection, as limited as it had been, was over.

"Next time," Ava said softly.

"Next time, Ava," Ms. Rae said, her eyes flickering briefly before she shut the door behind her.

The door clicked just as the realization washed over Ava in a cold wave.

Ms. Rae hadn't called her *Mel* just now.

She'd called her *Ava*.

Chapter Eleven

Either Gray had been fucking with Jack, or they just hadn't known where Ava had gone, because there was no sign of her in the room at the end of the hall. There was a swing suspended from the ceiling, and a bench with empty cuffs, and a spreader bar hanging delicately on a little hook on the wall beside an array of floggers and paddles.

Any other day Jack would take more than a cursory look around. But today he was here on business, and that business was Ava fucking Cavalcante.

He tried the next three doors—two were locked, though people told him *not now* and *coming, darling* at both. The third swung open.

A small black purse was sitting on a chair abandoned. A very familiar purse.

Jack lifted it. It was heavier than he had expected because . . . was that his damn gun? And Ava had just *left* it lying around?

For *fuck's* sake.

Fear washed over him a moment later. She wouldn't have left her purse. Would she? She was chaotic enough that she just might have, but it seemed . . . odd to leave the gun, too.

Though he had already been wrong enough times about Ava that he really couldn't say. She was impulsive one minute and calculated the next, obsessive and chaotic in equal measure.

He carefully wiped off a smear of Dove dark chocolate and holstered the weapon in his own waistband with a sigh.

"Can I help you, honey?"

The woman who had entered moved quietly, despite her heels. She was wearing a sleek black dress and vibrant red lipstick, and she was carrying a flogger in one hand, smiling at him with an air of complete assurance. This was the Snapchat dominatrix Ava had saved in her phone as *daddy domme*. Ms. Rae.

Jack didn't startle visibly, didn't show fear, or surprise, because he had long ago schooled his body into a semblance of calm, no matter the situation. "I sure hope so," he said. "My wife was here."

"Ava?" The woman's smile faltered. "She's quite the popular girl tonight."

Of course Ava had given her real name. Jack sighed again.

"Is she?"

"You're not the only man who came looking for her," she said. "In fact, she just left with a *different* man who claimed to be her husband."

Jack swore under his breath. "Did she now?" He shook his head. "Well, she's a wild one. Though I'm sure you know that."

"See, I thought Ava was a wild card," Ms. Rae said. "A spitfire. Everyone notices her, even in a place like this, where plenty of people try to fly under the radar. But she's never had someone with her before."

"Are you supposed to be sharing this much about the people you meet here?" Jack asked icily. "And where did she *go*?"

"Out the back." Ms. Rae's eyes bored into him unrelentingly. "And Ava isn't like most of the people here, is she?"

Jack had no idea what she meant and wasn't about to stay to find out. He moved past her, but she slid into his way, blocking the door.

"I know what she plans to do." The woman's dark eyes flickered with something Jack could not quite name.

"Here? I assume it was get her ass beat," Jack said, nodding impatiently in the direction of the woman's flogger.

"If you know her at all," Ms. Rae said slowly. "Then you know exactly what I'm talking about. I know what she's doing. I know why she was here. I know what she wants. And I don't think she can do it without getting killed, do you?"

Jack stepped forward. "Why don't you move out of the way so I can go find my wife and get her out of whatever trouble she's gotten herself into?"

"Nobody," Ms. Rae said, "would move through the world with that little care for her own safety if she had someone at home who gave a shit. So either you're a shitty husband, or you're not her husband at all. But whichever it is, she seems like she deserves better."

And then she moved out of his way.

Ava was going to have to help him untangle what all this meant, but if this domme knew what Ava was up to, then other people could, too—including Cale. And *that* meant all this was over before it had truly begun.

Jack ran, following the flickering exit signs and thinking again of Jay, squinting against the flashing lights and grinning back at Jack as he did. When Jack pushed open the back door, which read *Emergency Exit Only*, the night was darker than before, rain pelting him from above. He was in the alley behind the club, cars flashing by where the road intersected.

A black SUV was parked but running, the windows tinted so dark Jack couldn't see anything inside.

He hesitated, hand lingering on the gun hidden beneath his jacket.

Had Ava looped back around and stolen the car again? It was the best-case scenario, honestly. Better than her leaving with someone who was going to hurt her. Or someone too eager to hear what they were planning.

As if on cue, Jack's phone buzzed.

Much like Ava, he didn't save friend's numbers. Just Jay's, after all this time.

Clients were just clients, and were saved as such (Cale's was *Client–Collective*), and each job had a new burner and a new phone number along with it.

Progress update, the text read.

Reconnaissance stage, Jack texted back. Disruption today at place of employment.

Forty-eight hours. Please. The response was immediate. Our needs have changed.

It will take at least three weeks to do this well, Jack responded, and then silenced his phone.

One SUV rolled toward the street, the other falling in behind it.

Jack hesitated—he had Ava's purse, which contained her phone, so he couldn't even call her and scold her for this goddamn lunacy.

Now he was behind a sex club, holding a woman's purse, two handguns strapped to him, feeling like a fool who had been played by Ava from start to finish today.

As the SUV reached the street, a taillight at the back shattered.

Jack dove for the cover of the dumpster, waiting for his mind to catch up, to find the shooter he'd missed, when he saw a hand reach out through the place where the taillight had broken, waving frantically at him.

Jesus.

"Ava!" Jack called.

Chapter Twelve

Maybe Ms. Rae's message had been a warning—maybe that was what she had meant when she'd dropped Ava's real name.

Either way, Ava hadn't read it correctly. Which, story of her life. Any messages she had to read between the lines were left firmly on read—

And now she was in the trunk of some fancy SUV driven by some big broad-shouldered white men who looked as though they would like nothing more than a chance to swing those meaty fists of theirs. She had kicked out the taillight as soon as the SUV started moving, and now she was reaching one arm through the back taillight, waving it frantically.

There was a man in the alley—a potential ally? Someone who would call the cops?

Shit, it was Jack.

Jack, whose car she had both keyed and hot-wired, all in a twenty-four-hour period.

Ava waved at him anyway, but her heart sank. Her ankles were tied, the paracord digging sharply into her skin, her feet already tingling from the lack of blood flow. Her shin was bleeding, a jagged cut from kicking out the glass taillight. They hadn't bothered to tie her wrists, maybe for the sake of time, maybe because they thought the knots at her ankles were enough to hold her. They hadn't gagged or blindfolded her, either.

Maybe because they fucking underestimated her.

She tugged at the knot holding her feet, which did not budge. If only Ava had this kind of knot-tying skills, she'd never trip over an untied shoelace again.

If circumstances were different, she would be delighted to be immobilized by rope this way.

But these men were not Ms. Rae or Ari or anyone pleasant. A man claiming to be her husband had entered first, followed by a menacing entourage of security guards. These men had dragged her out of the back room at Dynamo into the dimly lit alley and then tossed her unceremoniously into the back of the SUV. She would remember the sound of the trunk slamming shut for the rest of her life.

However long or short *that* was.

Ava waved for at least three city blocks, but when they turned down a quiet road with no streetlights and no cars, she lay back on the floor of the trunk with a little thump. Her heart was thundering in her chest, her head pounding.

Had she had anything to drink at Dynamo? She couldn't remember now. It was all hazy and getting hazier. Or maybe they'd hit her over the head.

Why couldn't she *remember*?

In the distance, the roar of a motorcycle cut the night. The SUV swerved, and when Ava peeked out the back light again, fighting the droopiness of her own eyelids, the SUV had turned off its lights.

Far down the road, a motorcycle swerved, avoiding the *pop pop pop* of gunshots.

Gunshots?

And then Ava's eyes blinked shut.

<>

When Ava woke, her head thundered painfully and her ankles and wrists were tied to a chair. An experience she *usually* found stimulating, arousing, and a damned lot of fun.

But, in this context, utterly terrifying.

Everything else was dim—one single light bulb hanging above her head.

"You're so cliché," she said. The words came out a little slurred. They must have drugged her, then, but she couldn't remember how, or when, or even having a drink to begin with. "Whoever the fuck you are."

"That's no way to greet your host," a man's voice said.

Ava blinked, her vision clearing a little. She was in a warehouse—wow, even more cliché—that had nothing but a few men with guns at one door, and another man in a chair a few feet away from her. He was not dressed in the plain clothes the men who had dragged her away had worn. He was tall and white, looked to be mid-thirties, and had a square, clean-shaven jaw and icy blue eyes. He was also wearing a suit, and he had those cold blue eyes locked on her.

"Your henchpeople were very rude," she told him. "Why am I here? Did that awful man send you?"

"I'm not sure which awful man you mean," he answered. "My name is Devin, and I'm the head of security for a private firm. We've been hired to get some answers, and *you* have them, Ms. Cavalcante."

"Are you one of Cale's henchpeople, then?" Ava asked. "How much did he pay you to kidnap me? Isn't kidnapping still illegal if you're a billionaire, or are they just allowed?"

"Have you ever worked for Jacobson Health?" Devin asked. He sat back in the folding chair, setting his ankle on his opposite knee. He looked very relaxed.

Maybe he did this often. Kidnap mostly innocent women off the street (or in the club) and drag them away to shady warehouses to engage in the most cliché intimidation tactics in the books.

"You couldn't have picked somewhere with a better view?" Ava complained. Her head was clearer now, and she'd taken enough ropes courses—even topped during some of them, though topping wasn't really her thing—to know how most knots were constructed. In her panic in the SUV, or in her drugged state, she hadn't been able to summon that knowledge.

She eased her ankles side to side, covering the motion by leaning forward a little in her chair, and then back again. Keep his eyes firmly up here.

"Tell me, what view would make you happiest, Ms. Cavalcante?" Devin pulled a handgun from a holster at his waistband and set it on his knee, his hand still resting on it, the barrel facing her.

If Ava was normal, if Ava was good, if Ava had anything at all left to lose, she wouldn't have laughed.

But Ava Cavalcante had watched a heart monitor go flat in front of her, had held the hand of the person she loved most as that hand went cold and slack in hers, and there was nothing, *nothing* here that scared her. Somewhere along the way, she'd broken too completely to ever be whole again. Certainly to ever be scared.

"Do you think I won't use this?" Devin leaned forward, hand still resting on the gun. "What do you know about the investigation?"

"The—wait, what?" Ava's left foot was almost free of the knot, the cord loosening. She laughed again, the sound echoing in the empty warehouse. "You think I know anything important?"

The second the words left her mouth, she regretted them. If they thought she knew something they needed, they would keep her alive. And while the bullet waiting for her in that gun didn't scare her, not anymore, she *did* need it to wait at least until she'd taken everything from Cale Jacobson.

A flicker of confusion crossed Devin's face before he schooled his features into that mask of calm. "The investigation is public knowledge," he said. "The Jacobson family has been accused of insider trading, and the DOJ is investigating. *You* seem to be holding a grudge about something, which is why Mr. Jacobson has a restraining order. Which you have now violated, of course."

Ava bit back a comment about how her glitter bomb and threatening letters were nothing in comparison to what Cale himself had done. "You think I'm mad at him for insider trading?" she asked.

It was such a wild leap, but of course they had made it. If she could laugh about this with Ari—

Ava stopped the thought short. She'd had a good, good life. Not an easy one, but so good it had left her breathless with gratitude.

And then it had all been gone. And maybe she hadn't ever been a good *person*, not really, because as soon as that goodness was gone from her life, she'd become . . . well, this.

"Do you have another reason you'd like to share?" Devin asked.

"Not particularly."

His foot hit the floor with a thump, and he was on his feet before she could really register how quickly he moved, the gun leveled at her forehead.

The barrel was cold where it pressed against her skin.

"Is this motivation sufficient?" Devin asked. "Or should we add pain?"

"If you'd done your homework, darling," Ava said. "You'd know that pain would be a *reward*."

Disgust wrinkled his face. "I can make sure it's not," he said.

"I do love to test my limits," Ava told him. She couldn't say that her strategy was working, exactly, but it was both buying her time and horrifying him, if only mildly. A stay of execution, *and* she got to annoy a man in the process? 11/10 strategy, would use again if the opportunity presented itself.

Though somehow she thought that using this strategy on Jack might backfire on her.

"Not the way I do," Devin growled.

"Oh, does it make you feel more masculine?" Ava asked. "Growling like a little doggie?"

He moved like lightning again, kicking out the leg of her chair.

She tumbled forward, catching herself with her face on the unforgiving concrete floor.

Blood spurted immediately from her nose, coupled with a crunch Ava would worry about later. If she lived long enough to *have* a later.

"Is that the kind of pain you like?" He towered above her, his hefty leather boots at eye level. "I could break every rib in your body. Is *that* the kind of pain you like?"

"Well, I haven't tried that sort of thing yet," Ava managed, blood running into her mouth as she did. And *fuck*, that hurt, but the anger burning through her like a wildfire remained brighter. "I'm sure we could, just to—"

Her words were cut off with the kick to her ribs that robbed her of breath.

But—her left leg was free.

Another kick to the ribs, another *crack* that left her breathless.

Devin's phone rang sharply, and he stepped away, shoulders angling away from her. "She's close," he said into the phone. "I'll get what she knows and then—"

Ava fought for a strained breath, her ribs aching, and then returned to the task of untangling herself from the paracord.

A few feet away, someone was speaking to Devin on the other end—the voice was garbled and unnatural, but they were saying something about *cut the losses* and *knows too much* and *shouldn't have been able to make that escape*—

And then Ava's right leg was free, and Devin was still angled away from her.

Ava rolled, her ribs screaming in protest as she did, and then staggered to her feet as Devin spun toward her. She swung the chair, still attached to her wrists, as hard as she could. A third sickening crunch echoed in the warehouse, but this one belonged to Devin's nose.

Blood streamed down his face, and the gun went off, and then she was running, running for the exit on unsteady legs in her stupid tight-fitting dress, the chair still attached to one of her wrists, thumping along beside her. For fuck's sake, this had to be one of the stupidest things she'd ever done, and that was saying something, because she'd once sledded down a ski hill on a pizza pan and nearly taken out a group of senior citizens doing a "skiing for beginners" class.

A rough hand grabbed her shoulder, and she spun, swinging the chair as she did. Another thump, but not nearly as effective, and then the door to the warehouse slammed open, and so many things were happening at once that Ava couldn't keep track of it all.

A hand on her shoulder, and then nothing, and guns were firing, and the chair had somehow come detached from her wrist, which was aching, and she was still staggering toward the door, and then, and *then*—

Jack's hand closed around her wrist.

She caught a painful breath—she had a broken rib, or at least a badly bruised one—and started to cry.

Which was dumb.

But the relief coursing through her was complete, because Jack was here. She'd lied and stolen and run away from him, so Jack was probably going to kill her himself, but he was here, and there wasn't a Devin in the world that could stop him.

Jack's dark eyes flamed as he took in her injuries—the blood on her face, the ragged breaths, her probably crooked nose. "Who did this to you?" he asked, his eyes sweeping the room.

The two guards at the door were lying on the floor, likely unconscious because there was no blood pooling around them, and Devin was—Devin was shouting *you* in a tone of disbelief and he was—

Lunging for them.

One shot.

Another.

Another.

And Devin was lying flat, eyes wide, staring back at them.

A fourth shot, Devin's body twitching where it had fallen, and then two more. And then silence.

The gun was steady in Jack's hand.

For a moment the whole world slowed down around them. There was nothing, *nothing* but the sound of Ava's thundering heartbeat and Jack's ragged breathing, one of his hands outstretched with the gun, the other, somehow, wrapped around Ava's waist.

"You're here," Ava breathed, because—because what *could* she say?

"So are you," he said, but his tone was uneven, that endless calm broken. "He hurt you?"

It was a question. It was, somehow, something more.

"We—we have to go," she said. "Right? I'm sorry about the car."

Darkness flickered in his eyes, but his arm stayed firmly around her waist. "Can you walk?" His eyes swept up and down her, as if looking for injuries. "Can you *ride*? I have a motorcycle for us."

Dimly, the memory of a motorcycle dodging gunfire returned to her. "That was *you*?"

Jack nodded, his eyes sweeping the dim warehouse for threats. "Are there more of them?" he asked. "How many were in the SUV?"

Ava was stuck on the memory of Jack—Jack on the motorcycle, tearing down the road after the SUV, dodging bullets as he came to rescue her.

"A few people," she said finally. "I—I think they drugged me. These men carried me to the SUV, and then tied my feet together, and—"

Jack was towing her toward the door, hand still firmly on her waist. "We have to get out, and we have to get rid of this gun," he said. He looked down at the weapon in his hand as if he couldn't quite believe it had gone off. "Maybe the body, too."

"Slow down," Ava managed through gritted teeth.

Jack stopped abruptly, and Ava crashed into him. He was all hard muscle and concern, staring down at her, waiting for an explanation.

"Ribs," she said.

His hands were on them immediately, his gun stowed, his touch gentle. "Broken, you think?" he asked. "Does it hurt to breathe? If you've punctured a lung—"

"I'm fine," Ava cut him off. "We can go, just—just slower."

"I would go get one of their SUVs," he said. "But I don't want to risk leaving you."

He stopped and hesitated, as if considering.

"I could take a gun," she said.

"You did that already," Jack retorted. "And then immediately left it behind at the club, with your entire purse and your phone and your whole identity, just waiting for anyone to snatch it."

"Well, good thing the only person who found it was you," Ava said. "I'll go with you to the SUV. Do we have to take him? When will those two wake up?"

Jack shrugged one shoulder. "Any minute," he said.

And then, without another word, he lifted her off her feet entirely. "Tell me if you see anyone with a gun," he said. "And I'll put you down so I can shoot."

Ava wrapped an arm over his shoulder to hang on. "I can *walk*," she said.

"I can walk faster," Jack told her shortly. He pushed open the door, peering out cautiously before he broke into a slow run. One of the SUVs was sitting empty.

Ava opened the door to the back for him, and he deposited her gently on one of the seats.

"I'm getting the body," he said. "You stay low—all the way on the floor—and out of sight."

"I want to sit shotgun," Ava complained.

"Tough shit," Jack said. "This is the place to sit if you don't want to get shot."

"We're not getting shot at right *now*," Ava said, just as a bullet ripped through the glass in the back. Her timing was astonishingly bad. She had once insisted to Ari that she'd followed assembling instructions at the exact moment an IKEA shelf had fallen to pieces behind her—but this, now, a bullet chasing her insistence that she was safe. This really took the fucking cake.

Jack tossed Devin's body in with a heavy, wet thunk.

Ava shuddered, bile churning in her stomach at the sight.

And then Jack was in the driver's seat, pushing the button to start the car, and they were tearing out of the industrial complex, shots echoing behind them.

Chapter Thirteen

Jack swerved as a bullet shattered the glass of the windshield. Ava shrieked, covering her ears with her hands. She was still lying on the floor in the back seat, her body trembling.

"Stay down," he snapped.

This was an unholy fucking mess. A stolen, stripped car. A stolen motorcycle, abandoned near Jacobson's warehouse, and no guarantee that Jack hadn't left DNA on the bike somewhere. And Devin, the sharp-eyed security guard who had insisted that Jack stay and talk to them, had recognized him, moments before Jack had killed him.

And now—Ava, hurt. Devin, dead in their back seat.

Jack bit back the wall of frustration that was bearing down on him like a wave. This woman. This *woman*.

And when he had seen the blood running down her face, seen the way she curled over her injured ribs, something had snapped inside him that he still didn't understand. When he shot that man, he had none of his usual control. None of that slow, careful calm he had built, brick by brick, over years of doing this work.

No, he had just fired. Not once. Not twice. He had emptied the magazine.

Just because Ava was hurt.

She was—

Currently trying to clamber over the barrier into the front seat.

Jack put a hand out to indicate she should stay put, and Ava high-fived it.

"Go team," she said wearily, dropping into the passenger seat and groaning when she made contact. "Shouldn't have done that. Why didn't you stop me?"

"I tried," Jack gritted out, whipping the SUV left, lights off in an attempt to lose the SUV that was rapidly gaining on them. "You wouldn't stay put."

"Oh." She pinched the bridge of her nose. "Fuck, that was a bad time. I mean, I never feel *good* the morning after going to the club, but I don't usually feel so . . ."

"Broken?" Jack supplied. "Shot at?"

"Both," Ava said. "Where are we going?"

"Away from the people with guns," Jack said. "Now let me focus."

Did she think this was a time for conversation? When they were driving around with a busted-up windshield and a body in the trunk and gunmen in hot pursuit?

"How did you find me?" Ava asked. "I thought I'd lose you for sure when, uh." Her glance slid to him, a little abashed, if only for a moment.

"When you stole my car," Jack said, cranking the wheel to the right and speeding down a dark residential street. "Yeah. I know."

"Where did you leave it?" she asked. "Should we go back and get it?"

"I *wouldn't* have left it if you hadn't gotten yourself kidnapped in front of me." Jack pulled off the road into a dark parking lot for some riverside park. They were nearing the edge of the city, far enough from the warehouse district that he could afford to stop and get his bearings. "I had to leave it near Dynamo. And now I've had to leave the motorcycle."

It was a trail of chaos, leading straight back to him. He never left a mess like this.

Never.

And part of him thought he should have just let her stay in the back of that SUV, that he should never have chased her down and rescued her. That he should let her go down for this, let her be another body found along the river weeks from now, nobody to look for her.

But the thought of that, strangely enough, had been unbearable. She made him think of Jay. She made him think of a different world, a different life. A different version of Jack O'Sullivan, even.

"Jack?"

"Hmm?"

Ava was staring at him out of those impossible hazel eyes. "Where'd you go?" She laughed, despite the mess she'd gotten them in. "I said your name, like, three times."

He wanted her to say it again.

He wanted her to get the fuck out of this SUV and never see her again.

"We have to get rid of this car and this body. I think we need to drive far outside of the city and burn both." He took a breath and leaned back against the seat, bracing one hand on the armrest, the other on his gun. Fuck, he'd need to print and build a new gun, too.

Nothing connected to this most recent scene could be used on Cale Jacobson. There could never, ever be threads between one event and another. No trail to follow.

Nothing.

"Don't tell me you ate any Dove chocolates at *this* scene," Jack added.

Ava snorted. "No," she said. "Because *you* had my purse."

She said it like an accusation, as if it was Jack's fault Ava had left her purse behind and he'd had to rescue both her purse and her ass.

He reached into the back seat and grabbed it for her, holding it out to her wordlessly.

"If you ate my chocolates," she said with a shake of her head.

"Then you can consider it payment for saving your sorry ass," Jack said.

"*My* sorry ass?" Ava scoffed. "It was worth it. I was getting *intel* from that guy, and I had actually already escaped from the ropes when you finally got there, thank you very much."

And just like that, every ounce of calm he had spent years forging was gone, burned away by the flame that was Ava Cavalcante. Anger, white-hot and fierce, melted the space between them.

"What the *hell* were you thinking, running off to a club where people knew you? Where you could get dragged away like that?" Jack snapped. "What were you *thinking*, going out as if half the city wasn't hunting for you?"

For the first time Ava truly froze. He had not seen fear on her, he realized. He had seen anger, spades of it, and a grief deeper than that. But he had not seen fear, even when he had been sitting on her hostel bed, waiting for her with a gun.

Then, slowly, a grin twisted across her face. "Oh, Jack," she said. "Don't start sounding like you *care*."

"I care," Jack ground out. "When you are jeopardizing my *job*."

Ava snorted. "You could have let them kill me," she said. "It wouldn't have stopped you from killing Cale Jacobson."

"We've been over this."

He'd been clear: He needed information she had, because she knew things, knew *people* he didn't. And he needed to control the collateral so that she didn't ruin his damn job.

"You've rambled a lot, yeah," Ava said. She leaned across the center console, her chest heaving, her eyes crackling. "In fact, you never shut the fuck up."

Jack took a deep breath. And then another.

He was angry with Ava, so angry it was burning him alive. But he couldn't afford that. Couldn't afford anger, or anything else, not when there was chaos to manage. A body to get rid of. A *body*.

Usually Jack didn't worry too much about the body. There was only one, a clean hit, something that looked like a random mugging. Untraceable bullets. A piecemeal gun, easily deconstructed, the parts abandoned in dumpsters and gas station trash cans.

And then he was in the wind, long gone until the next time he resurfaced with a job to do.

One of these days it would catch up with him. He had always known that. He had just not quite expected it to be *today*.

Finally, he sighed. They could drive this SUV out of the city, stop along the way for a few gas cans—he had the cash for that—and burn the SUV and the body. By the time it was found, there would be little the cops could learn beyond, maybe, the identity of the deceased. But that meant hiking all the way back into the city, which limited his radius. Or they could drive back for his motorcycle, banking on his hope that Jacobson's people had cleared that warehouse by now, and he could ride behind Ava while she drove the SUV out of town.

Or option three: Drive back downtown toward Dynamo, through the heart of the city, where a blown-out windshield and a bullet-riddled car would have any cop with their eyes open rushing to pull him over.

"Your *thoughts* are loud," Ava complained. "Are you thinking of murdering me again?"

"I haven't ever thought about murdering you," Jack returned.

Thought about framing her for one, sure.

But that was entirely different.

"Why are we sitting in this dark parking lot by the river, Jack?" She reached across the center console and punched his arm, hard.

He flinched.

An automatic reaction, one he hadn't planned. He thought he had gotten rid of all those automatic tells, the stories his body told without his permission.

Ava, who had been slouched against her seat back, looking absolutely destroyed from the night at the club and everything that followed, sat up a little. "Are you . . . okay?"

Jack startled.

How many years had it been since anyone had asked him that, and meant it? Since—since Jay, probably, and Jack couldn't think about that.

"I'm good," he said. "We have to go back to the warehouse, Ava."

She groaned.

"Buckle your seat belt."

"No."

His gaze snapped to her as he started the car again. "What do you mean, *no*? Do you want to die in a car accident?"

"Are you going to crash the car?"

"Ava, we're driving back to a place where there might be armed men, if we're unlucky," Jack said. "Cops or Jacobson's hired assholes. So buckle your damn seat belt."

"And if we're lucky?" Ava leaned back against the seat again. "What then, Jack O'Sullivan?"

"If we're lucky, Jacobson's people have cleaned everything up so that it's spotless *and* didn't find where I concealed my motorcycle," Jack said. "*And* the cops haven't been through yet."

"Why would the cops come at all?" Ava asked as Jack pulled the SUV slowly back out onto the road. "We were so far from anyone. You don't really think anybody could hear gunshots way out there, do you?"

"Rule number one," Jack said as he rolled to a stop. It was getting dangerously close to dawn now, and that meant more people out, more people looking, more questions asked. More cops called. "Assume there is always someone watching, and assume there is always someone listening. And assume people always know more than you want them to, and more than they should."

"That's a paranoid way to live," Ava said, but her usual bite was missing from her tone.

"It's a good way not to die," Jack told her, and then the rest of the drive was in silence.

When they reached the warehouse district, Jack slowed the SUV. There was no sign of conflict as they approached—no cars, not even a trace of broken glass or blood. Like most things when it came to the ultrarich, they could afford to wipe the slate completely clean.

Jack breathed out.

Jacobson's men would have ensured that there were no cameras recording when they brought Ava here a few hours ago. But the cameras *would* be recording now, and it was imperative that whoever replaced Devin did not see Jack side by side with Ava.

Jack pulled his ball cap from his pocket and jammed it on his head and then pulled on his mask.

"Are you worried I'm contagious?" Ava asked him. "I mean, no shade if you're COVID cautious. I've just noticed you wearing that a lot, but not in the house."

He didn't grace her question with a response, just got out of the car and came around to her side, offering her a hand.

She took it, eyes sweeping up and down as if she was taking in new details, seeing something she hadn't before. "Are all hit men such gentlemen?"

"We prefer the term *contract killers*," Jack reminded her dryly. "It's more gender inclusive."

Her hand was warm in his. It was the first thing that made him realize his hand ached, the knuckles scraped and raw from hitting the guards he'd knocked out. How long had it been since he just made a fist and *punched* somebody? His MO was usually more removed, distant, weeks of planning followed by a single bullet.

"Let's be quick," he said, even though he had been the one lingering.

They found the motorcycle where he had left it, parked in a narrow gap between two long, low warehouse buildings.

By now the sun was well and truly starting to rise, and their window to leave the city was rapidly closing.

"I'll drive the motorcycle," Jack said. "I'll be right behind you, and you'll take the SUV. That way if we get—"

"Do you *know* how many stop signs I run?" Ava asked. "Give me the motorcycle key. I'll draw way more attention by driving the SUV over every curb in the Pacific Northwest. Also, I'm *not* driving the body. It's gonna start to stink."

"*That's* why you don't want to drive the body?" Jack shook his head. "No, Flight Risk, I'm not handing you the key to the motorcycle so you can take off and try to fight Cale Jacobson in broad daylight again."

"I could do that either way," Ava said, practically pouting as he walked back to the SUV with her.

"You can't," Jack said. "Because I'm taking the SUV key with *me*. If you behave, I'll even disable the alert so it's not beeping at you the entire time. And then I'll drive close enough to you to make sure it stays running."

Ava groaned. "I *hate* push-to-start," she complained. "They're way harder to steal."

This woman. This *fucking* woman.

"Stop stealing cars," Jack told her sternly. "Now we need to *go*. The SUV has enough gas to make it outside the city. I'll follow you, and you'll stay close. Is that clear?"

"And if I decide to eliminate the competition?" Ava asked as he helped her into the driver's seat. She groaned, pressing a hand to her ribs.

"And by *competition*, do you mean the person who saved your life?" Jack reached out impulsively, his hand closing over her wrist. "Drive *safe*, Ava. And don't pull anything wild."

"Okay," she said. Too easily, which meant she was planning something, but this would have to do. "I got Ms. Rae's phone, by the way."

Jack shook his head. "Who *aren't* you stealing from? And it seemed like Ms. Rae knew you pretty well—you've been going to see her there for a while now?"

"Well, she's been my domme for . . . a while, I guess? As long as I've been in Portland," Ava told him, as easily as breathing.

Most people, in Jack's experience, were a lot more hesitant to talk about kink and the role it played in their lives, however large that role may be. But Ava shrugged her shoulders to shame as much as she dismissed fear, and Jack couldn't tell if he respected it or feared what could happen to her.

Maybe a little bit of both.

"I think she tried to warn me," Ava continued. "Or threaten me? I couldn't really tell. But because it was one of those undercurrents—the messages under the things people say, the ones you're just supposed to automatically know or guess—I didn't get it, and then she left and those men came and put the cloth on my face . . . and oh that means they *did* drug me! And then they dragged me to the truck, and I think I bit one of them?"

Well, her face was going to be all over the news for yesterday's incident, so her DNA being on one of Jacobson's people was hardly making anything *worse.* But still. Biting?

"The phone could be useful," Jack curtailed the Ava ramble. Having the assistant's phone was going to be even more useful than having the copy of Cale Jacobson's calendar, but they needed to go, not stand around talking about it.

And Ava needed to *sleep*, but that wasn't an option now.

"Is your rental car a bust, then?" Ava asked. "What about the rental house?"

"Rule number two," Jack said. "Always leave the house knowing you might never come back, and pack accordingly."

"Well, I left with one Dove chocolate, some gum wrappers, and your gun," Ava called after him. "I don't even have a pair of underwear. Like, at all. You can't wear underwear in this dress."

"Just drive, Ava," Jack called without turning back. "We have places to be."

He had checked and double-checked and triple-checked that he still had the key to the SUV as he was walking away. Still, when he got back to the motorcycle, relief washed over him when he found he *still* had it.

He let her lead as they left town, but he drove slowly, cautiously, stopping fully at each stop sign so that Ava would be forced to do the same. Once they were on the highway, he drove beside her, scanning for threats as they went and ignoring her attempts to talk to him through her open window.

They stopped for gas cans and a few gallons of water once they were well outside the city, and when they finally pulled off the main highway, down a long, winding road that led deeper into the forest outside the city, Jack felt like he could finally breathe—as long as he avoided looking at the bright-eyed, red-haired mess in the driver's seat of the SUV.

The second they stopped, Ava had lots to say. About the location, about having to pee, about his chosen career field.

And Jack's phone had a single text from his client:

> There's been a wrinkle. We've encountered a second problem we need you to solve for us.

Jack was grateful for their ability to veil what they actually meant. There was nothing quite as stupid (or as likely to make him walk away from a job) as a client who wrote, in detail, what they wanted done. Anyone who said "I want to hire you to kill someone" over text was either a dumbass or a cop, and Jack wanted nothing to do with either.

He replied as Ava fussed at him about finding a place with a bathroom.

> Our agreement was clear. Limited in its scope.

Their response was immediate, too.

> We'll triple your original payment plan. We're in a tight spot with this wrinkle.

Jack's finger hesitated over his phone. He needed the money. He always did. And this job had paid so well he thought it would be smooth. Simple, even.

But he'd lost the rental car, the rental property, all of it in one fell swoop, and that had been an important investment of his cash to begin with. And this job reeked of complications, but to blow it—especially with a job as big as this one, with a price tag as high and a hit as high profile as Cale Jacobson—might mean that Jack's reputation would be so damaged he'd never work again.

He texted back:

Tell me more about the wrinkle.

He breathed out.

"Jack!" Ava was saying his name insistently. "Don't look at me. I'm going to go pee in the bushes."

Considering he'd seen her naked more than once, seeing her pee seemed like an unimportant matter at this point, but Jack left that argument for a different day and turned away politely.

His phone buzzed again.

A picture this time.

Staring back at him from his phone was a woman in a red dress, her fist raised above Cale Jacobson outside that café.

The mild morning felt suddenly stifling, the air in the forest dead and still. Jack's pulse was a drumbeat as he stared down at his phone.

His clients wanted him to kill Ava Cavalcante.

Chapter Fourteen

It hurt to pee, which was not a problem Ava had time for. When she reappeared from the forest, Jack looked a little sick to his stomach—not what she would have expected from someone who was supposed to be a seasoned killer.

"I told you he'd start to stink."

Jack looked at her distractedly. "What? He hasn't yet." He grabbed one of the gas cans and started splashing it across the seats and the body.

Ava shuddered and looked away. Despite her determination to kill Cale, this body was . . . a lot. Honestly, she hadn't put much thought into how *gross* it was all going to be. Her plan ended when Cale's life did, and she hadn't bothered too much with what came after. Certainly not living with the fact that she'd taken a life.

"Grab the other gas can," Jack said shortly.

"Who died and made you king?" Ava asked, masking a wince. "Wait, unless you've actually killed a king? Have you killed a king, Jack?"

Jack caught her flinch, despite her effort to cover it, his eyes flickering as he paused pouring the gasoline. "Never mind," he said. "Probably best not to lift something when you're injured. Just stand back and let me work, then."

"I want to know if you *have* killed a king," Ava repeated.

"I'm an O'Sullivan," Jack said. "Plenty of us *would*, if we had the chance. That isn't even special to me or my line of work."

"What the hell does that mean?" Ava wiped the back of her hand over her brow, where sweat was beginning to bead. Even that motion hurt, the pain in her ribs feeling as sharp as if she was being kicked right this minute.

Jack didn't answer, just splashed the last of the gasoline over the body, tossed the gas cans into the trunk with him, and held a lighter out toward the edge of the car, leaning slightly away.

"It would look cooler if you lit it and tossed it in," Ava observed.

"Don't believe the movies," Jack said. "Tossing the lighter wouldn't work."

"That must mean you've *tried* it," Ava said. "And when it didn't look cool, you've been salty ever since. But I bet I could get it to work."

The flames poofed up, and Jack stepped back.

Within seconds, the heat from the car was overwhelming.

"Should we be worried about a forest fire?" Ava asked suddenly. "I don't want to be like those dumbasses a few years ago who threw fireworks over the side of a cliff and lit half the state on fire."

"I damped down the soil first with the water from the gas station," Jack said. "And that's the best I can do. Now you and I are going to get a motel room somewhere."

"Oh, I thought you were too good for motels or hostels," Ava said. The Airbnb they'd stayed in had been fancy, at least by former-librarian-from-Iowa standards.

Jack grabbed her wrist and began towing her toward the motorcycle, which was parked far from the flames engulfing the SUV. "No, I just prefer not to stay in the places the police check first," he said. "Have you ever ridden a motorcycle before?"

"I—of course I have," Ava lied.

She'd had a pretty boring, law-abiding existence before this. But you couldn't really tell that to the wall of muscle who just saved your life, could you? If there was one thing Ava couldn't do, it was admit she wasn't good at something to an expert in the field.

"Just hold on to me," Jack grunted.

His eyes fell on her and then darted away again, like he couldn't quite bear to look at her.

That was new.

Even when she had been stark naked, and he had sometimes averted his eyes politely (not that he had to—his hungry look was kind of fun, if Ava was being honest with herself), he hadn't looked this . . . *nervous*.

"Do we need to wrap your ribs first?" Jack turned to her at the motorcycle, his face unreadable. He took her face roughly, his calloused hand eclipsing her jaw.

Ava's knees weakened at the touch. *Get it together, Cavalcante.* "My ribs?" she asked. She pressed a hand there, gasping when it hurt. Never breaking eye contact with Jack as she did. "No," she managed shakily. "No, I think they're fine."

He grunted and pushed her hand out of the way, his touch still rough but controlled. "Let me see."

"It's not a T-shirt, Jack," Ava said when he motioned for her to show him her ribs. "I can't just move it out of the way."

"Are you shy now?" Jack asked, looking almost surprised. "I'm not going to force you to undress, Ava. I just didn't think you minded if your ass was out."

She gaped back at him, the heat of the burning SUV overwhelming. Or maybe she was just blushing. "At the motel, then," she said. "Also, that's rude. Of course I mind if my ass is out."

"In front of who?" Jack asked, looking around the little clearing. "Never mind. Here, wear the helmet."

"I don't do that."

"Of course you don't," Jack said. When she didn't take the helmet from his hand, he reached out and placed it on her head with more care than she would have expected. "Or you wouldn't, if you'd ever ridden a motorcycle before."

"Hey! I told you that I *have* been on a motorcycle, actually." The *nerve* of this man.

Jack cut off her argument by mounting the motorcycle and tugging her on behind him.

She straddled it, an inch or so of space between her body and his, because come *on*. How was she supposed to be pressed against his body and not make bad choices later? Her library romance book club girlies would have classified this one as a *danger bang*. Which Ava had always thought was theoretical, until she was on the back of a motorcycle clinging to a hit man.

Jack tugged her forward. "Let's *go*." His voice was an impatient growl, something Ava felt all the way down her spine.

Across the clearing, the flames were reaching higher.

"Is it going to explode?" Ava shouted through the roar of the motorcycle. "I want to stay and watch if it's going to explode."

In answer, Jack revved the motorcycle, and then they were off, Ava clinging to him as they went.

<>

Jack didn't bother to tell her where he was going, or what motel he had found, or his plans around transportation. Or anything else.

They didn't return to Portland. Instead, Jack stopped at the edge of South Scappoose for gas, and then at Deer Island, a tiny thing nestled in towering pines, the elevation higher here than it was in the city. Even this late in spring, there was a chill in the air.

Jack looked like he could fit in anywhere, with his jeans and T-shirt and nondescript ball cap, the boots with no logo on them. Ava felt about as out of place as a polar bear on the beach, dressed in her tattered little red dress, which still clung to her skin.

Jack pulled into the parking lot of the motel and offered Ava his hand. Which was a good thing, because her head was pounding and her legs were jelly, and she wasn't sure she could have gotten off the motorcycle at all without his help.

"I'm going to pay for our room," Jack said. "And then I'm going to get you some clothes and get us a new rental car. *You* should stay here."

"What's wrong with my dress?" Ava managed, but it sounded half-hearted even to her ears. The dress was digging in everywhere, and Ava would *kill* for some sweatpants right now.

Jack ignored her, helping her to a bench outside the stretch of rooms.

It was a cozy little place, daffodils and a few early-blooming lupine nodding merrily from well-tended garden beds that stretched the length of the motel.

Ava's vision swam. She rubbed furiously at her eyes. The motel sign had a rose above script she couldn't quite decipher. *The Rose—the Rose* something.

There was a stretch of . . . twelve rooms, maybe? The garden was nice, and there was no cracked or patched glass, and the curtains all looked neat and clean.

A few minutes later Jack reappeared, holding out his hand to her.

She took it, despite herself.

"We're here for one night," Jack said.

"Just one?" Ava groaned.

The sun was high in the sky, around midday—her phone was dead, so she couldn't tell exactly what time it was. She needed to sleep for at least twenty-four hours.

Jack shrugged and unlocked the door, helped Ava to the bed, and then, when she flopped dramatically down onto it, stood there, surveying her with his hands on his hips. "How are your ribs? Your head?"

Ava grunted in response. She was too tired and sore to be appropriately verbal.

"Can I look at them?"

He was impossible.

"No. They're fine."

At least, they were fine-ish. Fine *adjacent*. They would be fine someday.

Right now she could breathe and move—and run if she had to, honestly. And that would have to be enough.

"All right. I'll check on them when I get back, then. I'm going out to get you clothes," he said. "Anything in particular you *don't* want?"

"What is your obsession with making me wear more clothes?" Ava rolled her eyes at him.

"I don't care if you're naked while we carry out this job," Jack told her abruptly. "But it *does* draw unnecessary attention. Which we already have way too much of, thanks to you."

Ava sat up swiftly, regretting it as the room spun rapidly, Jack's face distorting as her vision wobbled. "Excuse me?" she said. "Which one of us *shot* a man and had to do away with the body?"

Jack crossed the space between them so swiftly it disoriented her for a second time, his hand covering her mouth and forcing her back down onto the bed. "Keep your voice down," he snapped into her ear. "Do you know what the hell you're saying, Ava?"

Jack was all hard muscle, the hand pressed to her mouth strong and broad.

Ava let out a low moan, and he nearly jumped off her, his eyes flashing.

For a moment they stared at each other, chests heaving, breaths caught.

And then Jack was gone, hands clenched into fists at his sides.

Chapter Fifteen

Jack couldn't stay in the room with Ava Cavalcante a moment longer, not when she was staring at him out of those fierce hazel eyes, her dress ruffled and her hair messy, all fury and hunger and a fire he could hardly bear to look at.

Because all he could see when he looked at her was what his client was asking him to do. Pull the trigger. Put out the fire.

And a few days ago, he would have, wouldn't he?

He reached the motorcycle with a few long strides and was racing away from the motel a moment after that. There was a practical piece of this—he needed the motorcycle gone, he needed a new vehicle, he needed clothes for Ava, and food for both of them.

He needed to catch his fucking *breath*.

Jack pulled over outside town, his chest still heaving wildly.

The area around the town was densely wooded, the trees towering, the air cool in a way that comforted him, slowed his racing heart. It wasn't like Jack to lose control, not even in the version of his life when he had been happily married, when he had been Jay's beloved husband. Jack was careful, controlled—and that had translated well when he'd lost everything and ended up in *this* career.

So why couldn't he pull it together and do what needed to be done?

He'd planned to keep Ava with him until the hit was finished, mostly so she wouldn't get in his way. And then frame her, probably, or leave her behind to fend for herself while he lay low somewhere off grid, maybe back on his property in Montana, where nobody asked questions or looked too closely or even, really, knew his name.

Jack pressed a hand to his racing heart. He needed to get a grip, and then a plan. Briefly, wildly, he considered leaving Ava in that motel room, her auburn hair splayed across the pillows, and just abandon this altogether.

But there was a promise he had made, long ago. A person who needed the money he was going to make from this job.

Jack drew in a shaky breath and then drove slowly back toward town. When he was at the outskirts, he pulled off the road again, leaving the motorcycle underneath a bridge that led into the town. There was a small car rental agency a few blocks in. He could walk there and get a cheap rental, regroup from there.

His heart was still stuttering in his chest, beating an uneven pattern. As he reached town, his pace steady, his phone buzzed.

Another text:

Will you do it?

Jack hesitated before shoving the phone back into his pocket. This was going to take some finesse—he couldn't piss off his client, because pissed-off clients were dangerous, especially mid-job, and he couldn't overpromise when he didn't know what the fuck to do. If he could only make it to the damn gala, hold out for three weeks, things would be simpler. If Cale Jacobson was dead, this would *all* get easier.

Jack crossed the parking lot at the car rental center, scanning as he went. There were only a few cars—a small electric car, a sleek Suburban, a handful of sedans that looked at least a few years old, and a minivan that looked as if it had seen better days. Jack sighed. It wouldn't draw attention, sure, but it wouldn't be the smoothest ride he'd ever had.

The attendant at the desk inside was an elderly man who barely looked up when Jack entered, but waved him over with one wrinkled hand.

Jack asked for the minivan and paid for it with the prepaid card he used for jobs like this, wincing when it took most of the remaining balance on the card. By the time he was finally out of the parking lot, on his way to get more of the things they needed, his heartbeat had slowed.

There was a Safeway across town. He could take his time, get groceries and do some more research on Ava, on his client, on Cale and the gala Jack was going to be attending against his will. When he reached the parking lot, there were two more texts from the client.

Need update, the first one read.

Time sensitive. Please advise.

The client was still careful with their language, something that was unusual for even the more cautious people Jack had worked with.

Why? Jack almost asked. Instead, he typed and retyped and finally settled on:

First the primary job.

There was typing on the other end, and then:

This is critical. Please reconsider.

Jack closed the text and returned to the private browsing app he used to do much of his research. He preferred his laptop, of course, but the portable option was often the best one. Customers streamed by him into the store, most barely noticing the man in the minivan—people should really notice their surroundings more—and Jack dug in further to Cale Jacobson.

The three siblings were public, had been most of their lives. The oldest, Clara, was less public-facing than the brothers, but no less powerful—just harder to find. Carson, the man Jack had spoken to after he'd saved Cale's life, was in the background of every press conference Cale had ever done. And Cale himself?

Spoiled, rich, just like most men in similar positions. But now when Jack began his search, the first dozen articles were on the recent attack, including a particularly unhinged celebrity gossip column that had headlines reading "Bombshell Psycho Leaves Billionaire Reeling" and "Heartthrob or Heart-Stopper?" Jack sighed, pinching the bridge of his nose where the tension was beginning to build into a headache.

Leave it to Ava to go viral for looking hot while trying to murder somebody.

He sent the client a text:

Looks like she'd be an easy cover. Lots of media coverage about her.

It was true, even if the idea of framing her for the job was feeling more and more unpleasant. So why *did* this client want her dead? They had told Jack early on that they were a small collective of people who had been wronged by Cale Jacobson, and while Jack never took things a client said at face value, this had at least seemed realistic—Cale's company had had increasing PR issues in recent years, with more and more complaints of unfairness in claims denials and a recent investigation into insider trading.

The client typed for several minutes before responding:

Too much heat. Need it gone.

Jack sighed and closed his texts, returning to the research on the gala, and then combing the calendar Ava had duplicated for him. The address for Cale's mansion up north was difficult to find, but Jack combed satellite images on his map app until he found the general location. There would be no other event where Cale wasn't swarmed with security guards, especially with the high-profile, unsolved attack. The gala would be crawling with security, of course, but Cale would be less likely to be personally surrounded at all times—and even so, that was weeks away, the delay dangerous in Jack's line of work.

Unfortunately, for better or worse, Jack's client was right about one thing: The only way for this heat to die down would be if Ava Cavalcante were out of the picture.

Chapter Sixteen

Ava couldn't manage to get that fucking dress over her head, so she fell asleep with it still on, the dress holding her together. There was blood on her—some her own, some maybe belonging to Cale Jacobson's hired muscle.

When she woke, it was overcast but still light out. Her whole body ached, especially her ribs, but she pushed herself up as the key clicked in the lock.

Jack reentered, a new car key in one hand and several paper Safeway bags in the other. He set the keys down on the table near the door, locked the door firmly behind him, and then set the groceries down, all without speaking to her.

There was a small refrigerator humming in the corner of the room, which Jack arranged groceries in meticulously. As meticulously as he shot the man who had hurt her. As meticulously as he poured gasoline on a truck and a body. As meticulously as he *touched* her.

"Hi," Ava said. "Do you usually avoid greeting the people you're sharing a room and a murder with?"

Jack crossed the room, stopping directly in front of her. "Get up," he said, because social norms apparently meant nothing to him. "Let me help you out of that dress."

"First you want me to put clothes on," Ava complained. "Then you're demanding I take them off. What's next?" Surely he could see why this was confusing.

Jack hooked a hand under her arm and scooped her off the bed with unnerving ease. "Do you ever stop flirting?" he asked, turning her slightly so that he could reach her zipper.

Ava's stomach flipped violently.

"Oh," she said, peeking at him over her shoulder. "Is *that* what we're doing?"

His warm, heavy hand stilled at the nape of her neck, chasing shivers down her spine. "Ava."

"Jack."

"What we're doing," Jack said, then cleared his throat. His voice had dropped an octave, the way it had when he'd found her in the warehouse and left six bullets in the man who'd hurt her. "Is serious. It's deadly fucking serious, Ava Cavalcante. And you need to stop forgetting that."

Jack eased the zipper down and then tugged the dress off, helping Ava as she shimmied out of it.

When she had extracted herself from the dress, he did not release her, his hands still on her shoulders, her dress pooled on the floor.

Every bit of her skin felt like it was aflame, every ounce of her *alive* in a way she was not sure she had ever felt. Maybe in her life.

Jack's index finger trailed a path down her shoulder, tracing the curve of her body. "He hurt you," he said softly.

Ava shivered. At his touch, at his words. "I'm all right," she said. "Jack, I—"

He spun her to face him, his hands rough. She wished they had been rougher. "I would have killed him slowly," he said. "If I had known. Those six bullets were a mercy."

Jack's dark eyes flared dangerously. He opened his mouth like he wanted to speak, but then his eyes swept up and down her body, slowly, consuming every inch of her.

Ava drew in a shaky breath. The pain had faded into background noise. *Everything* had faded into background noise—this job, this motel room, all of it. "You're . . . you're staring," she said.

You're seeing *me,* she wanted to say. But she found, despite this, that she couldn't bear to pull away from him.

Jack tilted his head, the look that flickered in his eyes all danger. "Do you want me to stop?" he asked.

Time slowed, the little motel room falling away until the only thing that existed was this moment, was—

Jack.

"No," Ava breathed. "No, I don't want you to stop."

Jack's hands tightened on her arms, and he moved her away from the bed, toward the center of the room. He paced slowly around her, his eyes never leaving her.

"Jack," Ava said. She needed—she needed him to stop staring like he could see right through to her *soul.* To all the damage she carried.

His steps slowed, his eyes flashing to meet hers.

"Ava."

His voice was low.

He was—a bad idea. A danger to her, to others. He had killed before and he would kill again, and again, and again.

He had saved her life. When he touched her, it was electric.

"I want—"

What *did* she want?

She wanted so few things these days. She wanted Cale Jacobson dead, and she wanted a shower and another nap, and she wanted some chocolate, and she wanted Jack to be so rough with her that she forgot everything else in the world. She hadn't fucked anyone since Ari, and what did it say about Ava that the first sex she'd wanted after losing her wife was with a violent, dangerous criminal?

Ava took a step toward him, and the pain rushed back in.

In an instant the hunger in his look evaporated, concern replacing it before the mask settled over his face again. There was not much use for concern in a business like his, she supposed. But she had seen it, brief as it was.

"Before—anything else," Jack said, clearing his throat again. "Before anything else, let me help you get a shower and see to your injuries. Come on."

"That's not what I want." Ava's voice sounded whiny, even to her own ears. Bratty, Ari would have called it. But Ari was always calling her a brat. Ava's chest ached at the memory.

"Mmm," Jack said. As clear a dismissal as anything Ari ever did when Ava's brattiness got the best of her. "Do you want to take my arm? Or I could carry you."

He was fully dressed and Ava was completely naked. Again.

It wasn't *fair*.

"You should be naked," Ava blurted as she took Jack's arm.

Jack's dark eyebrows shot up. "You want me naked?" he asked, a slight grin tugging at his mouth.

The carpet beneath Ava's feet was soft, and she focused on that sensation, focused as hard as she could so she would not have to feel the muscles of the arm she was leaning on or feel the weight and heat of his gaze.

"I just mean it's not fair that you're always clothed and I'm not."

She wasn't making sense. It was the vulnerability, that she was always vulnerable, always a mess, and he never seemed to be either of those things. And she had always hated vulnerability, even when she'd had a loving wife who never held it against her.

Oh, it was definitely a smirk on his face now.

"I'm sure I can oblige you, Ms. Cavalcante," Jack said. "I wasn't planning on getting in the shower with *this* on. Though in fairness, I do think your nudity has been *your* choice."

"Not when you were waiting for me at the hostel," Ava groused as Jack pushed open the bathroom door. "*That* was an ambush."

"You walked right in," Jack said. "I wasn't hiding. It's not much of an ambush if the danger is in plain sight."

"And that's you?" Ava asked as he laid a towel down and then helped her to a seat on the closed toilet before he started the water. "The danger, in this equation?"

Jack's eyes found hers again, dark and unbearable and unsettling in a way she felt . . . well, in all the places that mattered. "Do you think I'm not, Ava?" he asked. "Do you think I'm *not* the most dangerous person you've ever met?"

Her stomach flipped, though not entirely in an unpleasant way. It *should* be in an unpleasant way. But the feeling was warm, and curious, and . . . yes, hungry.

"Am I not the most dangerous person *you* have ever met?" she asked. "I attacked Cale Jacobson in broad daylight."

"That makes you infinitely less dangerous, actually," Jack said practically, dumping most of the motel body wash into the bathtub. "Do you like roses? I hope you like roses, because this motel has roses on every-fucking-thing."

"Don't change the subject," Ava said. "I *can* be dangerous." She *could* and he should take it seriously. But it was strangely comforting, too, to even now be cared for as if she were *not* an infinitely destructive force.

He turned back to her, rolling up his sleeves. "I'm going to lift you and put you in the tub," he said. "Unless you have an objection."

"I *always* have objections," Ava said.

In her library days, she had taken to saying *Objection, Your Honor* during staff meetings whenever she felt things were going awry. In retrospect, that was probably one of the many factors her former colleagues disliked about her. She'd had only one friend, a kind older woman named Lizbet who used to remember Ava's birthday and bring her a plate of snickerdoodles every year.

Jack waited patiently, crouched at the bathtub, those sleeves rolled up to reveal infuriatingly well-toned forearms.

"Yes," Ava said in annoyance, when it was clear that the bratting had gotten her nowhere. "You can put me in the bathtub."

Jack lifted her, more carefully than he had any right to, and set her in the growing heap of rose-scented bubbles.

The warm water burned in some places, where her skin was scraped, but her sore muscles eased almost instantly.

The shampoo was far out of reach, but Ava reached for it anyway, grunting a little as she scooted forward.

"Let me," Jack said.

"Didn't you promise to be naked?" Ava asked. "Why are you still clothed?"

She had always been bold—in fact, when she was fourteen, she'd had sex for the first time when she'd pointed at a boy leaning against a locker in her school and said *You, with me* and brought him back to a quiet place behind the bleachers. But this version of her was something past bold.

Reckless, maybe.

Racing toward danger just to feel something.

It was an instinct Ari had helped her curb, back when there was an Ari. Back before Ava's entire world had been ripped to shreds.

"If I do take off my clothes, you're going to behave yourself while I see to your injuries," Jack said. Not like a negotiation. Like an ultimatum.

Ava *humphed* loudly even as her heart raced faster in her chest. "I never behave," she said. "It's what makes me charming."

"I was going to use the word *bratty*," Jack said calmly. "And you badly need your scrapes cleaned and your ribs wrapped, and I'm going to do those things before—"

"Before anything fun," Ava repeated with a sigh. She couldn't take her eyes off him—the corded muscles in his chest, visible through his shirt. How was she supposed to listen to a *lecture* on wound care right now? "I remember."

"How can you be in this much pain and still be this . . . sassy?" Jack sat back on his heels and looked at her with a flicker of amazement on his face.

"I'm good at pain," Ava blurted before the full meaning of her own words caught up with her. "Now take off your shirt. Please."

Jack hesitated for a moment and then shrugged off his flannel, his eyes never leaving hers. "What is it you want from this, Ava?" he asked softly.

He dragged the thin cotton tank top over his head next. He was fully shirtless now, his chest and abs as tightly corded as she had imagined they must be.

"What we all want," Ava shot back, her eyes sweeping up and down and lingering at the bulge pushing against the front of his jeans. "To have a good fucking time before I die."

Jack's expression shifted, some of the intensity masked again. "Is that what's waiting at the end of this for you?" he asked.

"Oh, hell no," Ava said. "This isn't therapy. I was planning to ride you until I can't think, Jack, not have a heart-to-heart about our feelings. Unless you wanted to talk to me about why your emotional baggage pushed you into a line of work where you're making money from killing other humans?"

The mask slid firmly into place again. There was no emotion, not a hint of it.

"No heart-to-hearts," Jack said with a nod of his head. "Let me wash your hair."

He cupped the back of her neck with one hand and lowered her into the warm soapy water.

Ava was weightless, held by the water, held by Jack. *Held.*

He ran his other hand slowly through her hair, untangling the knots gently. His calloused fingers traced lines on her scalp, the headache that had been clinging to her for days finally receding.

When Jack pulled her up out of the water, Ava couldn't quite look at him.

No heart-to-hearts. Just fucking, and killing, and running for their lives. And more of that tomorrow, until it all ended.

But still, but *still*—his hands were so gentle as he washed her hair.

He massaged the shampoo (also rose scented) into her scalp and then lowered her under the warm water to rinse. When he conditioned her hair, he used more than she would have, rubbing it in all the way to the ends of her curly auburn hair.

Ava found she didn't have the wherewithal, or the spirit, to comment on Jack's lack of complete nudity. Not when he was looking at her like *that*.

"I didn't want to know," Jack said after a long silence in which he gently rubbed soap up and down her arms and legs. "Why you're doing this. Why you ended up here. I looked into you, because I look into everyone. I know about the medical debt and the credit card debt. I know about the 5Ks you used to run, and the club where you meet with your domme. I know about your library science degree, and I know about the job loss, and I even know what your coworkers say about you on the internet."

"Was it Linda?" Ava blurted, because this was veering dangerously close, again, to the kind of vulnerability her life no longer had space for. "It's always fucking Linda."

"It was someone named Lizbet, actually," Jack told her.

That stung more than it should have, but Ava squared her shoulders anyway.

"But what I don't know is the *why*," Jack continued. "I don't know what you lost or who you lost, or why you think it's Cale Jacobson's fault. But I don't think death is the only thing waiting for you at the end of this, and if *you* think that, then you're too volatile to do this with me. You'll get me as far as Cale Jacobson's party, and Ava . . . the rest I'll have to do alone."

Chapter Seventeen

Ava braced her hands on the tub and pushed herself to a sitting position, her spine straight.

"You'd have to kill me," Ava said.

Jack arched an eyebrow at her, a look that said he very much *could* stop her, and quite easily at that.

It was more serious than she had ever been with Jack, and she could tell that he could see it, too, could see the wildfire in her eyes, ready to burn everything down.

"I'm not going to kill you, Ava Cavalcante," Jack said firmly, but he was not looking at her when he said it. "But you're not going to ruin this for me. I have reasons, too. Do you understand?"

"I do speak the same language as you," Ava snapped. He was an asshole. He was an asshole, and controlling, and she knew all this—*she knew all this*—so why was it hitting her this hard now? Why was the anger so fierce she was shaking? "You should get the fuck out of the bathroom. I can do this alone, since you're all about that now."

Jack hesitated, suds dripping lazily from his hands. "Ava, I—"

"Get the fuck out!" She wanted him gone as badly as she wanted him inside her. She wanted to wrap her hands around his throat as badly as she wanted *him*.

He stood, wiping his hands and arms on one of the towels, and nodded to her before stepping back.

He was halfway out the door before Ava pulled herself to her feet with a small, pained grunt. "Wait," she said. She'd have him, have *this*, if she could have nothing else.

Jack turned, his look guarded. "Do you need—"

"Fuck you. I don't *need* anything," Ava said. "I want—I want *you*."

He crossed the space between them so fast Ava lost her breath, and then he was in the water with her, his hands at her waist, lifting her off her feet, pressing her against the wall so hard it rattled her.

"Ava," Jack breathed against her mouth. "Ava, we *shouldn't*."

"Yeah," Ava said, her hand fumbling at his zipper. "But we're going to."

Because fuck it all. If this was what it took to stop feeling the miserable cocktail of grief and fear and anger, to stop *feeling* at all, Ava was going to jump at the chance.

And then his mouth was on hers, hard and rough and bruising, and his tongue was in her mouth, and Ava couldn't tell where she ended and he began.

When he drew back for a moment, his chest heaving, his pupils dilated so much she could barely see the brown of his eyes at all, Ava laughed, tipping her head back and letting it thump gently on the wall behind her.

"I need to rinse," she said. "Jack, I'm all soapy."

He grunted, nudging the faucet so that it sprayed above them, blinding her momentarily.

Ava sputtered, but he pressed in harder, ignoring the water. "Whatever you want, little firecracker," he said. "Are you wet enough now?"

A moan escaped her lips, something feral and hungry and sharp. "Jack," she gasped. "Get your clothes off."

She tugged his zipper down, and then shoved at his jeans, which were wet now, too wet to easily drag off him.

Jack set her down briefly, peeling his jeans and boxers off and kicking them aside before he lifted her again, pressing her back against the wall. He was—bigger than he'd felt when he'd pressed against her.

Ava stared for a moment, and then caught his gaze, the twist of his lips, and blushed.

"Fuck you," she whispered.

"Working on it," he said, and then he kissed her again, slower and softer and crueler, and Ava could think of nothing else. There was here, there was right now, there was Jack's skin on her skin, and his hands holding her up by her hips in a grip that would leave bruises.

"I want you inside me," Ava snarled.

He laughed, a sound she hadn't heard from him yet, something that made her feel warm all the way through. "You can learn to be patient," he said.

"No, I can't," Ava said. "Fuck me right *now*."

"I know you go to that domme to get tied up and topped," Jack said into her ear, in that low voice, that half growl that made Ava's insides twist. "I just didn't know how much you needed it."

Ava squirmed, his words, his tone, all of it going straight to her clit. "Fuck you," she said. "You don't know what I need."

"You need to be fucked hard and spanked harder," Jack said. "But that last part will have to wait."

Ava gasped as he slid inside her—she was slick with cum, but the stretch of taking him so fully still hurt, hurt in the best way. Hurt in a way she never wanted to stop. "Fuck me hard," she whimpered. *"Jack."*

He thrust inside her, slamming into her so hard she hit the wall behind her with a hard thump. "Anything you want, Ava."

"Anything?" she asked.

He freed one of the hands holding her up and slapped her ass so hard she knew without looking that he'd left a handprint. "Anything," he said.

Ava had no space left for words after that, as he thrust, hard and fast, no space left for anything but moaning, no space left for anything but *him*, inside her, filling her.

The water was still falling, steam still rising, and he was the only thing she could see—his face, inches from hers. His chest heaving, his arms tense where they held her up.

Unbidden, the image from last night returned—Jack's face when he saw her injured, Jack turning on the man who had hurt her, Jack firing three rounds with unerring accuracy. Unexpectedly, Ava's body responded in kind, and she contracted around him, her body trembling from pleasure as wave after wave of her orgasm rushed through her.

He finished just as the last waves of it were coursing through her, her clit still trembling.

Ava's ears were ringing as Jack set her on her feet and turned the water off. Her knees felt wobbly, too.

Jack grinned down at her as he helped her out of the tub. "You good?"

"Am I *good*?" Ava shook her head at him. "You're incorrigible. And insufferable. And some other insulting thing that I can't think of right now, because you fucked the thoughts out of me."

Jack arched an eyebrow at her again, humor still twinkling in his eyes as he grabbed her a towel and wrapped it around her carefully. "How are your ribs after that?"

"You did *that* to me and you're still worried about my ribs?" Ava stared back at him, dumbfounded. "No, don't cover that up. Stay naked."

Jack tipped his head back and laughed, a sound so warm and bright it took Ava's breath away for a moment. "*You* are incorrigible. And yes, I'm still worried about your ribs. That's why I didn't lay you out on the bed. I thought your ribs wouldn't respond well to me on top of you."

"Everything else would have," Ava told him, drawing another laugh.

"Am I not allowed to dry off?" Jack asked, holding the towel in the same hand that had smacked her ass.

She twisted to look at it. The outline of his handprint was still there, and firmly so. "No," Ava told him. "You can dry off, but you can't get dressed. That's my rule for the evening."

Jack lifted her unceremoniously and carried her back out of the bathroom. He set her on the bed, ignoring her noises of protestation. "Do you make the rules, then?" he asked.

"I *always* make the rules."

"What does your domme say when you tell her that?" Jack asked her conversationally, running the towel through his hair.

"Not much," Ava told him. "Usually she's too busy tying me up."

"Or gagging you, I assume," Jack added, drying himself with militant efficiency. "Are you going to dry off and get dressed, or lie there all night?"

"What do you have against rest?" Ava said. "And excuse me, who said anything about gagging? You don't even know if I'm into that."

"Are you *not*?" he asked.

Ava was into most things. She'd been into everything, when it came to Ari. Her kink was just Ari, honestly, the way her wife had been able to make Ava feel it all. But now that Ava was alone, kink was a good distraction.

Jack was a good distraction.

And if both the kink and the desires for Jack were embarrassing, well, she was a little bit into that part, too.

"I'm not *not* into it," Ava admitted. "What about you? Have you played this way much before?"

They had just had sex, not particularly kinky, but his bossiness—Ari would have called it toppiness—seemed well practiced.

Jack shrugged one broad shoulder as he started pulling things out of the refrigerator. "Sometimes," he said softly, his voice a little distant. "I've played around with it before."

"Do you always top?" Ava asked, slowly massaging the towel through the ends of her hair.

Jack looked at her over his shoulder, grinning. "With you?" he said. "Yes, always."

Ava pulled her wet towel off and flung it at him.

He caught it easily. "I assumed you always bratted your way to the bottom," Jack said. "But feel free to correct my assumption if I am incorrect."

"No, Your Eminence," Ava said. "Though you can spare me the pretentious language."

Jack brought her a paper plate with a sandwich—turkey and Swiss on rye bread, with a neat slice of tomato and lettuce—a small handful of carrots with hummus, and a few strawberries.

"Dinner," he said. "You haven't eaten in—I don't know how long."

"What time is it?" Ava squinted at the motel clock. In bright-red numbers, it read 6:57 p.m. "Maybe twenty-four hours, then?"

She hadn't felt hungry until he held the food out to her, though how he had known, or guessed, that she loved a turkey and Swiss on rye was beyond her.

"Does this work for you?" Jack asked. He was still naked, standing in front of her with his arms folded, watching her carefully.

"Unfortunately, I love turkey and rye," Ava told him. "I do hate for you to be right, though. And strawberries are ideal. Though I won't be eating a vegetable."

Jack turned away without responding to that assertation. "I'm making myself a turkey and provolone," he said. "And try the hummus before you rule it all out. It's an olive tapenade."

"You're an olive tapenade," Ava told him, but she tried it anyway. When his back was turned, so he wouldn't know if he happened to be right about that, too.

He returned a few minutes later, taking a seat in the one chair in the room as he ate his sandwich. "Don't get crumbs in the bed," he told her.

"Don't tell me what to do unless you're fucking me," Ava responded through a mouthful of her sandwich. Her carrots and hummus had been decimated, but she was hoping he wouldn't notice that part.

"Mmm," he said.

"Don't *mmm* at me, you oaf."

"All right, *please* don't get crumbs in our bed," Jack said.

"Wait," Ava said. *"Our?"*

"You just demanded I get naked and then rode my cock while I had you up against the shower wall," Jack said. "Are you shy now? And do you see more than one bed?"

"Right, I don't care if you're balls deep inside of me, but I *do* like to have my space when I'm sleeping," Ava said. "So don't you dare cuddle me, understood?"

Jack mock saluted her, but his eyes were serious. "When you're finished eating, we should talk about what comes next."

"When I finish, I was thinking about getting on my knees on the carpet over there," Ava said.

Jack nearly choked on a bite of his sandwich. "Oh."

"Yeah, *oh*. But if you have super-serious important updates on our murder date, we can of course do that first." She said it in the sweetest tone she had, which was not saying much.

"No," Jack said, leaning back in his chair and surveying her with a smirk. "No, I think I prefer you on your knees first."

Chapter Eighteen

Jack hadn't lost track of time like this in years. But Ava's mouth made that perfect round, red *O*, and her knees hit the motel carpet with the softest thump, and her hands were on his thighs, and the way she looked swallowing for him was—

Well, it was fucking celestial.

And that was how he lost hours, time slipping away until it was dark out, hours evaporating like water before he really returned to himself.

He was sprawled out on the bed, Ava tucked against the crook of his arm despite her earlier insistence that they would *not* be cuddling.

"We should rest," Jack said, turning over and looking at the clock. It was past ten now. "Are you still hungry?"

"I'm always hungry," Ava said. "Do you have any chocolate?"

He had bought the family-size pack of Dove dark chocolates, just for her. He'd just have to make sure she didn't bring any along the next time they left the motel, leaving a trail behind her that anyone could follow.

And he wouldn't think too hard about what any of this meant. Couldn't think about the hit on Ava, either—about how he was going to handle his client, about *why* they would want Ava.

Whatever he decided to do, they would need to lie low for a few days. When he told Ava they would need a few days to regroup, she closed her eyes and leaned more heavily on his arm.

"I want that motherfucker dead sooner than that," she said. "But I won't say no to a few more days like this."

Because she thought she would die doing this. She was single-minded in her intention to kill Cale Jacobson, though not in the cold, detached way Jack was—she was all fire, pain and heat and longing bundled into one petite woman with a perfect mouth and eyes he kept getting lost in.

"We can't stay *here*, though," Jack said. "And we need to make sure nobody sees us, gets to know us, talks to us. Even this far away from the city, people are looking. Cale's people *and* the police. You even made the local news."

He could still do this—dig into his client, find out more about why they needed Ava dead, or if he couldn't find that, then some leverage to keep them off his case about killing her. Keep Ava with him until Cale was dead. Keep it all under *control.*

He could, of course, take the money and kill Ava Cavalcante.

Ava lifted her head and looked at him. "I did?"

"Don't sound so happy about that," Jack told her firmly. This was *bad* news. Many people thought they wanted their fifteen minutes of fame, until it happened—and Ava certainly didn't need that, not when the man she was after was as high profile and fucking *rich* as Cale Jacobson. "This isn't good, Ava. Everyone is looking for you."

"They wouldn't be," Ava said, her tone icing over, "if it wasn't *him.* If it was you or me or anyone else who was being attacked or harassed. They wouldn't care. There wouldn't be news, or a widespread manhunt, or anything else. Why does he get to be treated differently?"

That fury was back in her voice, the thing that usually stayed stuck at the edges, buried under the flirtiness and sassiness and refusal to take things seriously.

Jack shrugged as he pushed himself up off the bed. "That's the way it's always been," he said. "But regardless of why, that's the way it *is.* That's the reality we're working with. So we'll leave early tomorrow—"

"You lost me at 'early,'" Ava cut in. "No earlier than ten a.m., tops. Eleven if you keep talking my ear off like this. Besides, you said we had to lie low. So why not lie low *here*?"

Jack had never talked *anyone's* ear off, and certainly not Ava's, making her words even more ludicrous, but Jack just pressed on bravely. "We'll stay somewhere else, another town farther out of the city." He also wanted to scope out the location of the gala, see how close they could get before encountering obstacles, and then plan his way around whatever obstacles they found. Of course, once he found his way in, he could just leave Ava behind, which might be the least messy solution, all things considered. "We'll pay with the cash I have left—"

"What do you mean, the cash you have *left*? Can't you get more? Doesn't popping people for money make you, like, *rich* rich?" Ava made finger guns with her hands, mouthing *pop pop* as she did.

"It's not that simple, and it's not that easy," Jack said. "Part of flying under the radar means not withdrawing huge sums of cash at one time. Part of it also requires different banks, different names, different transactions over time."

"Well, and you couldn't have withdrawn enough before the start of this?" Ava threw up her hands.

"Ava."

"Jack."

"Do *you* have any cash?"

"No, I have a mission I don't plan to walk away from, remember?" Ava's laugh was hard. "*I* have maxed-out credit cards and a free checking account that's been overdrawn for weeks. You wanted to kick me off the team for the whole this-is-my-end-of-the-road shit, if I recall correctly."

"I don't want to kick you off anything," Jack said. "But, Ava, there *is* no team. We just *currently* have goals that are aligned. So we're working together on those goals."

"Like fucking me hard and spanking me harder," Ava said. She stretched, arching her back a little as she did.

Jack swallowed hard. She was impossible. And blindingly, brutally bold. The way she just came out and *said* it—

"Yes," he said. "Yes, like that. But you know what I'm saying. We both need to kill the same person, you for personal reasons and me because this is my *job*. I don't want you treating this like a mission that ends you, because that recklessness puts us both in danger, and I don't want you to be the reason I get caught."

"Right," Ava said. She sat up abruptly, pressing a hand to her bruised ribs as she did but suppressing the wince that must have tempted her. "And nothing matters to you more than your own damn safety. Living long enough that you can continue making money off shit like this."

Jack sighed and sat up, too. "Exactly," he said, though it wasn't true, or at least not the *whole* truth. "So we should talk about what comes next."

He stood and grabbed the bag of chocolates from the drawer he'd stowed it in, opened it, and handed her one.

"I start with at least three of those," Ava said, holding her palm out for more. "You need to know how this works."

"And you don't bring any when we gather intel or go to this party," Jack said.

"There are so many *rules*," Ava said. "How would you punish me if I disobeyed? Would you tie me up to do it?" She held out her wrists, eyes sparking at him.

"Take this *seriously*," Jack said. His headache had arrived in full force, the weight of the what-to-do-with-Ava question so heavy on him that he could hardly see a path forward.

"I'll take it seriously when I'm dead," Ava returned. "All right, whatever. Carry on with all the rules."

If she *didn't* treat this with more seriousness and less recklessness, then that was going to be sooner rather than later. Jack's hand tightened into a fist.

"We'll leave early tomorrow, find a different motel in a different town, and lie low for—oh, at least until next weekend. Then I'll make a few visits to some leads of my own, and we'll monitor Cale's schedule for any changes. The plan is still the party at the end of the month, but we need to solidify our way in, because this party will have ridiculous security no matter what—and it'll be tighter now that you've made a public attempt on his life."

"I want to be the one."

Jack paused, his body stilling at the weight of the seriousness in her voice. He stared back at her.

Ava had three wrappers balled up in her hand, the chocolates long gone. Her eyes were sharp and . . . haunted. "I want it to be me," she repeated. "I want him to know that I'm the reason he dies."

There was a whole collective of people who were going to be the reason Cale Jacobson died, but that was beyond the scope of what Ava needed to know.

"Ava," Jack said softly. "You haven't killed anybody. And you're angry at him, I can see that, but—"

"I'll do it," Ava said. "I'll do whatever you want me to do along the way, but you have to let me do that part."

When Jack hesitated, she swung her legs off the end of the bed and stood, squaring her shoulders as she looked up at him. It would be easier to just lie. To tell Ava that, sure, she could be the one to kill him. That they would make it there together after all, that they were a team.

"*Promise* me," she said. "Promise me I'll be the one to kill him."

The moment stretched out between them like a cord about to snap, all of it flashing in front of Jack—Ava darting out the café door, Ava dragged away at the club, Ava hurt on the warehouse floor, Ava on her knees in front of him. *Ava, Ava, Ava.*

"I don't know if I can give you that," Jack said softly. "When it comes down to it—"

"Then when it comes down to it," Ava said, those fierce eyes locked on his, "I'll do whatever I fucking have to."

And that, Jack O'Sullivan knew, was exactly the problem.

Chapter Nineteen

Jack woke early, before the first hint of dawn was visible outside their window. Sometime during the night, he'd crossed into Ava's space, and now her head was pillowed on his shoulder, his arm flung out across the bed, settled on her.

They were *cuddling*.

Jack eased his arm out from beneath her head, and she mumbled in her sleep, eyebrows furrowing. When he rolled out of bed and onto his feet, noiseless as always, she reached out one arm as if looking for him.

For *him*.

Jack had never been anyone's comfort. Not even when he'd had a husband who loved him.

He had been too isolated, too avoidant, too . . . too closed off.

Jack shook his head, as if that could clear the mental cobwebs. He packed their things—the small cooler he'd gotten from Safeway, the remaining groceries, the go bag he'd taken with him when he left the rental house outside Portland. They didn't have many next moves, at least not viable ones, but one thing he *could* do while Ava slept was get closer to Cale Jacobson's compound and do some scouting.

He shouldn't take her, either. She had heat on her unlike anything Jack had ever experienced. But she'd be *pissed* if he left her behind.

Jack looked down at her sleeping form and sighed before he moved quietly across the room to fish Ms. Rae's phone out of Ava's purse—how she had stolen it in the first place, much less held on to it through her kidnapping, was beyond him. He'd been able to guess Ava's passcode fairly easily, but with Ms. Rae, he had no place to start. Instead, he'd have to do his best at decryption, see if he could uncover anything useful still on this phone.

"You won't get in."

Jack startled, his shoulders tensing. He usually wasn't this easy to sneak up on, but Ava Cavalcante was constantly surprising him.

He turned.

Ava was wrapped in one of the motel sheets, leaning against the wall behind him.

"I thought ten a.m. was your earliest," Jack said.

"And I thought you'd just ask for the phone instead of sneaking it out from my bag," Ava said through a yawn. "Silly me."

"You're upset that I took a phone you *stole*?" Jack fought a smile. "If you have any ideas on how to get in, I'm all ears. I have some decryption software on my laptop, but that's lengthy, and it isn't my main skill set."

"Your main skill sets being murdering people for money and making me come," Ava said.

Jack choked.

"Am I wrong?"

Jack shook his head.

"Who's Jay?" she asked.

Jack froze. *"What?"*

"You say his name," Ava said curiously. "In your sleep. Who was he? Was—"

As if on cue, his own phone buzzed—if Jack had to guess, it was probably another increasingly impatient message from his client, telling him that Ava needed to go. He rarely felt anything but trepidation when clients texted him, but this—this was a welcome relief. Anything to avoid answering questions about Jay.

Who he apparently talked about in his sleep.

For a moment, in the predawn light, staring at Ava's fierce hazel eyes, Jack had to fight the urge to open his mouth and tell her everything.

Not just about the client, their proposed hit on Ava, but the rest, too. That he'd been married, once. That he'd been happy, once. That it was his fault Jay was gone, that it was his fault he was this way now. That if she had any sense, she'd leave now before he destroyed her like he'd destroyed every good thing he'd ever had.

Jack shook his head, clearing the cobwebs away. That was madness. He couldn't tell her that, not ever. He'd get through this and then leave her behind to fend for herself, and of all the things he *could* do, that option was probably the kindest.

"Earth to Jack," Ava called, waving the sheet at him.

"Sorry," he said softly, and meant it. "We need to find a way into this phone, so if you know anything, tell me now."

"Only if you take me with you instead of sneaking off," Ava said sharply. That look in her eyes was no longer playful. Instead, the undercurrents there were deadly.

"I wasn't—"

"Going to go scout around Cale Jacobson's mansion today?"

Her words stopped him in his tracks. That was exactly what he'd been planning.

Ava let out a long-suffering sigh. "Why would I help you, Jack?" she asked. "Why would I help you with that phone, or anything else I know, if you're going to run off and leave me first chance you get?"

So I don't have to kill you, Ava Cavalcante.

That was what he wanted to say. Wanted to blurt it right out and watch her eyes widen. Wanted it all out in the open.

But instead Jack cleared his throat and said:

"Can you be ready in ten minutes?"

"Definitely not, and getting from naked and sleepy to ready and out the door in ten minutes is an unreasonable ask of *anyone*," Ava told him from under the sheet, but he could see the outline of her ass as she wiggled it at him. "And you didn't answer my question."

"I bought you clothes," Jack told her, pinching the bridge of his nose. Clearance Walmart sweatpants were going to have to do, since she hadn't given him any guidelines when he'd asked the day before. He tossed the bag to her and ignored her question a second time, because what could he say?

Ava wrinkled her nose. "You got me sweatpants that say *Dog Mom* on the butt? And are these . . . did you get me granny panties, Jack? Tell me your real full name so I can full-name you. You need to feel the extent of your shame."

Jack *had* told her his real name, though he couldn't blame her for thinking that was another stretch of the truth.

"I didn't know you *wore* underwear," Jack told her honestly.

Ava punched him in the arm, hard. "Get out of here."

"That's the plan," he said. "Get dressed. Underwear or not. And are those really called 'granny panties'? Or is that just a horrible name *you* gave them?"

"Everyone calls them that," Ava said, rolling her eyes as she swung her legs over the side of the bed. "And don't look at me, I'm naked."

"You were naked when you were riding me last night," Jack said, leaning against the wall behind him and folding his arms, surveying her with a grin. "And when you got on your knees for me like a good girl. And when you cuddled me all night. But if it really matters to you now—"

"Excuse me, *I* cuddled *you*?" Ava snatched the underwear and started pulling on a pair—which was honestly a shame, because covering that ass seemed sinful to Jack. "You wouldn't let me *move* last night. Every time I rolled around, you'd reach out with those big long arms of yours and yank me against you. I couldn't have snuck out of here if I'd wanted to."

Jack arched an eyebrow. Why hadn't he considered, last night, that she might still try to leave? It gave him pause. How sure he'd felt that she'd stay.

Only one night after she'd given him the slip, hot-wired his rental car, and nearly gotten herself killed.

"Did you want to?" he asked. "Leave?"

"No," Ava huffed as she pulled on the sweatpants. "But you're buying me a thong today. Maybe a few. And you're buying me a nice dress because I'll need a name-brand cocktail gown to get close to a billionaire. Which you would *know* if you were any good at this."

"I've never had to buy a dress to do my job before," Jack said. He'd never considered working with a partner, not even once in the long, winding journey that had brought him here. "Get a shirt on, and we'll go."

"I'm assuming you didn't buy me a bra," Ava continued complaining. "Really, Jack? Are my tits just supposed to be free balling in my shirt?"

"Free balling?"

"You heard me." She pulled on a soft yellow T-shirt that read *I'm Not Bossy, I'm Just the Boss* above a coffee cup. "And now I'm dressed like a dog owner who lets her dog shit in somebody else's peonies and then leaves it there. Who also wears slogan T-shirts. From Walmart."

Jack opened his mouth to respond, but a heavy knock on the door stopped him in his tracks.

"Police!" a man's deep voice sounded at the door. "Police, open up."

Jack hooked an arm around Ava's waist and hauled her back into the bathroom he'd fucked her in yesterday.

"What the fu—"

Jack clapped his hand over her mouth. "Shh," he snapped in a hushed voice.

Another series of heavy knocks rattled the windows of the small motel room.

Ava's eyes were wide, but at least she understood the stakes now. Jack released her, stepping back slightly.

Fuck.

If they breached the door, there was no way out. Not without killing a cop, and that would bring a federal manhunt for Jack and Ava. That would be heat that was impossible to stay ahead of.

Fuck, fuck, *fuck*.

How do they know? Ava mouthed at him.

Jack shook his head. You had to always assume they knew more than you wanted them to. You had to *always* assume that you were closer to being caught than you should be. You had to *always* keep moving.

Jack *should* be long gone.

The loud knocking paused, and Jack breathed out. Then it resumed, but farther away.

Jack let out his breath, dropping to a seat on the edge of the tub. "They don't know, not for sure," he said softly. "Or they'd already be in here. But they know they're *close* to finding us, so they're going door-to-door to see if they can get a lead. Ava, we have to *go*."

Ava's face was pale, but somehow she looked less daunted by this turn of events than she should, less afraid. "You're still buying me a thong today," she said. She almost looked defiant as she said it.

Jack shot to his feet, his heart pounding. "I could go open that door right now, Ava," he said softly. "Tell them I picked you up at the bar last night, that I didn't know you were dangerous until I saw your face all over the news. Should I? Give me one reason to think you're taking this seriously enough, Cavalcante. That you're not going to get us *killed*."

It took everything he had to moderate his tone, to keep from snarling the words at her.

"I give good head, O'Sullivan," Ava shot back. She tipped her chin up and met his gaze, unrelenting. "And I know how to get into Ms. Rae's phone."

Jack grimaced. He *did* need that fucking phone—or it would at least be helpful. If they managed to make it out of here at all, that is.

He had decided, somehow, not to kill Ava. He'd decided to keep her with him until the job was done, to keep her from snitching on him in favor of a plea deal—because whether *she* knew it or not, she was one of the only people alive who still knew him by his full name.

Jack had even, stupidly, decided to fuck her. A decision that was beginning to complicate things.

"Fine," he gritted out. "Let's go. Take only what you can carry. Wear a hoodie, keep it low, and wear a mask. I have a box with the groceries—that'll throw off facial-detection software, and out here there are still enough people masking that people don't really think twice about it."

"Try masking in Iowa," Ava said. "Everyone stares at you like you have two heads."

Jack grunted, moving past her.

"Jack—"

"Go."

They didn't have time for more of her banter, her quips, the humor that melted him until it felt like he was defenseless.

Jack shoved his recent grocery purchases back into their sacks—some into his duffel, so there were fewer items to carry—and grabbed his bags. He kept them packed. He'd had luggage packed even when he and Jay'd had that little apartment in Atlanta, back when Jack O'Sullivan was still trying to convince himself that he was someone who could stay in one place.

"I'm ready," Ava said, a little breathlessly.

Despite her defiance, her refusal to do this on Jack's terms, she was darting around, grabbing her belongings and shoving one foot into the sneakers he'd bought her.

The cops were a few doors farther down now, still knocking on doors. An elderly woman shouted at them to go away, and more voices were mingled now. Jack thought he recognized one of the owners, the nervous but flamboyant man with an impeccable sense of style who had checked Jack in the previous day.

"We'll have to be careful," Jack said. "And no, you're not ready. You're still running around. Finish *up*."

This would be tight—the odds of escaping without detection of any kind were low. The growing commotion outside could help, because it would be easier to get lost in a throng of people than sneak out with nobody else outside.

An insistent, flustered voice sounded sharply outside—

"You can*not* interrupt our guests' beauty sleep!"

Yes, it was the owner. Jack breathed out.

This could work. Maybe. If the cops were distracted by the owner fussing at them, Jack could get into the van without drawing attention. It sounded like there were two, maybe three, police officers, which meant they couldn't be *that* sure Ava was here. Crimes against billionaires always brought out an absolute army of cops.

"I could fit out the back window."

Jack stopped, one hand on his duffel bag. "I can't," he said. "And besides, I have to get the van or we'll have no way out of here."

"Come pick me up around back," Ava said. "You could leave out the door. They're not looking for you."

Jack hesitated. The look on Ava's face was guarded, cautious.

But she was offering this like a lifeline: her trust.

He could walk out that door, drive north out of town and up to Cale Jacobson's mansion. Leave Ava Cavalcante behind completely.

And she, impossibly, was trusting him not to.

Chapter Twenty

Ava could only hope that her own fear didn't show on her face. Why *would* Jack want to keep her around? He was probably already certain she didn't actually know Ms. Rae's passcode, and she'd proved to be nothing more than a liability so far.

A running theme in her life.

Jack stared back at her as red and blue flashing lights lit up the parking lot from the other side of the thick motel curtains.

The moment crackled between them like a live wire, Jack's fierce gaze meeting Ava's.

"All right," he said softly. "But be *ready*, Ava, because if I'm seen looping back, police are going to have questions. Lots of them. And get into the back seat."

She was never going to get to even ride shotgun, let alone drive one of their getaway cars.

Though upon reflection, that seemed like it shouldn't be at the top of her list of worries.

"If we're lucky, they haven't set up a perimeter yet," Jack said tightly. "Open the window. Be ready."

"And if we're not lucky?" Ava felt her heart flip in her chest.

She knew the answer. Of course she knew.

The cops would find her. She'd be done.

There would be no justice for Ari, no moment with Cale Jacobson dead at her feet.

And—

She'd never see Jack O'Sullivan's burning brown eyes again or feel those rough hands on her bare skin.

Jack shut the door behind him with a quiet click, and Ava nearly sprinted for the back window at the far side of the kitchenette. She pried the window open, hands shaking, and peered cautiously through. At the far end of the motel, near the corner, two cops stood, one leaning against the wall. They looked bored, and a little sleepy, but if they saw the woman they were looking for dive headfirst out of a motel window, they'd be onto her.

Ava looked desperately around her for something. Anything. When she looked down, she was clutching her bag so tightly her knuckles had gone white.

And Jack was nowhere to be seen.

Of course he wasn't.

She'd trusted him. She'd stayed last night, even though she could have slipped out from under his arm—despite what she'd told him. She'd actually stayed because being curled against his body felt *good*, and how stupid was that? That she'd stayed because she'd wanted to feel something, anything, for one more moment?

And now it was too late for her.

Well, Ava had no choice but to run for it—the cops would be back to her door, and it was only a matter of time until they checked security footage and saw her coming into this room, still in that tattered red dress. She had to run for it.

There was the squeal of brakes and then some shouting, and then the two cops who had been standing at the corner jogged away, rounding the corner to see what the noise and fuss were.

Ava's pulse pounded in her throat. Had that—had Jack—

There was no time to wonder. She tossed the bag Jack had bought for her—a Hello Kitty backpack, of all things—out the window and scrambled after it, just as Jack's minivan came tearing around the corner. He screeched to a halt as she sprinted for the van.

He was driving before she was fully in, at full speed before she managed to get the van door shut behind her.

Ava had to stay down, had to get out of sight, and she would—she would. But first, she reached up, closed one hand over Jack's arm.

"You came for me," she said.

Jack's gaze caught hers in the rearview mirror, though he didn't turn his head. "I promised you," he said finally, a weight behind his words that left Ava breathless.

Chapter Twenty-One

You came for me.

Ava's words haunted him through the long drive north later that day, to the little cottage rental he'd secured for them. They haunted him that night, and the next after that when they were lying low and avoiding talking about the fact that they'd fucked and weren't sure what to do next, and the night after that, and he worried, as he pored over yet another incomplete map of Cale Jacobson's compound, that they'd haunt him forever.

They haunted him when he watched the news reports around Ava only grow, instead of fade, when he dove into more research and found she'd been married, once. Widowed.

They haunted him when she avoided his eyes, and when she met them.

They haunted him, because they were the same words Jack's husband had said the day he died. The only words, when Jack found him. The last words Jack would ever hear, and they weren't even true, because while Jack had come for his husband, he hadn't come in time.

Now Ava was reclined on the couch in their small living room, staring at her phone, and Jack had the printed map in his hand, turning it absentmindedly.

"I don't want to be here forever," Ava told him.

She'd told him that every day they'd been here.

Jack grunted. "You know why we're here."

"You look extra murder-y," Ava told him. "Though you've looked like that all day."

Jack's client had been hard to pacify this week, too, asking many too-pointed questions about the delay and the fact that he'd been dodging their request to add Ava to his hit list. "*Ava.* I need to focus."

"*Jack.* I need to get started on the murder." She was mocking his tone—he knew she must be. Most shifts in tone were harder for Jack to read, something that had been hard to navigate in his relationship with Jay, even, but certainly with the world around him. He had not been good at predicting when someone's friendliness shifted to sourness or when kindness had burned away into irritation, and it had always cost him. But Ava, somehow, made sure he knew exactly where he stood with her.

It was both a blessing and a curse.

"If we could just get into the phone, which you *said* you could—"

"To be fair, I only said that because you were thinking of betraying me," Ava said, cutting Jack off. "It was, like, a freebie lie. Because it was for a good reason."

"That's not how that works."

"Are you a hit man or a self-help coach? Anyway, I know you're thinking of going into that little town—Gable? Mable? Maple? Oooh, I want pancakes. I want to come with you to the store, Jack." Ava swung her legs over the edge of the couch and dropped her feet onto the floor with a thump. "I pinkie promise not to talk to any cops."

Jack sighed. This was nonnegotiable, not that that would slow down Ava's impulse to argue with him about it. "For the hundredth time," he said. "No, Ava. You're staying here, out of sight. Aerial footage could pick you up. There are drone cameras so far away that you'd never see, and they'd be able to pick up your face. There are talkative townspeople. There are nosy local cops. There are extra patrols, because people are starting to look at you like—"

Like she was some folk hero. There were dozens of social media videos full of people saying things like *Actually, she was with me helping me and my cousin move* or *So I actually know this girl, she was with me doing our makeup and she totally has an alibi*, a joke Jack'd had to google to understand.

And there were more, too, videos talking about the inequities in Jacobson's company, videos criticizing the Jacobson family—Cale in particular—for shutting down any public negative feedback or calls for reform for years now. There were headlines calling Ava an impulsive, deranged woman. And there were headlines, fewer but still there, wondering why people loved her so much.

"What are they starting to say? I know *TikTok* likes me," Ava told him, running her fingers through her dense curls. "They're calling me a hero. I think they just think I look hot in the red dress, though, and TikTok is, like, one hundred percent just thirst trap videos these days. I think it used to have more library content? But now it's just Pedro Pascal and that one singer the gays love, even though *I'm* gay and don't get the appeal—"

Jack had to look away, because the sight of her running her hand through her hair like that made him want to do the same, but rougher. The thought made his cock twitch.

"Don't let it go to your head," Jack said instead, wrestling for control of himself. They hadn't fucked since that impulsive moment at the motel, and Jack needed to keep it that way, keep himself clear of distractions. "Attention is a bad thing, even if it's positive attention. And no, TikTok is only one hundred percent thirst trap videos on *your* algorithm. That's about you and how you scroll, not about the app."

"Damn, are you defending TikTok?"

"Did you hear the important part?" Jack asked, exasperation seeping into his tone. "About not attracting attention?"

"Yeah," Ava said. "But it *is* a good thing, right? If people start talking about billionaires like Cale. If people start noticing the way men like him can get away with *anything*. If . . . if it gives people hope that things can be different. That billionaires aren't untouchable. That we aren't powerless."

Jack stared at her. She was confusing, and she was mesmerizing, and she held on to hope even when it didn't make sense. Because from here, it still looked like they were pretty fucking powerless.

"What will it take to get you to lie low for a few more days?" Jack asked.

Ava hesitated, a grin spreading across her face.

Her eyes sparked, sending warmth through Jack until he dropped her gaze.

"A thong," Ava answered, holding up one finger. "A decent breakfast. And—" She paused again, grinning wickedly. "You have to teach me your murder skills. Though I'm still disappointed I won't get to use the cool backstory I invented when we go into town."

Jack stood, brushing his hands against his thighs. Cale Jacobson's mansion could wait, at least for now. He was getting nowhere with it, anyway, and the gala was drawing closer. "My murder skills?"

"Yeah, the pew-pew. The punchy-punch. The—"

"Things have names, Ava," Jack said wearily.

"I know," Ava told him. "You're very easy to annoy. So you'll teach me?"

Jack's phone buzzed insistently. He jumped—he was losing his edge, jumping over the buzz of his phone. But he couldn't talk to the client who wanted Ava dead *and* look at her brilliant hazel eyes as he did it. "I need to take this."

He stepped outside.

The voice on the other end, as it had been during all communication he'd had with them so far, was garbled. "I need an update."

"The gala," Jack told them tightly. "Still the most logical next step."

"I want to talk about *her*."

Jack froze.

Ava was at the window to the cottage, dressed in a Walmart T-shirt that said *live laugh loaf* with a corgi on the front. It was small on her, just a little, accentuating the curve of her body.

"I told you," Jack said, "she's not part of the deal."

"She *needs* to be. This is imperative. As imperative as—" The client hesitated, maybe searching for the right words. They were good at this, almost as good as Jack was, good at making the words so vague they couldn't be used as evidence. "As imperative as our original objective. Maybe more."

"Why?" Jack blurted it out before he could call the word back.

Why Ava? Why now?

If Jack's client had been honest with him—and that was always a big if in a line of work where his clients were hiring him for murder—then they were a small collective of people who had been *hurt* by Cale Jacobson. Ava, then, should be an ally.

The internet certainly thought so. There were even, as Ava had proudly showed him, video edits of her grainy CCTV image to songs like "Solidarity Forever" and a popular new Taylor Swift song Jack had somehow never heard.

There was silence on the other end of the phone. Just breathing, harsh and distorted.

"While she's in the picture," the client answered finally, "the focus will be on her. Not him. That doesn't . . . align with our objectives."

Alarm bells had gone off for Jack from the very beginning of this job, not least because of how *good* the client was at this. But the precision of their language, the addition of Ava to this job . . . Jack needed to know more.

"I need more time," Jack said. "And I need more insurance."

Silence.

Ava rapped on the window, holding her hands up to him and mouthing *What the hell?* through the glass.

"What kind of insurance?" The gravelly voice at the other end was quieter. Careful.

"I'm sure our priorities are aligned, but—"

"A generous sentiment," the client interrupted him. "We'd like to see—"

"I need a way out." Jack cut them off. Too clear, too direct.

"A way out," the client repeated.

"Yes," Jack said. "A rented helicopter, or a boat headed south. Something."

"We can arrange that. The night of the gala." The response was immediate, clipped.

This client had no concern about coming up with money, then—for an escape plan, for a higher fee. For any of it.

"And the woman will be part of it?" the client prompted.

"After completion of the primary objective," Jack said, and then he hung up.

When he went back inside, Ava's eyes swept him up and down. "You look like you've seen a ghost," she said. "What the hell was that?"

"An important phone call."

"No shit."

Jack couldn't look at her. Couldn't look at her and imagine pulling the trigger. Couldn't look at her and imagine her without that light in her eyes, that bold, impossible light.

"If you want *me* to trust *you*, then *you* have to fucking trust *me*." Ava's words were sharp.

She was right. Of course she was right.

"Ava," he said softly. "I don't want you to get hurt." The words came out breathless. Soft. Uncomfortably genuine. "I just—my client is dangerous. And the less you know, the better."

It was true, as much truth as he could offer her, because she already knew too much. He was becoming more like her, bleeding truth before he could stop himself, littering details of himself in every interaction. It was fucking *dangerous*.

When she was dead silent, Jack looked back up at her.

Ava wasn't looking at him. "Let's go back to talking about the murder skills you're going to teach me," she said. Her voice was cold, distant, her eyes fixed on some point out the window. "Or I can tell you about the cover I made up for us."

Jack sighed. "I'll teach you to shoot," he said. "And I'm going to work on my cross-stitch while you tell me about the cover."

They definitely didn't need a cover. In fact, it would be better *not* to have some complicated story to stick to.

Ava's jaw was set, determined, belying the lightness in her tone as she spoke: "We're a young couple, wildly in love—"

Jack pulled his cross-stitch from his duffel. What kind of life had Ava been leading, that one single mention that Jack *cared* what happened to her was enough to shut her down? And since when did Jack care what happened to anyone but himself? "No, we're not wildly in—"

"In lust, then." Ava waved her hand airily, but her eyes remained hard. "Nobody can ever tell the difference. We're honeymooning on the Oregon coast. My name is Amélie Belle—very sophisticated, very fancy, there's definitely an accent on the *e*—and your name is Greg."

"Why do I have to be *Greg*?"

"Gary, then." Jack settled opposite her with his cross-stitch.

"*Gary?* Do I look like a Gary?"

"Would you prefer Gilbert?" Ava asked him cheerfully, sliding her sweatpants down and stepping out of them without a second thought. "Because that's where we're headed next. I'm determined that you're going to have a terrible name."

Jack focused his gaze on his needlework. "What do you have against names that start with *G*?" he asked her. "And do you walk around naked *all* the time?"

"Clothes are too loud," Ava said, and flopped onto the couch on her stomach in her underwear and T-shirt, facing away from him.

"Well, if you're done, we can talk about what else I can teach you," Jack said, ignoring that particular baffling comment. "Shooting, like we talked about, but you need more self-defense skills, and I can teach you some. We'll work on some basics of striking today, since we'll need to lie low a few days, and—"

"I know how to hit a man, Jack," Ava said. "And I'm frankly offended you don't think I do."

Jack opened his mouth to say he had seen her in that warehouse, but—she *had* hit the man who was holding her hostage. And she'd hit Cale hard enough that he'd still had a bruise the next day when he did a pitiful TV interview to talk about how he was strong despite how many challenges he had faced—challenges like being a billionaire. "All right," he said. "Have you done martial arts?"

"Kind of?" Ava said. "I watched a lot of WWE."

At his look, she burst out laughing, so loudly she snorted halfway through and clapped her hand over her nose and mouth. It was frighteningly precious, and if Jack didn't look away, she'd see how he felt about it, right there on his face.

"I'm fucking with you, Jack," Ava crowed. "I know WWE isn't the place to learn how to fight. That's where you learn how to *perform*. I've boxed for a few years. I know how to hit."

"Good," Jack said. "Do you know how to throw a man?"

"Does it have to be a man?"

"You can throw anyone you want, Ava, but you asked me to teach you some skills. Some of these could save your life."

"Who says I want it saved?" Ava turned her head and looked at him over her shoulder.

"I do." Jack heard the change in his voice before he really knew he intended to make it—the drop, the growl, the sound that made her body respond . . . well, like that.

He could see the shiver pass through her, see the blush creeping up her neck, and he moved his needle faster. *Focus on that, O'Sullivan,* he told himself firmly. *Not on the way her tits bounced while she squirmed at the change in your voice.*

"You're so bossy," Ava said. "But I'm still wearing the bossy shirt." She looked down, tugging at the hem of her shirt. "Oh, never mind, it's the stupid corgi one. I don't really get why people are obsessed with corgi butts, by the way."

"Ava."

"For the love of God, let's not do the Ava–Jack game again," Ava said. "Honestly, even *I'm* sick of it, so you're going to have to learn to stop saying my name like that."

"Do you want me to teach you or not?" Jack asked. "Because *you* brought it up."

A new realization slammed into him, one that took his breath away.

If Jack *didn't* take the hit on Ava, his client could very well hire somebody else. And she might need these skills to survive this—not just the police and the private security team after her, but another person like Jack. A person who could look ordinary and forgettable until the very last minute.

"*You* were the one who said I need it, Mister Smarty-Pants?" Ava's voice turned mocking, a little hard, knocking him back to the reality of their little cottage. "You act like you know everything. Has anyone ever told you how insufferable that is?"

"Many people," Jack said. "Many times."

"Women must tell you that at least once a day," Ava said. "And we should."

"Not just women," Jack said.

Ava rolled over and sat up. "Oh," she said. "Really? I wouldn't have pegged you—ha ha, get it?—as a bisexual queen."

"I don't know what label I'd use," Jack said cautiously. This was more new territory—sharing. Sharing anything, at all, with anyone. "But I know I like beautiful people."

"Cheers to that," Ava said.

"And I don't think I know everything," Jack told her. "I just—I have this one specific skill set, Ava. Which is making people *hurt*."

He didn't even mean for that one to affect her, but he could see by the way her pupils widened, the color all but disappearing, that it had. He should have guessed, based on what he had seen of her Snapchat and what he had seen of Dynamo.

"Usually I just prefer people use their skills *on* me," Ava said after a moment of taut silence. "But yes." She cleared her throat, recovering.

"But yes, *fine*, okay. I do very much want you to teach me your moves, pretty boy."

"You got it," Jack said wearily. "Boss."

Ava's eyes lit up. "So you admit it! You agree! I'm the boss forever and always, no take-backs." She punched him in the arm, harder than he would have guessed based on her size. When he rubbed at the spot, her eyes widened with delight. "*See?* I can hit."

"I did see you try to cave in Cale Jacobson's face," Jack said wryly.

"So you're going to teach me to throw," Ava said. "Do I have to be wearing pants?"

Jack's throat clenched strangely as he set aside his cross-stitch. He was supposed to be annoyed. Sighing at her antics, rolling his eyes at her endless stream of banter. But instead the annoyance was veering toward fondness, the eye rolls not even half-hearted.

And of all the things that could have proved dangerous to him on this job, Ava Cavalcante might be the biggest threat to him yet.

Chapter Twenty-Two

Ava didn't think she'd been the same since Jack had looked at her out of those intense dark eyes and said *I don't want you to get hurt.* Or maybe she hadn't been the same since he came for her at the motel, at the warehouse before that. In the alley. It wasn't like he cared about her, not really. He couldn't.

Could he?

But the very next morning, he was up well before dawn and returned as she woke with an iced flat white, strawberries, and cinnamon buns.

She met him in the small kitchen, a room with blue-checkered wallpaper and a round dining table with two chairs.

"How did you know?" Ava asked him, as she stretched and realized her ribs were still sore, but not nearly as bad as they'd been when she'd fled the city with Jack. "That this is my favorite breakfast in all of existence?"

Jack avoided her look. "There isn't a good way to say this," he said. "But when I first was . . . thwarted by you, I looked you up. All your social medias are public, and you have a whole post on Instagram dedicated to a flat white, strawberries, and a cinnamon bun."

Ava froze.

She knew the post.

It was the last time she'd been happy. Maybe in forever. The next day they'd gotten Ari's diagnosis, and then—then it was over quickly after that.

Jack could sense, maybe better than most people in her life, the shift in her mood. Generally, people didn't see past the bubbly exterior, the refusal to be serious. Silliness was a good mask, but it never seemed to work for long on Jack.

"You okay?" he asked.

"I'm good," Ava said. "Groovy. Peachy. Perkalicious."

"That last one is a made-up word," Jack said. "Did I make you sad?"

It was unexpectedly thoughtful, *again*, for a man who was really only interested in fucking her hard, keeping her from ruining his hit, and killing people for money.

"I'm always a little bit sad," Ava said. "Isn't everyone?"

Jack pulled one of the chairs away from the small table, turned it around backward, and straddled it, his eyes intent on hers. "No," he said. "No, I don't think so."

"Oh," Ava said. She turned away from him, taking a large bite of the cinnamon bun so that he wouldn't see her expression. But the cinnamon bun tasted just like a sunlit day in the small Iowa backyard she had shared with Ari, like the first truly warm day of spring, like little sprouts in their garden bed and the sun on her, warm as Ari's hands, which had not yet begun to tremble. "Oh, well, we can pretend I was joking."

But her eyes were misted over, and her throat was rapidly shutting.

Jack scooted the chair closer, his eyes unreadable. "I won't," he said. "You can, if you want. But I won't."

It was strangely comforting, though it shouldn't be.

"That's because you're an asshole," Ava said through a bite of cinnamon bun and maybe a few tears.

Jack shrugged one shoulder and then settled in, leaning his forearms on the back of the chair.

"Are you just going to watch me eat?"

He shrugged his shoulder again. "Do you want me to stop?"

It was always an effective method to interrupt Ava's fussing. He was asking, directly, for her preference. Which was annoying of him. "No," Ava said. "But I don't understand why it's so interesting."

"Has nobody ever told you how interesting you are, Boss?" Jack cracked a smile now. "Because you might be the most interesting person I have ever met."

He'd had a series of nicknames for her. Sunshine. Firecracker. Flight Risk.

She liked *Boss* best so far.

"Thanks, O'Sullivan," Ava said. "Good to know I haven't bored you yet."

"Has anyone, though?" Jack pressed as Ava devoured a handful of strawberries in one go.

"What?"

"Told you that you're interesting."

Not since Ari. And only ever Ari.

Ava hadn't been good at *friends*. She'd moved too many times as a kid, was too addicted to being the comic relief so that nobody would ever really know her, and unfortunately the result of that was that nobody had ever really known her. Fucked how things worked that way.

Ari had seen straight through the bullshit, though, and loved Ava anyway. More than Ava ever deserved. That kind of love was once in a lifetime, and Ava had gone and lost it already.

"Yeah," Ava said softly. "Yeah, once."

"Good." Jack nodded. "Now, today's lesson is on weaponry. There are some important rules about guns, but first I want to know what *you* know."

"Thank you for acknowledging both my expertise and my role as boss of this duo," Ava said. "But, unfortunately, I know nothing about guns. Is that treason in America? I feel like it must be."

"I'll save you from the treason charges," Jack said, so seriously Ava choked on her next bite. "There's a range just outside of town. I drove past it this morning. We'll pay in cash, and the guy who owns it will fuck off, so we can practice in peace. I grabbed a few boxes of ammo, and we'll head over there when you're done with breakfast."

"Is that why you're watching me so intently?" Ava asked, polishing off her cinnamon bun and licking her fingers. Maybe with a little more tongue than anyone *really* needed.

Jack responded to the tongue—and the eye contact—as the invitation it was. He stood, shoving the chair out of the way, and pulled her abruptly to her feet. "What do you want right now, Ava?" he asked, those dark eyes of his sparking dangerously.

They hadn't fucked, not since that whirlwind night in the motel. That particular day was blurry, faded at the edges from how exhausted and adrenalized she'd been. But the memory of his hands on her—she had that in vivid fucking detail.

"I want—" Ava began, a blush heating her face. Did she have to spell it out for him? "You?" She said it like a question.

"Hmm." Jack shook his head. "No, that's not good enough. I'll make you come if you want, Ava. But you have to tell me, in *exact detail*, what you want. Maybe you'll decide to do that later, but I guess now we're going to the gun range."

He was walking out the front door, shoving the ammo boxes in his pocket as he went. He didn't look back, either, just walked straight to the minivan as if he expected her to follow.

"You're an asshole," Ava yelled after him. "And insufferable. And I hate you."

She pulled on some pants—this time a pair of yoga pants with *Wine not?* bedazzled across the ass—and pulled on one of Jack's tank tops, a ribbed white one that was soft to the touch. And also, coincidentally, made of a clingy fabric that would accentuate her nipples. Which Jack deserved to see and not touch for being the most insufferable man in the history of the universe.

Jack was waiting in the minivan, his left hand on the center of the steering wheel, his right arm slung over the back of *her* seat. "You ready, Boss?"

"Yes, O'Sullivan," Ava told him. "Though you're in trouble."

Jack met her gaze evenly. "Yeah? Because you didn't want to say what you wanted?"

"It's *embarrassing*," Ava retorted. "Have *you* ever had to admit that you wanted to be . . . choked and tied up and bossed around?"

"Yes, actually," Jack said easily. "But of course you don't *have* to. But if you *did* tell me exactly what you want right now, I would fuck you right now. Right here in this car. Right here on the side of the road. You could already be feeling—*this*."

With his free hand, he pressed two fingers lightly against her clit, through her yoga pants.

She gasped at the contact, and then nearly growled when he withdrew his hand. "Keep touching me, you fucker."

Jack grinned at her. "Ask nicely, then."

Ava considered headbutting him but decided a car wreck *before* they completed their murder plan would only derail things further. She flipped him the middle finger instead as the minivan accelerated onto the highway.

They reached the shooting range about fifteen minutes later. It was outdoors at the end of a dirt road, nothing more than a little clearing in the woods. There was a padlocked gate—Jack got out and opened it—and beyond it, six stations were set up, six targets several yards downrange, and a steep hill backing up the targets. Any stray bullets would hit nothing but dirt.

Which was a good thing, because Ava was uncertain she should be trusted with a gun. "Can I call it a pew-pew?"

Jack laid three handguns out on the table in front of them, neatly placing a box of ammunition behind each of them. "You may not."

"Can I use *can* instead of *may* or will you correct my grammar like an uptight English professor?"

"We can do a professor roleplay if you want," Jack said. "You would have to tell me what we would do, though. Boss."

Before she could respond, Jack stepped up to the edge of the stone platform they were standing on, lifted one of the handguns, and aimed at the target.

One. Two. Three shots.

And then there were three even holes in the target in front of them.

"That's hot," Ava said.

Jack shot again, three more times. Three more perfect holes in the target downrange of them.

"That's six," Ava said, but she avoided looking at his hands when she did. "Is that an empty magazine?" *Focus, Ava,* she wanted to shout at herself. *On the guns. Not on Jack's hands.*

"For this one," Jack answered. "Other guns might have more in a magazine. This one has six."

He showed her how to reload the weapon, where the safety was. Where the trigger was, too, though that part seemed apparent.

"Let's talk about weapon safety," Jack said, with the same sober aplomb as the head librarian who used to start staff trainings by droning on in a complete monotone about policies and procedures.

"I mean, that's pretty obvious," Ava told him. "Don't point it at stuff unless you want that stuff to have a hole in it."

Jack nodded. "Yes, keep your muzzle down and your finger off the trigger until you intend to fire."

"No fingering the gun? Is that what you're saying?"

He didn't even give her one of his trademark stern *Ava*s this time. Just moved right along, ignoring her attempt at rage-baiting him.

"This next rule"—he pointed to the weapons on the table and then at her—"is the most important one. Do you understand me?"

Jack waited for a long moment until Ava realized it was not, in fact, a rhetorical question.

"Sir, yes, sir!"

"Treat every weapon as if it's loaded. Every single one. Every single time. The wrong one could go off, and you could lose everything like that." Jack snapped his fingers, making Ava jump.

"Got it," Ava said, because Jack had sounded more serious than usual. And he was always serious. "Anything else, or can I start blam-blamming?"

"We'll start with this one." Jack lifted a larger handgun. "This is a Glock, and it has less kick than the handgun I made. It's quicker to load, too. Here, you try."

"I just want to do the fun part," Ava said. "Can I just do the fun part?"

"No."

"But I'm the boss. Wait, did you say you *made* that gun?"

"You're not the boss of this. And yes, I 3D printed it."

Somehow *that* was hot, too?

Maybe Ava was losing it. Or maybe it was just that *Jack* was hot, and that bled into . . . well, everything he did.

"Ugh." Ava leaned her head back dramatically. "Fine. Show me how to load the gun, so that I can treat it as if it's loaded no matter what."

When she'd first met him, he'd begged her to be serious at least once every fifteen-minute interval. Now, though, her attitude didn't seem to faze him—he just breezed right on through, acting as if she was treating this as seriously as he was, and didn't seem to mind her derailments.

Which was refreshing, honestly. Ari had been like that—seeing Ava for exactly who she was, no matter how silly Ava had acted. And it was terrifying, too.

If she had a choice—which she really didn't, not if she wanted Cale dead—she would have gone running the first time she'd ever seen similarities between Ari and Jack. Because the way Ava'd felt when she lost Ari . . . she was never going to feel that way again. She wouldn't survive it if she did.

She took the gun from Jack and stepped forward. He moved behind her, adjusting her hips with his hands, his fingers digging in. For a moment, just a moment, she nearly forgot the weapon in her hand.

Then he reached around her and settled one hand over each of her arms, adjusting her grip and her aim. That was the moment she realized, weight settling in her stomach, that she had seen this gun in Jack's hands before. He had used this gun to kill the man who had kidnapped her. This one, the one heavy and cold in her hands. He hadn't gotten rid of it like he'd said, either. He had emptied *this* clip into someone and ended a life.

And Ava wanted to fuck him, right here and now.

Jack returned his hands to his side, but remained behind her, so close she could feel the warmth of his body, even though they weren't touching.

"Now," Jack said, his voice soft against her ear. *"Fire."*

One.

Two.

Three.

Jack was precise, careful. Until *her.*

Ava breathed in and fired again.

Four.

Five.

Six.

Gun emptied, just for her. Jack, standing over a man's body, firing even after it was clear Devin was dead.

Ava's breath came in raggedly, went out worse.

She set the gun down and turned to him. "I want," she began shakily. "I want you to fuck me. I want you to fuck me right here, right now. I want you inside me. I want it to be rough, I want it to be hard, and I want to be walking stiffly until at least tomorrow. I want you to bend me over this table . . ."

Her voice lost its strength as she looked up at him.

Jack's posture was similar to the way he'd stood while he was shooting earlier—his stance wide and commanding—and he was looking down at her with wildfire in his eyes. "Keep going, Boss," he said. "We'll do everything you want."

"I want you to bend me over this table, and I want you to pull my hair. I want you to keep going unless I safeword and tell you I'm *red*," Ava continued. Her knees were trembling now, the immensity of it all sweeping through her body until she could hardly stand. "Or if you're red, of course. I want you to choke me, and I want you to spank my ass the whole time, and I want—I want—"

Jack's hand trailed slowly up her arm, his touch slow and controlled. His index finger carved a line along her collarbone, and then, suddenly, his hand closed around her throat. Just hard enough to make Ava gasp. Not hard enough to leave her unable to.

"What else?" he asked softly, his eyes boring into hers.

"I want you," Ava gasped. "I want you to decide when I come. I want you to decide . . . *if* I come."

Was her face red from the embarrassment of having to say all this out loud, or was blood just rushing to her face because she was being choked? It didn't matter anymore. Nothing mattered except for Jack's hands on her.

"I want you *now*," Ava said, pushing forward against Jack's fingers.

He moved so quickly she barely knew what was happening, one rough hand settling on her hips and spinning her to face the tables. Her yoga pants were yanked down the next moment, one of the little bedazzled jewels falling to the ground with the force of his tug.

"No underwear? Again?"

Ava could hear the humor in his voice, and then every thought was erased because he brought his hand down across her ass, hard. She yelped, lurching forward, as a fiery, delicious sting spread across her skin.

Jack peeled her tank top—*his* tank top—over her head the next moment, one hand reaching around and cupping her breast.

"You should never cover these," he said. She heard the zip of his fly coming down, and then Jack tossed her clothes onto the edge of the table. "If I had my way, you'd never have a bra on again."

Ava opened her mouth to respond. What she was going to say, she had no idea. But something, anything, to maintain her sass, to maintain her control. But he wouldn't fall for that, because she'd laid out every single thing she wanted him to do to her. And because he *never* fell for that, no matter how insistently she teased him.

And then Jack's hands were on her hips again, lifting her up.

The table was just tall enough that, bent over, Ava's feet barely touched the ground. Jack was standing behind her, feet firmly planted, yet again maintaining his control while Ava lost hers, inch by inch.

"Jaaack," Ava whined.

He brought his right hand down on her ass again. "You'll behave," he said. "Or I'll come, and you won't."

"Jack!" Ava twisted her head to look at him. "That's not *fair.*"

"No, it isn't," Jack said, a grin breaking across his face. "But it's what you want."

She couldn't even argue with that, not when she'd spilled her guts and asked him for the kind of steamy, kinky fucking sex she'd wanted with everything she had.

Jack pushed against her entrance, not as carefully as he had that first time, and then he was inside her. Ava was wet enough, desperate enough, that when she stretched it hurt only a little, a delicious ache and fullness that made every thought in her head stutter to a stop.

"Like this, Boss?" he asked her, leaning over so that he was close to her ear.

When she didn't answer, he slapped her ass, harder than he had before.

Ava clenched on him involuntarily, a wave of pleasure rolling through her. "Like this," she said. "Keep going."

He thrust into her again, his hips slapping her already-sore ass, and then he reached one hand to cup her throat. "Color?" he asked firmly, slowing his pace.

"Green," Ava said. "You?"

"Green," he said, and then his hips slammed into her ass again, his cock so deep inside her it was the only thing Ava could think about.

"Jack," she whimpered. She was close, she was close *already*, and she wanted to come more than she had ever wanted anything in her entire life. "Jack, please. I've been so good. Can I—can I—"

She couldn't say it.

He laughed roughly, his hand shifting from her throat to sink into her curls and tug, rough enough pain spread across her scalp, but not so rough her neck itself jerked. Jack sank into her farther, letting out a soft sigh that made Ava's heart stumble dangerously.

"You're stunning," Jack said softly.

The words caught Ava off guard.

"Shut up," she told him.

He laughed. "You can't come if you can't take a compliment," he decided, and he was fucking her harder and faster now, his hand moving to the back of her throat and squeezing. His other hand was all over her ass, slapping it a few times before he reached around to finger her clit.

"Jack," Ava gasped his name. "Jack, let me *come*."

"When you let me compliment you."

"Fine," Ava said raggedly. "Fine, say nice shit about me, just let me—let me fucking *come*."

"Language," Jack reproved her, pulling his hand from her clit so he could squeeze a fistful of her ass again.

Ava sucked in a sharp breath of air, as much as she could manage with his hand wrapped around her throat. She was looking up now, at that fucking target with six new holes Jack had left there. An empty magazine. For her. That gasp in his mouth. For *her*. "Jack, please, Jack—"

His voice dropped an octave as his hand tightened. "All right then, Ava," he said softly. He reached his hand around her, fingers settling on her clit again, and then he increased his pace. "Come for me, Ava Cavalcante."

The moan that ripped from her mouth was half pain, all pleasure, the orgasm racking her body so intensely it felt as if it would never end. The world was floaty, a hazy, sunlit place where nothing bad had ever happened or could ever happen. She was sensitive, almost painfully so, as Jack finished while the last waves of her own orgasm shuddered through her.

And then he was lowering her gently down, her feet finally flat on the earth again.

"Jack," she said softly.

He was smiling, a soft thing she hadn't seen before. "Ava."

"I can't stand up."

"I can carry you."

He lifted her and carried her to the van, setting her carefully on the passenger seat.

"I can't drive naked," Ava said.

"A shame," Jack said. "I'll go get your clothes."

Ava shifted. She was sore—sore in more places than her ribs. Sitting like this, even for the twenty minutes it would take to return to their motel, was going to be the sweetest of agonies.

When Jack returned with her clothes, the ammunition, and the handguns, Ava felt a laugh bubble up through the pleasant haze that still enveloped her. "This is ridiculous," she said. "Look at us."

Jack grinned at her. "You need anything?" he asked. "I brought Gatorade. There's some in the back. And I can help you get dressed."

"I *would* say that I can do it all myself," Ava said. "But you fucked that out of me. For now."

"Are you saying hyper-independence can be solved through a rough lay?" Jack asked thoughtfully as he crouched to put the yoga pants where she could stick her feet into them.

"I'm not *not* saying that," Ava said. "Why, did it solve your avoidant personality?"

Jack looked up at her wickedly. "I'm not *not* saying that," he told her.

For as roughly as he had fucked her just now, he helped her into her clothes so tenderly it made a very different part of her ache.

"Who knew contract killers gave such good aftercare?" Ava said. But she waited until they were both safely in the van, with the windows and doors shut, and well on their way, before she said it. Because avoid detection, everybody is always watching, blah, blah, blah. Ew, he really was rubbing off on her.

Or maybe she was just still so deep in that hazy post-scene, post-sex, post-power-exchange glow.

"We're gonna have to do that again," Ava told him. "When we get back to the cottage—"

"Wait." Jack's voice hardened. "Duck down. *Now.*"

Ava unbuckled and slid down in the passenger seat, her body obeying before her brain caught up. "What the fuck is going on?" she hissed at him. That had *hurt.* She was sore, damn it, and her ribs were still aching.

"There are cops," Jack said. His face was a mask, but she could see his knuckles were white around the steering wheel. "There are six squad cars. Outside of our cottage."

"Shit." Ava poked her head up, and Jack pushed her gently down.

He was still driving slowly, maintaining that cool despite it all. For the first time, Ava was glad that he was driving and she was on passenger princess duty, because she would be pissing herself and blowing through stop signs and looking wildly in all directions, and the cops would snap her up like that.

Actually, they would have probably snapped her up a long time ago if not for Jack. Jack, who'd emptied his gun into someone on her behalf and fucked her until she couldn't walk.

"What are we going to do?"

Oh, *fuck* how scared her voice sounded. Fuck how scared she *felt.*

She wasn't supposed to feel anything. That was the deal, after Ari died. She wasn't supposed to feel anything except her desire for *revenge.*

But fear was pulsing in her throat, driving every other thought out of her head.

"It'll be all right." Jack's voice had returned to steady, calm. Even and low and smooth.

Ava's heartbeat slowed, just a little.

When had she started to trust his words the way she did right now? When he'd fed her dinner? When he'd brought Dove chocolates back for her? When he'd returned with cinnamon buns and her coffee order and strawberries? When he'd demanded she tell him what she wanted, and then given every bit of it to her?

"I trust you," Ava whispered.

His eyes locked on hers.

"Thank you," he said softly.

And that was when the red and blue flashing lights of the cop car lit up behind them.

Chapter Twenty-Three

Jack O'Sullivan was a fuckup long before his husband died. But for one brief second, when Ava Cavalcante had looked up at him from the floor of his stupid rental van, he'd felt like he had a chance at *not* letting someone down.

"Jack," Ava said. The fear was a live wire in her voice. "Jack, what are we going to do?"

"Hold on," Jack told her. For the first time in his life, he didn't have a plan, not exactly, but he *did* know he wasn't letting Ava go. Not today.

"Oh, *fuck*." She reached up and clung to his hand. "We're going to run for it?"

He could stop, of course. He could pull over and say he'd just picked this woman up while she was hitchhiking, and show them an ID that said Reed Grant, so when Ava indignantly said *Jack*, he could say she was also hallucinating.

The Jack O'Sullivan he had been even a few weeks ago, before he had encountered the wildfire that was Ava Cavalcante, would have done that easily.

But this version of Jack put his foot to the gas pedal. He jerked his hand back from Ava's, rougher than he wanted to, but he needed both hands now. He spun the wheel, turning sharply left off the county road onto a dirt road that led toward the river.

"Where are we going?" Ava asked.

"Get up and buckle in," Jack ordered. "*Now*, Ava."

"It—they'll see me."

"Yes," Jack said. "But they're trying to pull us over anyway."

The cop surged behind them, nearly closing the gap. More sirens wailed in the distance, the net around them closing so quickly Jack was furious with himself that he hadn't seen it coming.

He'd only had one other job come this close, a hit he'd done in Arizona one February, on a new retiree who had pissed off both his mistresses enough to get them working together. He'd been rich, too, though not as wealthy as Jacobson, and cops had swarmed the area so fast that Jack suspected, long after he'd made his escape, that the mistresses may have double-crossed him.

But they hadn't caught him that day, and he'd be damned if they caught him today. If they caught *Ava*.

"Buckle," he snarled at her.

This was going to get . . . bumpy.

The narrow road he was driving curved sharply through the forest, but Jack took the turns at full speed, his knuckles whitening from gripping the steering wheel so hard.

"What are we going to do?" Ava asked again. "Jack, we have to ditch this van."

They did. There was no other way.

He had his go bag—he *always* had his go bag—which had his cash, ID, and weapons. Some food. Extra clothes, for both of them. He'd have to get a new cross-stitch kit the next time life slowed down enough to allow it.

"As soon as I stop the van, get out and *run*." Jack rounded another corner, whipping into the small trailhead for some park.

Ava flung the door open, and Jack followed, snatching his bag with one hand and tossing it over his shoulder. He grabbed Ava's hand with the other.

Just as they reached the cover of the trees, the cops tore around the bend and into the trailhead parking lot, sirens screaming.

Fuck, they were too close.

Jack dropped Ava's hand and drew his Glock, loaded it.

One.

Two.

Three.

A dead shot to the van's engine, and the *boom* it made going up in the forest hit him so hard his ears rang.

Then Ava's hand was in his again, dragging him forward into the forest.

"Keep moving," she insisted.

Jack was still getting his bearings after the explosion, but she yanked him onward, deeper into the forest toward the river.

"That was brilliant," she said when their pace finally slowed. "You bought us time."

"They'll realize we weren't in the van," Jack said wearily. "I don't know how *much* time I really bought."

"Enough to get here." Ava stopped and looked around. There were tall fir trees surrounding them, early lupine blooming at their bases. "Where *is* here?"

He could hear the Willamette from where they stood. They had traveled steadily north, nearly parallel to the river as they went farther from Portland. He should have gone farther, much faster. He should have been states away, regrouped somewhere. Maybe even retreated to the black hole he lived in out in Montana.

It was practically a bunker, a far cry from the apartment with the balcony garden he'd shared with Jay.

But he'd stayed. He'd stayed with Ava, with this wild hope that they'd actually be able to pull off this hit.

"We can take a boat," Jack said. "Farther north, up to the perimeter of Cale Jacobson's compound."

Ava's head jerked up. "We're going back? *Now?* What happened to lie low and wait until the party?"

"Lying low didn't work," Jack told her grimly. "I don't know how close we are to the nearest dock. We can walk the coast and hope we stumble upon some private marina or make the trek a few miles into town and get a boat from the marina there."

Ava groaned. "Can we go back to you carrying me?" she asked. "I don't hike. Just so you know."

She was back to coping with it all through humor, but that didn't mean she was no longer afraid. Jack reached over and squeezed her shoulder gently. "I'll carry what we have."

"I wish we had snacks. And that it was still this morning, when I thought it would all be cinnamon buns and orgasms."

Jack nearly opened his mouth to say he could still give her the orgasms part, but that would have been a deranged use of their limited escape window. Still.

He chanced a look down at her.

Ava was looking back at him expectantly.

"You're dead serious, and that scares me," Jack said. "Come on. Let's start walking."

<>

It was midday before they found anything remotely suitable, after at least three miles walking through dense forest and thick undergrowth, constantly stopping to listen for the sound of search parties or cops. A few times, a police helicopter circled nearby.

When they did finally stop at a quiet marina at a little inlet along the river, Jack told Ava to sit down while he figured out how to hot-wire the boat.

"I'm better than you are at hot-wiring things," Ava said. "I think we already decided that? When I stole your rental car?"

"Don't remind me," Jack said wryly. She probably *was* better at most petty crimes than he was, despite having no criminal record that he could find. He didn't so much as run a stop sign, especially when he was on a job. "All right, sure. Go ahead and try hot-wiring it. We're also going to need to not look like . . . well, us. If the helicopter circles and they have our descriptions, they'll lock onto us immediately. And I really would rather not blow up a second vehicle today."

"I mean, I'm sure there are solutions to escaping on this boat that don't involve blowing it up?" Ava said. "But what do I know?"

She set to work on the boat, fussing with wires he didn't recognize.

"How many things have you stolen?" Jack asked as she worked, his eyes scanning the forest and the sky above. "And how did you know how to do it all?"

"There are reference manuals for *anything*." Ava shrugged one shoulder. "And sometimes the circulation deck got boring, so I'd watch YouTube videos about hot-wiring cars. Anyway, what kind of disguises can we even manage?"

Someday, in a moment when they were *not* running for their lives, Jack was going to want to know more about that.

But at present, they had bigger problems.

The speedboat was small, but it did have a canopy that would mostly obscure them.

"I, uh, have a fake beard," Jack said. He always had a rotating assortment of accessories to throw people off. Once he'd even worn a sleeve of tattoos that looked real. Police, when they finally managed to *get* a description of the mystery man who'd carried out the hit, were looking for someone with a nature-themed sleeve tattoo, round glasses, and a full beard.

Ava snorted. "Of course you do. Don't tell me you have a fake nose and eyeglasses, too."

"I do have glasses," Jack admitted. "Listen. It sounds cliché and goofy, but it works. People don't look twice at you if one little detail is different."

"Okay, Party City," Ava said.

"I don't even know what that is."

"They have good candy," Ava said. "Easy to shoplift."

"That's a . . . you amaze me," Jack said. "At every turn, you are making the worst decision possible. I assume that has been a trend for most of your life."

The boat roared to life. Ava turned to him with a triumphant grin. "You were saying?"

"Thank you, Boss," he said, and kissed her forehead.

She startled at the gesture, and then quickly stepped back. "I'm sweaty," she said. "And also, kiss my *mouth*. Weirdo."

"Are you red?" Jack asked her carefully as he stepped onto the boat, scanning the trees one more time for potential threats. "You really don't want a forehead kiss?"

"No," Ava said. "No, I'm not safewording. That was just . . . intimate."

That didn't make sense to Jack, who had been inside Ava only this morning, but he was too tired and sweaty and fed up with running for his life to question Ava's interpretation of the forehead kiss.

"All right, Ava," Jack said. "Mind if I take the wheel?"

She stepped back without a single question or sassy remark, which meant something was *really* wrong. "Do you want me to grab your costume out of the bag?"

"It's a *disguise*," Jack said. "Yes. Please. Thank you."

She dug around and then appeared beside him with the beard, glasses, and ball cap. "I sort of think I should be the one to wear the beard," she said. "I always thought I would look cool as hell with a beard. Have you ever tried those Snapchat filters that make you look like a middle-aged bearded guy? Lumberjack vibes?"

Jack shook his head, glancing up from the wheel. "You can show me later," he said distractedly. "Have you checked Cale's calendar recently? I want to know if he's made any changes."

Ava plopped onto the bench seat behind him as she opened the app. "He changed his regular shoeshine, canceled it, actually, for the foreseeable future. And—it looks like this weekend is completely booked off. His calendar doesn't say what it's booked for, though."

Jack considered for a moment. "No notes or shared invites at all?"

Ava paused for a moment. "No notes," she said. "Oh, shit, he has a flight scheduled on his private plane for Sunday, destination Spain. He won't be back for a month? What the fuck, Jack?"

Jack's stomach twisted. It was too late, way too fucking late, to extricate himself from this mess now and leave this hit behind. But *god*, it had just gotten a lot harder. "We have to get him this weekend," he said.

"But he's booked somewhere all weekend." Ava huffed in frustration. "How the fuck are we supposed to get to him?"

Her head snapped up, realization clearly hitting him at the same time as it dawned on Jack.

"You think—" she began.

"That they moved the gala up?" Jack asked. "So they could avoid further security breaches?"

"And also so they can get some good PR out there," Ava said, grinning up at him. "Their stock has *tanked* the last couple of weeks. That was an unintentional side effect of attacking Cale, but I'm not mad about it. Oh, *damn*, Jack, look at this."

Ava held up her phone.

Plastered across her news app . . . were their faces.

Ava's, a zoomed-in shot of her the day she'd tackled Cale Jacobson outside the café. And Jack's, his mask up and his cap pulled low, a grainy picture of him behind the wheel of that minivan.

Fuck, fuck, *fuck*.

"This is *everywhere*," Ava said in wonder. "Jack, we're fucked. How are we ever gonna get close to him now? We don't even know for sure they've moved the gala. We don't know that he'll be at his stupid mansion."

Running hadn't worked.

Hiding hadn't worked.

Jack's meticulousness had always served him before this, the extreme caution he used keeping him safely out of jail and ahead of whoever was coming after him. But it hadn't worked this time, and that might mean it was time for a change in strategy.

"I think we take a leap of faith," Jack told Ava slowly. "We go to Cale Jacobson's mansion, and we go now. And when we find him, we kill him. Together."

Chapter Twenty-Four

Jack looked positively ridiculous with his fake beard, but Ava had to admit it was doing something for her. Probably, if he went down on her with that scratchy beard, it would be—

"Ava." Jack was saying her name as if she hadn't been listening.

Which she hadn't.

They may be fucked, they may be running for their lives and freedom, but Ava was on a boat, in spring, with a very hot man she had been having mind-blowingly good sex with. So she was going to lie under the little canopy and watch the trees go by and enjoy at least that, thank you very much.

"Was I ignoring you again?" Ava asked. "You were probably using your 'Rules' voice again. That one is really easy to tune out."

"You're a brat, Boss," he said. "I'm going to dock the boat before we reach town, and I'm going to take out the drain plug so it sinks slowly, hopefully before anybody notices it."

Ava winced. "Hope the owner's got good insurance," she said, and then her face clouded. "Are you sure we have to sink it?"

"It would be safest," Jack said, but she could see that he was hesitating.

Staying alive in his profession must mean doing a lot of unsavory things and being pretty ruthless about taking a resource or leaving a resource—a car, a boat, a motel room, the clothes you'd woken up in, the sandwich you'd been planning to eat—at a moment's notice.

He hadn't mentioned the rental car she'd ruined, or the motorcycle they'd abandoned, or the SUV they'd burned in the woods. Or the van they'd blown up.

"We don't want the cops to be able to retrace our footsteps any more than they already will," Jack told her. "With this much pressure on them to find you—to find us, now—they'll be using every resource they have. Every camera, whether or not they legally are allowed. And I want to slow them down as much as we can."

"But somebody's going to be *really* fucking sad when you sink their boat." Ava and Ari hadn't had the money for a boat, but Ari had grown up on the water in coastal North Carolina and had been driving her family's little fishing boat long before she'd learned to drive a car. And this little boat reminded Ava too much of that one, the boat Ari loved like it was an old friend. "Let's just wipe down anything we touched and leave it somewhere it'll be found eventually. They won't even know it's us, not necessarily."

"You didn't have the same feelings about any of the vehicles you or I have ruined so far," Jack said as he steered the boat toward a flat patch of land along the river.

"Rental cars are just rental cars." Ava waved her hands. "And insurance for corporations always takes care of them. Insurance for *people* is just there to fuck you over."

"Are you ever going to tell me more than that?" Jack asked. "About why insurance, and why Cale?"

Ava stiffened, the sun beating down suddenly feeling oppressively hot. "I haven't demanded that you tell me more about Jay," she said. "You don't ask me for a *why*. Deal?"

He was quiet, controlled, even in sleep. But he always said the same name:

Jay.

Jay, please, said in a whisper.

Jay, come back. Measured and steady but so desperate.

Jay, Jay, Jay.

Ava shivered. You probably didn't get to a career as a hot hit man without going through something along the way. "Is this like a John Wick situation?" she asked, turning on a smile despite the way the mention of Ari, of the *reason*, fucked her up. "Or is that insensitive to ask?"

Jack grunted in response, not even stooping to respond. When they neared land, he jumped out, taking the rope with him, and towed the boat onto shore, where he tied it to a tree. "I still think we should sink it," he said. "But you're the boss."

Ava snorted. "Damn right I am," she said. "I'm going to remind you of that next time we fuck."

"Oh, did you want to top?" Jack called her bluff with such merciless precision, a glint in his eyes, that Ava had to take a step back.

"Why, are you going to bottom for me?"

"Tell me what you want to do," Jack said, his mouth twisting into a roguish little smile. "And we'll do it. If you're going to top me, Ava, I'll get you a cock myself."

Ava squirmed. He should be more of a gentleman and stop calling her bluff. "Maybe I will," she said. "Maybe I'll say *Jack, I want to bend you over and—*"

Jack's mouth was on hers, hard and bruising, a kiss that deepened. When he stepped back, he was still grinning. "If you say it, say it like you mean it, Boss."

Ava blushed from the base of her neck to the top of her forehead, which was an unfair genetic trait she would like to formally complain to her ancestors about. "Fuck you," she whispered, and kissed him again, moaning when his hand cupped the back of her neck and then slid up, tangling in her thick curls. "Kissing you with this dumbass beard is something, though," she added when he pulled away again.

"It's staying on," Jack said. "I wish I had a wig. I had a really good one once, with a man bun, and I had a very realistic tattoo, and all the descriptions centered on the man bun and tattoo, and I walked right by some police who were *looking* at the sketch they'd done of me, and they didn't even look my way."

"That sounds like risky behavior," Ava nagged him as he set off into the patch of trees. "Weren't you lecturing *me* about risky behavior and keeping a low profile? For, like, a hundred days in a row?"

Jack reached back and took her hand, his closing over hers with such firmness that she found herself blushing again. "And I'll lecture you about it for the next one hundred days," Jack said.

The words left Ava feeling unexpectedly warm. There was no *after* this hit, but when Jack talked about the future, in that tone, Ava could almost pretend there would be. "Well," she said. "Don't be stupid."

He just *mmm*'d at her in response.

Silence fell as they skirted farther up the shoreline, Jack shrugging his bag on like a backpack. "Do I look like a hiker who has wandered back into town?"

"No," Ava told him. "You look like a dangerous man who is very good at fucking. Who is currently wearing a goofy-ass fake beard."

"No respect." Jack shook his head, but he was looking at her playfully. "All right, we're only a few miles from Cale's property line—about thirty from the mansion, though, because his property is really fucking big. And I found us a hostel just at the edge of town. It's cheap, and they'll take cash. We should both keep masking up—I have extras in my bag—and you should wear a hoodie."

"It's hot as balls," Ava said, aghast.

"I imagine prison isn't comfortable, either," Jack said. "And I'd rather not go. Would you?"

"And you call *me* sassy," Ava shot back, but when Jack stopped to retrieve hoodies and masks for both of them, she put the hoodie on. It smelled like Jack. Pine and gunpowder and a musk that was just uniquely *him*. Her heart rate slowed for the first time since she'd been blissfully hazy postorgasm earlier that day.

Damn, how fast that had been snatched from her.

"The police really picked the worst moment to interrupt us," Ava complained as she trailed behind Jack. "I mean, who starts a car chase with postcoital—"

"You did *not* just use the word *postcoital* to talk about this," Jack said, shaking his head. "You're the most irreverent person I've ever met."

They had reached the main road—a county road with wide sidewalks and little tree cover, a few businesses lining the street. It felt strange to be back in civilization, this town—she didn't know its name—even smaller than Gable, the town they'd left behind. It felt the same, though: busy and dangerous and *waiting*.

Jack squeezed her hand, pulling Ava back to the present as a few cars rolled by.

"We're not *that* far from where we blew up the van," Ava murmured. "You don't think they're looking here?"

She hadn't seen helicopters for miles, the search probably still centered on the patch of woods they'd first fled into. Maybe they had time, but Ava had felt secure in that feeling before. In fact, she'd felt pretty damn secure up until the moment Jack had snarled at her to duck down to the floor of the minivan.

"They will be," Jack said. "Always assume that. Assume that wherever you are, there are eyes and ears, and that every action has a consequence, and everything you say to anyone can be remembered. Every interaction can be a way you are recognized, found, and caught."

Ava threaded her fingers through his as they walked up to a small two-story white building set back from the street, two fir trees bracketing the sidewalk leading up to the door. "I know you always say that. But that sounds lonely," she said softly.

Jack looked down at her, surprise on his face as he adjusted his mask. He pulled the door open after Ava adjusted hers, too. "I was lonely," he said. "Though I'm not sure I knew it."

Was.

He *was* lonely.

Did that mean he wasn't anymore? Did that mean—

Ava's chest squeezed as she walked inside. The air-conditioning was blasting, a welcome relief from outdoors, drying the sweat so quickly Ava shivered.

The person at the front desk, an androgynous person with pale skin and messy, short dark hair, did not look up from their phone. "Checking in?"

"Yep," Jack said. "Booked earlier today. We'll be paying in cash."

They held out their hand for the cash, then scribbled something on a list. "Name?"

"Gilbert," Jack said.

It took every ounce of control Ava possessed not to whip around and stare at him.

"And my wife, Amy."

"I only need one name," the desk attendant said, their tone bored. They scribbled *Gibbert* on the paper in messy handwriting, and then sat idly, chipping blue nail polish off their thumb. "Anything else?"

"Are there towels in the room?" Ava asked.

The desk attendant grunted, returning to their phone. "No amenities," they said. "This is a hostel, bucko."

Ava could respect the disinterest. She could even understand how it was objectively better for them. But she was eternally petty, so she opened her mouth to call the attendant *bucko* in response and start an altercation, because everything was raw and Jack's hands were so tender with her, and Ari was still gone and they had almost gotten caught by cops earlier that day and—

Jack's hand was so gentle on her arm as he pulled her away. "That's it," he said softly as they reached the hallway. "That's it, Boss. Let's go."

There was a sob in Ava's throat that hadn't been there a minute ago. She swallowed it down, but she leaned against Jack's arm.

He was unmoving. He was a rock. She was dangerously close to feeling something for him, dangerously close to having a reason to—

Stay.

Jack unlocked the room and ushered her inside. There were two single beds on opposite sides of the narrow room and nothing else.

"I liked your first rental house better," Ava said, her voice coming out shaky and a little watery. "Jack, I—"

And then the tears came, sudden and forceful as a spring rain, and Jack sat down on one of the beds and pulled Ava into his arms and just held her there.

"I'm not panicking," Ava said through the sobs that were quietly racking her shoulders. "I'm not *scared*."

And Jack just said *mmm* and closed those big arms around her.

There was nothing else in the world. There never was, not when Jack was touching her.

When her tears finally subsided, the exhaustion set in. "I don't ever want to live through a day like today again," Ava said. "How are you just . . . carrying on? I thought the cops were going to get us. And then I thought they might *kill* us. And I had to *hike*, which is honestly maybe worse?"

"You're from the Midwest, and you're in the PNW, and you hate hiking?" Jack pulled back a little to look at her in amazement. "Never mind. I know it's been a long fucking day. But we're all right, and this job can still be done, and you're safe. And that's the important thing."

The words dug down into Ava and unsettled something. That was the important thing, Jack said. But what was *most* important? That the job could still be done, or that she was safe?

That was a stupid thing to wonder, and Ava knew it. Contract killers didn't fall in love. Neither did angry ex-librarians still grieving a lost wife, though.

But when Ava closed her eyes, she saw cinnamon buns and an empty magazine and Jack, demanding she accept kindness about herself.

"Ava?"

"Hmm?"

"Let's get you rehydrated," Jack said. "I'm keeping the beard on, and you should keep your hoodie on, everything in place in case we have to run again."

"I hate the beard," Ava said. "I'm gonna be so honest. It doesn't quite match your hair, and if you *did* grow a beard, I'd love it, and I'd ride it twice a day and three times on Sundays, but this one doesn't feel like real hair, and that freaks me out. I don't want to ride a fake beard, Jack. Did you ever consider that?"

"I did not," Jack told her, very seriously.

He moved her gently to the bed and then stood and began rummaging through his bag. He withdrew a lukewarm orange Gatorade and a protein bar, both of which he offered to her. "Eat something and drink something," he instructed.

"What if I don't want to do as I'm told?" Ava said. "I'll drink the Gatorade if you take off the beard, though."

Jack raised an eyebrow. "I'll grow my own beard if you drink the Gatorade," he said.

"You'll *what*?" Ava stared at him in disbelief. "You wouldn't. No, you would. That's absolutely wild work, my dude."

"My dude," Jack repeated to himself, shaking his head. "I think I like *O'Sullivan* better. You manage to make my own name sound a little condescending."

"You got it, bucko," Ava said, since she hadn't gotten to call anyone *else* bucko.

He laughed. "I knew that got under your skin," he said. "Now, I have to—"

"Jack?"

He stopped, looking at her carefully, waiting for her to continue.

"Her name was Ari," Ava blurted. She didn't know why. Why now, why him. But she hadn't talked about Ari—she couldn't with Ari's aging mom, who wanted nothing to do with Ava after Ari was gone. She couldn't *bring* herself to with any of the friends she'd alienated—and now, finally, it was all catching up with her.

Jack sat down on the edge of the bed next to her, his dark eyes so serious. "Your wife," he said.

"You knew."

Of course he did. Of course he'd done his research.

"I knew you were married," Jack acknowledged. "But I don't know anything more than that."

"You know that I lost her."

For a second, just a second, she could see emotion in Jack's eyes, too. "I knew you had lost someone the day I met you," he said softly. "Because I know how it feels."

"Jay," Ava said. "You don't have to—if you don't want—"

Jack leaned in and kissed her, soft and slow. "I do," he said. "I do, Ava. He was my husband."

Ava felt her chest squeeze dangerously, and she reached out, took Jack's hand in hers. "Did he make you laugh?" she asked.

She didn't ask whether losing Jay had driven Jack to this line of work. She didn't ask who he had been before. She didn't ask how he'd lost Jay. Because she knew, she knew so intimately how much the pain of something like that *burned*.

Jack's eyes were distant, but he squeezed her hand. "He made me laugh every day," Jack said. "We fought about laundry and getting a dog. But mostly he made me laugh. He did this little—this little scrunch with his nose. You do it, too."

Ava's eyes snapped to his.

The look he gave her was electric.

"What about Ari?" Jack asked. "Did she—make you laugh?"

"It was always my job to make everybody laugh," Ava said. "And I did make Ari laugh, yeah. But she made *me* laugh. So hard my stomach hurt. We'd play cards every Saturday, like we were ninety-two or something, and I'd make fun of her for wanting to. But we'd always end up laughing, I don't know what about even. One Saturday night I laughed so hard I fell out of my chair and sprained my wrist on our kitchen floor."

She'd give anything for one more fucking day at their little card table.

Jack pulled her close, wordless but so steadily *there*.

They stayed like that for so long Ava's heartbeat slowed and her eyes even started drifting shut. When Jack gently pulled back, he helped her settle against the small hostel pillow.

His phone buzzed, and Ava sat up.

She was pretty sure he *only* talked to his client with that phone, so buzzing was probably not good news. Not that she was an expert. She dried her eyes and looked up at him expectantly.

"I'm sorry," Jack said. "I want to hear more about Ari, okay? But I think it's urgent that I respond to my client, so I'm stepping outside to make that call. You stay here, all right?"

"Last time you told me to stay somewhere, I went to Dynamo," Ava reminded him playfully, but the weight of what they had just talked about remained. She couldn't shake it—couldn't pretend in front of Jack, not when he'd *seen* her.

"Right," Jack said, running his knuckles along the ridge of her jaw lightly. "But I'm trusting that this time is different, Ava Cavalcante."

Ava closed her eyes, leaning into the softness of his touch. "Is that because you know I'll always come back to ride that dick?"

Jack shook his head, but when she opened her eyes again the look on his face was fond. "That's not why I trust you, Ava," he said. "But it is a definite bonus."

Ava waved him away. When Jack left, he shut the door behind him, turned the key in the lock carefully. Even the sound of his footsteps was measured and even, control in everything he did.

Ava leaned back on the bed, an uncomfortably thin mattress on a shaky bed frame that might break at the first sign of any excitement. Now that he had stepped outside, Ava had nothing to distract her from the most uncomfortable truth she'd ever discovered about herself:

She was falling for Jack O'Sullivan.

Chapter Twenty-Five

Jack took a breath when he stepped back into the mugginess of the spring day. Spring here hadn't always felt this stiflingly warm. It had been years since he had talked about Jay, but now that he had, it was like the floodgates had opened. He had forgotten, almost, that he'd been on this side of the country before—he'd vacationed here with Jay, back when they were young and hopeful and saved up their money for long weekends in beautiful places.

Jack had been many beautiful places now, but only for the work he did, which was a grim realization. For a moment, he thought about what it would be like to see those beautiful places—but with Ava at his side. Sighing, he pulled his phone from his pocket.

Updates, now.

That text was an hour old.

Another, thirty minutes ago:

I'll pull the plug on this. I'll go to the FBI.

And a third, as he looked down at his phone:

This needs to wrap up ASAP.

Jack ran a hand over his fake beard. Ava was right. It was a strange texture, definitely not real hair. Maybe some plastic substitute, despite its generally convincing appearance. I have a new plan, Jack responded to his client.

The money had been so, so good. And established in his work or not, Jack still had bills to pay.

Updates. Now. There are helicopters sweeping the Willamette. I've seen the news about the person, or people, who attempted to complete our shared goal.

Oh, this client was on the verge. Jack could read the frantic tone.

I've got it handled, he responded. The secondary piece of this job can temporarily be an asset.

No. Eliminate.

Jack's stomach twisted. This was dangerously close to being explicit about *what* they were doing over text, something he never did.

Call me, he typed.

Less than thirty seconds later, his phone rang.

At the other end of the line, a man's deep voice, slightly garbled by some kind of masking technology—one that Jack also used through an app he downloaded every time he got a new burner phone—sounded.

"You have five minutes."

"Asset is a distraction," Jack said. "Better alive and out of custody for now. Any attention will be focused primarily on containing and stopping her. This will allow other objectives to remain on target and proceed as planned."

Speaking in guarded, nonspecific ways in writing was always Jack's biggest worry, but wiretaps were a real threat, too—and some clients found ways to sneakily record phone conversations. Any client smart enough to use an app or other technology to obscure their voice was going to be smart enough to record their conversation if Jack gave them the opportunity.

There was nothing for a moment but the sound of the person breathing on the other end, the sound twisting and crackling through Jack's phone.

"That's unacceptable," they said finally. "This is time sensitive, and we've had an endless series of delays."

Jack rarely asked clients *why* they wanted a person gone when they hired him. It wasn't his business, and he took jobs without usually caring much why. Many times it was because a person had cheated. Other times it was because someone had hurt a family member. But the shared grudge this group of clients had was new. And possibly dangerous.

"I can accelerate the timeline," Jack said. "But you knew when you hired me that this kind of work was difficult, and something high profile like this can take time."

A long pause.

"How accelerated?"

"Done by Sunday," Jack said.

The person at the other end breathed out heavily. "Fine," they said.

"One more thing," Jack said. "You have a collective of people with the goal of the chief deliverable. For the additional deliverable, you'll send half up front. Can your collective manage that?"

There was a fierce, bright-eyed woman in the hostel room who Jack couldn't, wouldn't, let down. And if he wanted them *both* to get safely away, he'd need more money than he had.

There was another long stretch of silence.

"The payment's not a problem," the client said finally.

"You'll have your deliverables this weekend," Jack said shortly, and hung up.

The money hit his accounts within moments.

And that, *that* was the part that smelled foul to him. If Ava had hired him, he'd believe her when she said she wanted Cale Jacobson dead, because he had hurt someone she loved. It wouldn't be hard to believe that Cale had hurt people, either. Nobody got where Cale was in life without a trail of pain and victimization behind him.

But Ava also wouldn't have been able to scrape up the kind of capital in a year, or five years, or maybe even longer than that, that this client had just dropped into Jack's account in the space of fifteen minutes. The news was full of speculation about Ava—her life, her motives, how she'd escaped capture so far—but it was also rife with speculation about the investigation into insider trading Cale was facing.

Was this an investor—or group of investors—with deep pockets and deeper resentment for Cale's cost to their bottom line?

Jack shoved his phone in his pocket and went back inside, dread building in his gut. There was too much here that he didn't understand, and he couldn't both keep Ava safe *and* carry this job across the finish line.

Ava was asleep, sprawled across one of the twin beds, her curls falling across the pillow. She was naked—because of course she was.

Jack padlocked the door, an extra layer of security that was habitual to him in places like hostels, double-checked the windows were locked, and then lowered the blinds again before climbing in beside Ava. He would barely fit in a twin bed alone—his feet went past the end of the bed as it was—but the thought of being in the other one, *not* touching her, was somehow unbearable.

She sighed and curled against him.

He lay there, staring at the wall, while she sprawled across him. Like she'd trust him with anything.

It had been a long time since something like this mattered to him—but this, Ava's trust in him, might just break Jack's heart.

<>

Jack woke before Ava. He texted her that he'd be back with food and then unlocked the padlock before slipping out the door.

When he returned, it was with takeout from a small Chinese restaurant down the street from the hostel. He brought six different entrées, because they'd both worn themselves out fucking and running for their lives and fucking again. And then a double order of cream cheese wontons, because that seemed like something Ava would eat in large quantities. And *then* he'd stopped at the corner store and bought whipped cream in a can and strawberries, because if Ava had to go a day without strawberries, she lost her shit a little bit.

And also because he could probably find creative places on Ava's body to lick that whipped cream off.

Ava was on her phone when he entered, scrolling the news with a furrowed brow.

"What did I say about getting a new phone and ditching this one?" Jack asked, snatching it out of her hand and replacing it with the biggest strawberry in the package. "Doomscrolling is bad for you, too. Especially right before bed."

Ava sat up and glared back at Jack indignantly. "Who says I'm going to bed anytime soon? And I don't want to ditch my phone—oooh, strawberry."

She devoured most of the package, all the chicken fried rice (both containers), and the entirety of the cream cheese wontons before looking up at him a little guiltily. "Do you have your own order of wontons?" she asked.

"Not a cream cheese guy," Jack said.

"That's absurd," Ava told him. "And a red flag. Everyone likes cream cheese."

"Is the cream cheese thing more of a red flag than my chosen profession?" he asked, digging into a container of spicy noodles.

Ava poked him with one of her chopsticks. "You're sassy," she said. "Thanks for food. Is now a good time to talk about our plan? Because now that you basically forced me to talk about my feelings and take a nap, I have some ideas."

The feelings had been her idea to share, but who was Jack to argue with her about it? Besides, he'd wanted that, too.

Jack nodded. "Shoot," he said.

"Bad use of the word *shoot*," Ava told him. "But I digress. Okay, if the gala *is* this weekend, I'd never get in without looking the part. And if I wear a wig, do my makeup right, and have a nice dress, I might actually have a chance. You know how it is—a white woman in a dress that says she comes from money, and people don't ask that many questions."

"I'll wear a suit—I saw one down the street that I can rent—so we'll look the part as much as we need," Jack said. "But first we have to figure out how we're getting in. This guest list will be exclusive, and security will be on high alert."

Ava had many ideas—from calling Ms. Rae and asking for help to having Jack call Clara Jacobson and ask for an invite to the gala as thanks for saving her brother's life—but Jack's phone buzzed, interrupting her.

Confirm that you got the additional payment, his client texted.

Confirmed, Jack responded.

And confirm she won't be a problem after this weekend. Secondary objective must be eliminated.

Anger flashed through Jack. He had done this himself, reduced the people he killed to this cold, detached language. But seeing them talk about Ava this way . . . he wished the client was in the room with him.

Still, he did what he had to. He texted back:

Confirmed.

Chapter Twenty-Six

The next morning Ava woke up ravenously hungry. For more wontons or for more of Jack's cock, whichever she could get first.

He was already awake, poring over details in his notebook.

"Is this murder manual back in rotation?" Ava asked him. "And do you need to have a murder matcha to go with it?"

That was what he'd been drinking that first morning. He'd ordered before her at the café, asked for a matcha, unsweetened.

She should have known then that he was a violent criminal, honestly. Who didn't add sweetness to a drink?

"It's not a murder matcha," Jack said wearily. "I'm glad you're up. Let's get to work."

"Work? Before cinnamon buns?" Ava gave him her best pleading face, without any hope that it would work, and then came over and sat on his lap, naked, grinding her ass a little against him as she sat.

She was rewarded by feeling his cock stiffen beneath her.

Jack swatted the edge of her thigh lightly. "Knock that off and let me focus," he said. "Don't you need to get dressed?"

"If I don't do either?" Ava asked.

"Then I'll tie you up and leave you here while I go and get things done," Jack said. "And you hate being ignored above pretty much everything else, so. Knock it off."

Ava made a whiny noise, because otherwise she was going to open her stupid mouth and tell Jack her feelings for him. It was kind of dumb that she'd only figured it out yesterday, and unfortunately she'd woken up still falling for him today. Very inconvenient.

"I've been poring over the floor plan," Jack said. "I can see a few ways in—there's an entrance for waitstaff that might not be too difficult—but I'm not finding a way out."

"Unless we take the helicopter that'll be on the roof," Ava said.

Ms. Rae had talked about her boss having his helicopter parked on the roof anywhere he went, even if he hadn't used it to travel there. He always had an escape route, she'd said.

And that meant Jack and Ava did, too.

"Do *you* know how to fly a helicopter?" Jack asked her, shifting her on his lap. "And put some clothes on."

"So that you won't drop everything and fuck me again while we're in the middle of working?" Ava asked. "And anyway, I was assuming *you* knew how to fly a helicopter. Are you telling me you don't?"

"I do, actually," Jack said. "It just seemed like quite the assumption to make."

"Are you former military?"

"No."

"Former CIA?"

"Definitely not."

"Well, you're a badass," Ava said. "And you know how to drive a motorcycle. So I guess I just kind of assumed."

Jack patted her thigh again absentmindedly (which was rude, because gentle little pats didn't sting as deliciously—all they did was *tease* Ava into wanting more). "Those two are not the same," he said.

"Vroom," Ava said sagely. "Now get on with it. You get distracted so easily. You have a way to get us in, and I have a way to get us out. If we're right that they moved the gala up, Cale will probably be at the mansion already? So we need to get ready."

She had spent so many months working to get this close, but now that it was just a night away—Ava shivered. Tomorrow, everything would change, one way or another. Cale would be dead, and Ava likely in jail at best, or dead at worst. Or she would have failed, Cale would still be breathing, and this would all have been for nothing.

But, either way, it was all going to be over soon.

"Ava," Jack said slowly. "But, Ava, there's a very real chance we don't walk away from this. I want you to know . . . I'm willing to walk away. If you are."

Ava nearly jumped off his lap. His words had scrambled her brain hopelessly. He couldn't mean that. He *couldn't.*

"You're right, I do need clothes for this conversation," she muttered. She crossed the room and pulled on one of his shirts, and then his hoodie, which went down past her ass, the sleeves so long her hands were buried in them. "What the fuck did you just say to me?"

"I don't want you to get hurt," Jack said. He couldn't look at her, either. "I—I have my own reasons for choosing this work. For needing to do this job. But I've never had a job go like this, and I'm not one hundred percent sure I can get us both out safely. So I'm willing to walk away, if you are."

Ava hesitated.

Was she? Could she be?

She hadn't thought that was possible, even a few weeks ago. She couldn't imagine a version of herself without the fury, the grief, the thing holding her together and pushing her forward. It had kept her *alive* after Ari.

"Come here," Jack said softly, and that was how Ava realized she had started pacing.

Jack was still sitting on the opposite bed, but he had set his phone and notes down and his arms were open to her.

She accepted the invitation, settled next to him, tucked against his side.

"You could tell me," he said softly. "If you wanted."

He said it so simply. An invitation to share her *why*, the thing that was driving her so inexorably onward despite every obstacle, every danger.

And oh god, she *did* want to tell him everything she had started sharing earlier.

After months of talking to nobody about this, of letting nobody in, it was Jack O'Sullivan who had worn away the walls around her heart and made her want to talk about it.

"Her name was Ariel, but she went by Ari," Ava said softly. "And she was my whole world."

Jack sat up, looking down at her, his full attention fixed on her, just like before. "Ari," he repeated. "Ari, who made you laugh."

It meant something, talking about Ari without talking about all the grief and loss. Talking about the good, the laughter, the games of cards that all felt like a lifetime ago now. It was freeing not to have to tell the awful details.

Ari's symptoms, building slowly and then all at once. Ari's doctors, not listening until it was too late. The diagnosis. The one single hope they had, an experimental drug that might have saved her. Denied by her insurance, Cale's company. The appeal delayed and delayed and delayed.

Ari, gone.

The appeal coming back the day of Ari's funeral. Treatment approved. Full coverage.

But Jack wasn't asking her to bleed for him, to share details that opened her like a wound.

She could talk about who Ari had been. That, Ava could do.

"I met her in high school," Ava said. "It was so cliché. I was a loner. I hung out in the library at lunch, and she was an all-star athlete who played lacrosse, and one day she was in there studying for a test, and she said—she said I had the most magnetic eyes she'd ever seen."

Jack nodded. "You do," he said softly. "She was right."

Ava couldn't even tell him to shut up. She'd dropped the walls she'd made out of banter and humor and teasing, and now it was too late to put them back up. "And that was it. I loved her so much. We started dating senior year, got married at the end of college. We bought a house just outside of Cedar Rapids, and we grew tulips in the front yard and tomatoes in the back every summer. We went to the skating rink together every Friday and played cards on Saturday. I became a librarian, and she became a groundskeeper for the conservatory, and then, three months after her diagnosis, she was—"

She was gone.

Ava didn't realize tears were running down her face until Jack reached out and caught them with his thumb, swiping them away.

"I'm sure you've had enough people tell you they're sorry for your loss," Jack said softly. "So I won't say any of those meaningless words. But I know the kind of love that burns you down when it's gone. And I wish there was anything I could do to take that kind of pain away from you."

Ava leaned heavily against him. "You only know that if you've felt it," she said. "You must have, with Jay. You have to love someone an awful lot for it to ruin you like this."

And they were ruined, weren't they? Ruined beyond any hope of rescue. A hit man and an ex-librarian with a grudge, both gunning for the same man.

For a moment Jack stiffened, and she thought he would refuse, say he had shared all he meant to earlier. But then he leaned his elbows on his knees and leaned forward with a heavy sigh.

"His name was Ajay, but he usually introduced himself as Jay," Jack said slowly.

AJ.

The name Jack had given her first. Who knew that it had been weighted with so much history?

Ava threaded her hand through his arm and squeezed.

"We met at a bar, and he asked me to dance," Jack continued. "Jay loved to move—he did salsa and swing dancing and even dabbled a little in Irish dancing. We got an apartment in Atlanta together, and . . ."

Jack's voice trailed off.

"You don't have to talk about this part," Ava told him. She could feel Jack's grief as palpably as her own. He walked around with his mask up to the whole world, literally and figuratively, but she could see every impossible, beautiful layer of this man unfolding in front of her. "You can talk about the part where he made you laugh and you argued about laundry."

Jack shook his head. "Do you ever forget?" he asked. "Do you ever forget the good things? Like they're so far away—"

"It's almost like you can't remember they happened at all," Ava finished for him. "Yeah. I do. I used to sit at a kitchen table with Ari and steal strawberries off her plate, and now I'm not sure I remember what her laugh sounds like."

"Yeah," Jack said. "I was going to marry him. I—I called him my husband, but we never got that far, not officially. I was meeting him at a park north of the city to propose to him. I left early, even though he wanted us to drive together because he was an anxious driver. But I wanted to get there before him to set everything up. And Jay never came, because a drunk driver in a pickup T-boned his car and left him to die. When I found him, he said—*you came for me.* He died before knowing I wanted to propose to him. I'd set up the park for our proposal when the EMTs called me, and I just . . . I just left it all there. I couldn't bear to go back and get it."

Ava couldn't help the sound that escaped her. "Oh, Jack."

It was unfair.

Ava didn't care who Jack had become, what he was now. This, *this* wasn't fair. Loving someone so much you transformed a city park to show them and losing them before they ever knew.

"Jay was the first person I killed," Jack said softly. "When I knew it was too late, that he was gone, that I had nothing left, I found the drunk driver. I planned. And then I carried it out, and it was so easy to do that it scared me."

Ava's hands were shaking when she wove her fingers through Jack's. "You didn't," she said softly. "You didn't kill Jay. If he was here, he'd tell you that."

Jack nodded, but the look on his face said he wasn't sure he could believe her. Not today, and maybe not ever, but Ava would keep telling him if she could.

"I—I take care of his mom," Jack added. "She doesn't want to see me. Never did, after Jay died, because I was a reminder of everything she'd lost. But I pay for her assisted living with . . . this. It's the least I can do."

Ava threw her arms around Jack, and he held her in return.

It wasn't fair. None of it was fair, not the hand Ari had been dealt or the hand Jack and Jay had been dealt. And despite it all, despite everything that had happened, Jack and Ava were still *here.* Messy and wrong and doing nothing they *should* do, she knew. But they were still *here.*

And that, Ava decided, was worth something.

They talked well into late morning. She told him about the silly inside joke she'd had with Ari about the endless garden center trips, and he told her how Jay sprawled across the whole bed and then dramatically claimed to only have a corner of the blanket. Ava even told him about Ari's infuriating insistence that she should let in *every* driver at the merge, even when all the drivers behind her were honking.

It was strange to remember the annoyance and foibles and negative things—and to love someone so much you ached.

To love *two* people now, though that was all still too confusing to parse out.

Finally, near lunchtime, Jack pushed a box toward her. "I forgot," he said. "I *did* get you cinnamon buns. But the corner store was out of strawberries."

Tears stung Ava's eyes. "Before you got me cinnamon buns," she told him through a mouthful, "the last one I had was one that Ari picked up for me. We got her diagnosis later that day."

Jack looked stricken at the news, but he just leaned over and kissed Ava's forehead, so gently it nearly made the tears spill.

"Watch it, O'Sullivan," Ava said. "Or I'll think my contract killer is going soft on me."

"Maybe I am, Boss," he said with a grin. "All right, after this I think I need to go and rent myself that suit—with cash—and you need to get yourself a dress. Also with cash."

"How much cash do we have left?" Ava asked skeptically.

Jack paused for a long moment, his face dangerously unreadable again. Withdrawn. "I can get some more out today," he said. "I try to be careful how much and how often I withdraw, but I've had enough time between transactions that it's probably all right."

"Good," Ava said. "There's a mall down the street and an ATM. I checked."

Jack nodded. "I'll reach out to a contact I have who can possibly help us get in as waitstaff. From there, we'll change and hopefully be passable as party guests. You ready?"

"You just have a contact who can help with that?" Ava asked.

"Don't you?"

"No, I was planning to fight my way in," Ava said. "My knuckles have healed. See?"

"That was one of the first things I noticed about you," Jack told her, grabbing her hand and pulling it to his mouth, where he kissed each knuckle, lingering on the ones with scars. "You had striking eyes and bloody knuckles and a pretty dress, and none of the puzzle pieces made sense."

"Do they make sense now?" Ava asked as Jack shrugged on his hoodie and reached for his fake beard and new masks from the box. "All the puzzle pieces?"

"No." Jack smiled at her as he handed her a mask. "Put this on. We don't want bucko at the desk to get a good look at either of our faces."

"Aye, aye, captain," Ava said as she snatched one of Jack's hoodies and pulled it over her head.

"Not even a shirt underneath," Jack muttered with a shake of his head. "Wild behavior, Boss."

She stuffed one last cinnamon bun into her mouth as she followed Jack through the door. He reached back for her, as if instinctively, and took her hand.

"Aren't you soft this morning?"

"I told you, Boss. Soft as a cinnamon bun."

<>

"You walk too fast," Ava whined as she trailed behind Jack's longer strides down the sidewalk. The little strip mall had *looked* like it was closer on Maps, but they'd already been walking forever.

Jack slowed his stride and offered her his free arm. He was wearing a small backpack, and he had at least one gun concealed in a holster on his back.

"Are you sure you should be offering me your weapon arm?" Ava asked as she took it, leaned heavily on him. "What if you need it for fighting?"

"I'm ambidextrous," Jack told her as he helped her effortlessly over a low point in the sidewalk, where muddy water had pooled.

He laughed, and then silence lapsed between them for the remaining walk, as their footsteps took them toward the strip mall a few blocks away.

They reached the shop Jack had mentioned first—a small, well-lit shop with a variety of black and navy tuxedos hanging neatly in the window. Jack held the door open for her, and when they entered, his free hand was firmly on the small of her back. At what point had this shifted between them, that Jack walked beside her as if she was his to protect? And at what point had things shifted for Ava that she *wanted* this?

They might be staying barely one step in front of the cops, they might be about to undertake the impossible, but Jack's hand was broad and warm on her back.

"The dress shop is just around the corner," Jack said. "If you want to get started looking at dresses?" His gaze raked up and down her body. "Be careful, okay?"

"You can trust me," Ava said.

"I do." His words were soft, and then he turned to the man at the front desk, who nodded a greeting at Jack.

"Hang on," Ava said. "Let me grab my phone out of your bag?"

Jack nodded, shifting the pack to one shoulder so she could reach the side pocket where she'd shoved her phone—carrying things in her hands was annoying, she'd told Jack earlier, expecting him to give her a *look* or an exasperated *Ava*. Instead, he'd taken her phone with a grin and zipped it into his bag.

Ava's fingers found the smooth case of her phone, and she pulled it out, shoving it into the pocket of her sweatpants.

"Be safe," Jack said softly.

"You too," Ava said.

It was just around the corner. What the fuck could happen in the amount of time it took to—you know what, never mind. Vans could blow up. Kidnappers could grab her and drag her to a warehouse. Anything could happen when Ava Cavalcante was involved.

The dress shop was small, but dresses from three different designers hung in the windows.

When Ava entered, the shop had air-conditioning blasting, and the tall blond woman behind the desk arched her eyebrows and looked down at Ava with open judgment on her face.

"Do you need directions somewhere?" she asked, her eyes darting toward the phone behind the desk. "Goodwill, maybe? Our restrooms are for customer use only."

If Jack were here, he'd be bracing for impact, just like he had when that front desk person had called her *bucko*.

"Yes," Ava answered the woman, pushing her hoodie back dramatically and letting her hair cascade down her back. "I need directions to someone who doesn't wear last season's off-brand at a store like *this*. Because that would be the person who can help *me* replace the wardrobe the airline lost. But that clearly isn't you. What is that you're wearing? Target brand?"

Ava wrinkled her nose.

Of course, *she* had never worn designer in her life. But fashion had been one of Ari's special interests—despite the fact that she wore cargo pants and boots for work. She knew trends, and brand names, and who made the fashion decisions that ruled the world. *And* she loved to tell Ava all about it. So despite never having worn designer clothes a day in her life, Ava knew her brands.

More importantly, she knew how to out-bitch a bitch, but that was her own personal specialty and had nothing to do with Ari. The woman at the counter stared at Ava. "Are you fucking serious?" she asked. "This is obviously Gucci."

"Sure, if Gucci was selling on Shein," Ava said, waving her hand. "Now, am I going to walk out of here in a Versace, or are you going to keep driving away customers, sweetie?"

The woman gave Ava the thinnest smile she'd ever seen. "I'm Mikayla," she said. "I'd be *so* happy to help you find the right dress for"—she waved a hand in Ava's direction—"all *that*."

"Oh, *thank* you," Ava intoned with brittle enthusiasm.

Mikayla nodded tightly, grabbing a white dress from the rack labeled *Versailles*. "Let's start with this one," she said. "It looks the most in line with your budget."

Ava followed Mikayla to the fitting rooms at the very far end of the store, relieved when the heavy curtain was pulled behind her.

Ava plopped down onto the bench, mindlessly entering her passcode, before she realized whose phone she had in her hand. Instead of hers, with the bubblegum pink case and the spiraling crack from the top left-hand corner, she had Jack's in her hand. It was thin, sleek, black, a newer model than hers.

But her passcode had worked. Why the hell was Jack's passcode *AvaO*?

She shook her head, clearing the cobwebs, and then a text message flashed across the bottom of the screen.

Updated timeline. She needs to be first. Confirmation requested.

Below that was a picture that was all too familiar now: the grainy CCTV screenshot of Ava in her distinctive red dress, fist raised above Cale Jacobson's face.

Ava froze, her thumb hovering over the unlocked phone. Jack was around the corner, still getting fitted for his suit, probably, or maybe he was already on the way. She should *assume* he was on the way, because she should always assume she was in more danger than she knew.

Because . . . because Jack was *still* the danger to her.

There it was, plain as day. Jack's client, the only number or text thread in the entire phone, asking him to kill her, too. And Jack saying yes, only a day after he'd saved her from Cale Jacobson's team.

Ava was on her feet before she realized where she was going, her breath heaving. Her vision swam, and she staggered, bracing a hand against the wall for support.

She'd been so wrong about everything. She'd been so wrong to trust him at all, to feel safe with his hands on her, to love the way he'd kept her safe and alive and out of harm's way. She'd been wrong to let herself fall for him, for his lies—had the story about Jay been a lie, too? Had her own grief kept her from seeing that Jack was lying to her? That the shared grief she thought they had in common was just hers, after all?

She'd been wrong to hope he might feel something for her, too.

Jack O'Sullivan wasn't falling for her.

He was plotting to kill her.

Chapter Twenty-Seven

Ava scrubbed at the tears that had appeared on her face, sudden and hot and fierce. Her breath came unevenly, the dressing room and the stupid white dress blurring around her.

And then—

The bell on the front door rang distantly from the other side of the store. And then Jack's voice, that low rumble of his, though she couldn't make out the words.

Think, Ava.

There was no window to smash. She could make a run for it, but he was fast, he was good, and he always, always, *always* caught up with her. She could make a play for his gun and use it to get a head start. She could—

There was laughter, both Jack's and Mikayla's, and then footsteps. His.

Coming toward her.

Ava scraped more tears from her face. She could do this. She *had* to do this. The footsteps were right outside the room, Jack's black boots visible below the heavy curtain.

For Ari, Ava told herself, and then she pulled back the curtain.

Jack was wearing his tux. He was grinning, a little wickedly, but his expression shifted abruptly. "Are you okay?" he asked.

Fuck him, *fuck* him for being able to read everything she tried to mask.

Fuck him for ever making her believe that meant he *cared.*

"Oh, you know," Ava said lightly. "I was just scrolling this year's trends to see which dresses might be the right fit, but *Mikayla* over here was being a real buzzkill."

Mikayla was at a rack nearby, two dresses slung over her arm. She looked at Ava with only marginally less venom in her gaze. "Your husband explained the situation to me," she said.

"That your luggage was lost by an incompetent airline," Jack filled in, but his eyes were still focused on Ava. "You sure you're okay?"

"Peachy," Ava said. "Perkalicious. The usual."

Jack arched an eyebrow. "All right," he said.

It was a *we'll talk about it later* sort of "all right," but Ava didn't intend to give him a later.

"How many dresses did you want to try on?" Mikayla asked.

"Two or three, at most," Jack answered. "We're in a bit of a rush."

"Oh, seven or eight will do." Ava smiled sweetly at Mikayla.

Jack caught her eye and shook his head slightly. It chased a shiver down her spine. Fear, yes, but longing, still. All of that, mixed with anger, a wildfire of it that would consume her if she lived long enough to let it.

That look on Jack's face said: *Rein it in, Cavalcante, or I will.*

And god, after all this, she still wanted him to.

"Do you just want to see Versace?" Mikayla asked. "We only have two dresses from them, and ordering some in would take a few weeks. We do have some Givenchy, which has a few similar pieces. What's the occasion?"

Well, Ava couldn't say *murder*, could she?

Well.

She did have free will. And free speech.

"I want to look like I could kill a man." Ava's voice dripped with sugar. She could *feel* Jack's eyes boring into the back of her skull. "Can you help me with that?"

Mikayla shrugged one shoulder. "You already look like you would," she said. There was a hint of respect behind the sharpness.

"Thank you," Ava said. Maybe she could be a girl's girl about this, after all. "So do you, honestly. I'm sorry I went the bitchy route."

To her surprise, the other woman startled and then smiled, just slightly.

"I can respect it," she said. "All right. Are you looking for a black dress or something with color?"

"A red dress," Jack said from the door.

When Ava turned, he wasn't even looking at her as he said it.

A few minutes ago, Ava would have eaten this up—Jack taking charge, Jack using that *look* and that low voice to make Ava feel like she was melting. Now she was seething. Seething because he'd betrayed her, because everything she had been beginning to feel for him had been built on *trust*.

Seething because Jack taking charge was *still* hot.

"Oooh," Mikayla said. For the first time, that hint of a smile looked conspiratorial. "Is he picking today?"

"He always thinks he's in charge," Ava said. "No, I'll be wearing black. Something sophisticated but sensual."

It was a fancy way of saying she wanted to wear a slutty little dress, but make it designer.

If Jack was going to betray her, Ava at least could get what she wanted here first.

Mikayla brought half a dozen dresses to the dressing room, but when she offered to come in and help Ava zip them, Jack stood without a word and came over.

"This is my job," he said.

He put his hands on Ava's hips and guided her into the single dressing room, pulling the curtain behind him.

And despite his betrayal, the touch *burned*.

"Jack," she said. She wanted him, she fucking *wanted* him, and she would have him.

One. Last. Time.

Jack put his finger on her lips, pushing her backward against one of the two mirrors affixed to the walls. “Shh,” he said. “Don’t make a noise. Do you understand me?”

He made short work of her hoodie and shorts, and then he gathered her wrists with expert ease, pinning them against the mirror above her. He looked into her eyes for a long moment and then repositioned her so that one hand was around her wrists, keeping them pinned, and the other was sliding down, down. Down.

And oh, Ava finally understood Jack O’Sullivan.

“I understand you,” she breathed.

“Good,” he said. “Then I’m going to fuck you, Ava. Color?”

“Green,” she gasped.

Desperately so.

“I’m going to go grab you some dresses in color,” Mikayla said from outside the curtain, just as Jack pushed a finger inside Ava’s slick entrance.

Ava held on to her gasp so tightly her vision blurred.

“Thanks,” she squeaked.

“No worries.” Mikayla’s footsteps faded as she left the cluster of dressing rooms and returned to the main store, and Ava’s body sagged with relief.

Jack was fucking her now, those hard, calloused fingers finding just the right spot inside her. Would he think of her, after all this was done?

Or would she be one more in a long line of people he had used and forgotten?

“Ava.”

Her body responded to his tone.

His pace had slowed, his dark eyes holding her gaze. “Color?”

“Green,” she said.

“You’re far away.” He increased his speed again, but more slowly than before, the pace unbearable.

“Then bring me back, O’Sullivan,” Ava said fiercely.

Jack's eyes sparked, and then he moved his fingers farther, the fullness pushing Ava closer to orgasm.

"My god," she whispered, letting her head fall back against the wall of the dressing room with a soft thump.

"My friends just call me Jack," he said, his eyes lighting in that familiar way she had been naive enough to fall for. And then he pulled his fingers out of her, tugged his fly down, and moved toward her. "Do you want me inside you, Boss?"

Boss.

The nickname stung now. Dug its claws in, replaced tenderness with anger.

And unfortunately for Ava, the anger only made all this that much better.

Ava bit her lip to keep back the noise. She'd send the cops after him when she left him behind. She'd send the Jacobsons. She'd send the fucking Navy SEALs. But first—*this.*

A gentle knock on the wall from the other side of the curtain made Ava jump.

"I've got a red dress if you want?" Mikayla said.

"One second," Ava called back breathlessly, glaring at Jack when his grin broadened.

"No worries," Mikayla said again. "You all good in there? Any trouble getting the dresses on?"

"No trouble," Ava called back, just as Jack slid inside her.

God, no matter how much he warmed her up with his fingers first, she was never quite ready for just how *big* he was.

"Okay," Mikayla called. "I have another customer to help, so call me when you're ready for the next dresses?"

"Sure thing," Ava choked out.

"That's good," Jack said wickedly, the words dropped right into her ear, her hands still pinned above her head. His other hand made circles on the outside of her clit, teasing her as he pulled back. Then he thrust again, pinning her against the mirror. "Look in the mirror, Ava. If you like being seen so much, *look*."

"I don't want to," Ava said in a whisper-yell.

But she did. She wanted to see them, together, to freeze this last image of them in her mind, to remember what it was like when they were pretending to be two people who knew how to *stay*.

Jack pushed deeper inside her, eliciting the tiniest of whimpers. "Ah, ah, ah," he said, his tone reproving. "Don't make a noise, Ava. You know the rules."

"I'm going to kill you," Ava hissed at him, and meant it.

Maybe he sensed the furnace of anger there behind her words, or maybe he mistook it for the anger she was always carrying.

"Promises, promises," Jack said, and then he took her chin in his hand, his calloused fingers rough on her skin, and turned her head forcibly to look in the mirror.

Ava was a sight—completely naked, hair wild, eyes half shut with pleasure. She was an absolute picture of hedonism, with Jack inside her, her hands still pinned even though her arms were aching now.

"Make me come," she demanded. "Jack, please."

He chuckled, and then he started fucking her harder and faster, holding her chin there, pinned just like her hands so that she was forced to look at herself in the mirror.

Just like every time this man had made her come, the pleasure hit her so hard she couldn't stand. Wave after wave, Ava clenching around Jack, clinging to his shoulders desperately as they rode out their orgasms together.

Ava was still trembling, her legs weak from what Jack had just done to her—and from what she was planning to do to him. Jack stepped back, grinning at her as if this had cost him nothing.

"Sit," he said. "I'll grab the next dress for you if you're ready."

Ava sat, her chest still heaving. "I need my underwear," she said.

"No, you don't," Jack said.

When Jack returned with another dress, Ava shook her head.

"No," she said breathlessly. "No, Jack, I want you. Again."

She would be dead—they might both be dead—within the next day.

This time, this last time, Jack moved slowly with her, his hands so careful, so tender, Ava could hardly breathe.

"This time," he said softly, "I want you to keep your eyes on me."

Ava caught her breath, and then hooked her arms around his neck, holding on to him.

There was nothing else.

Jack lifted her, her legs wrapping around his hips, and entered her without preamble or warm-up, his eyes locked on hers. "That's it," he said softly. "You're going to come for me, Ava. Harder than you ever have in your life."

He rocked his hips into her. She was so sensitive it was painful, but it was exhilarating. It was pleasure unlike anything she had ever known, the last she might *ever* feel, and his hands were crushing her thighs where they held her there, and his cock was filling her like she had never felt, and then—and then—

Jack's mouth was on her mouth, his tongue inside her, kissing her hard.

And Ava came apart.

Chapter Twenty-Eight

Jack secured waitstaff uniforms after they'd bought Ava's dress—a skintight red dress that made his mouth water. Ava, for her part, was strangely quiet as the sun set Friday evening.

He'd asked her—twice, maybe three times now?—whether she was okay. She'd redirected, joked her way around it. He'd tried to chalk it up to nerves, as they were less than a day away from killing Cale, but there was an undercurrent that worried him.

Jack was up before dawn on Saturday morning, only to find Ava already awake.

"T-minus twelve hours until the gala," she said, but she avoided his eyes as he flicked on the lamp at their bedside.

She was standing at the window, looking out into the predawn darkness.

"Ava," he said. "We should talk."

There was so much he needed to tell her.

That for the first time since Jay, she'd made him feel something. A flicker of hope and something else, feelings that were burning brighter than he knew what to do with. That he admired her courage and grit and that he thought she deserved better. That he thought Ari would be proud of who she had become.

"Let's talk on the way to the venue," Ava said. "We'll have about two hours, right?"

Jack let out a slow breath. "Okay," he said. "Yeah, of course. I'm going to do some last research, then. And I'll grab you cinnamon buns for breakfast?"

Ava nodded distractedly.

Jack changed into his tuxedo, packing his go bag carefully, before retreating to the lobby, where the Wi-Fi signal was stronger.

Jack had been combing the darker corners of the internet for hours, trying to find any gossip about the Jacobson family, their health insurance empire, but especially the insider trading scandal Ava had been interrogated about. What was it they thought she knew? What was it they thought she was *avenging*? Was there an investor, or group of investors, so worried about their bottom line that they wanted Cale *and* Ava out of the way? He couldn't protect her if he didn't know exactly what they were up against—and that meant learning exactly *who* was gunning for Ava.

It had been so clear to Jack from the beginning that Ava's grievance was far more personal than fraud like insider trading, even when he hadn't known her or what that was. Even before she'd told him, in that fierce, fragile voice, about the wife she'd loved so much and lost so brutally.

About the insurance claim that had been approved only after it was too late to help Ari.

She'd wanted to cost Cale what he took from her, and she'd go to any length to do it. That was the first thing he'd admired about her, if he was being honest. Her ruthless, blinding determination to see her goal to the end.

Of course, he was also worried it would get her killed, but that particular worry had come after he'd started to care about her.

Now he was wading through any news footage of the Jacobson family.

Jack pinched the bridge of his nose. The headache from too much screen use was always only about an hour of intense focus away, ever since he'd had a job that went badly wrong and left him with a TBI. Of course, he'd still finished the job, but now screens left his head aching.

He clicked play on a recent video in which Cale was speaking about Ava's attack on him outside his building. Jack closed his eyes, letting the sound come through his headphones and giving his eyes a break.

"We're shocked and horrified at this blatant attack that threatens *all* of our safety," Cale said into the microphone. "Jacobson Health values each employee and takes the safety of all its members seriously. Premeditated violence like this cannot be allowed to stand. We are working closely with law enforcement and providing our own resources to assist in the capture of this dangerous individual."

Jack rolled his eyes internally. Ava had a point—was her premeditated violence any worse than the kind of premeditated violence that refused to pay for lifesaving treatment? Ari was gone because Cale and his company had acted, in a premeditated way, to prevent her treatment.

Then another voice came on, and Jack's body stilled.

"Here at Jacobson Health, we are a proud *family* company. As a family-owned, family-run company, we consider every member of our community a key part of our Jacobson Health family," the second voice said. "Any attack on one of our employees would be treated with the utmost importance, and we are initiating new safety standards in each of our corporate offices."

The words were bullshit someone else had written, of course, the voice familiar because Jack had spoken to each sibling after Ava's failed attempt at the Portland café. But there was something else about this, something tugging at Jack's mind just below the surface.

Jack followed his instinct. He opened his eyes, and then flipped to a new tab, where he narrowed his search to *Carson Jacobson Health*.

As CFO, Carson's role was much less public-facing than Cale's, but he was a public figure nonetheless.

Jack scrolled through a few videos—a press release or two, a "meet the team" collection of micro-videos, and a company-wide statement at last year's acquisition of another small company—until he found a video of some holiday party, posted by an employee.

Jack closed his eyes again, listening. He picked up a few voices—Clara's, telling someone it was time to gather by the tree, Cale's, booming and loud as he joked with investors.

And Carson's, his voice clipped and measured.

Just like the person on the phone, their voice garbled by technology, demanding that Jack move up the timeline of the hit. That he kill Ava.

Jack jumped to his feet, slamming his laptop shut.

Even Bucko at the desk, forever unflappable, actually looked up. "You okay, man?"

"Yeah," Jack said distractedly. "Great."

He had to warn Ava.

This was even worse than a pissed-off investor, and he should never, ever have taken this job. Many hits came from inside the house, a family member hiring him to kill someone in their family they didn't like. A cheater, an abuser, a thief. There were infinite reasons for it.

But this was a different type of house, and a different type of family.

Cale Jacobson's brother had hired Jack to kill him, maybe to stop the investigation into his insider trading, and now Ava had drawn more negative PR at the exact wrong time, so they needed her gone as much as they needed Cale gone.

It was the perfect setup, and Jack had walked into it with his eyes shut.

He ran to their room, knocking first and then managing to get the key in the lock with a hand that was, somehow, shaking. They had to get out. He had to take Ava and get out of the city, the state, the country.

They could go south, cross the border to Mexico and then travel down through South America. He knew enough Spanish, he had enough cash, and there were plenty of countries farther south with limited extradition to the United States.

But when Jack got the door open, the bed he had left Ava in was empty. The window on the far side of the room was open, the screen missing, wind blowing gently through the gap.

Ava Cavalcante was gone.

Chapter Twenty-Nine

She'd taken her dress, her phone, and—and the gun he had built. The one he'd used to kill that man, the one he'd shot the van's gas tank with, the one she'd learned to shoot with at the shooting range.

Scratch that, *everything* was gone except for the bag he carried—his phone, one handgun, his passport, some cash. Thank fuck he had that, at least.

Concern washed over him first, followed rapidly by fury.

If Jack had had a vehicle of any kind, she'd probably have taken that, too. Just like last time, except now it was all immeasurably worse—because he had thought he and Ava had *had* something. He'd never talked to *anyone* about Jay. He'd disappeared from his old life, ignored Jay's friends when they tried to reach out, anonymously paid bills for Jay's mom at the assisted living center, and built new versions of himself over and over again to do the job he'd decided to do.

But he'd let Ava *in*.

Jack kicked the small table in their hostel room over so hard one of the legs cracked. He let out a stream of curses and began pacing the small space. Where the *fuck* had she gone?

He had trusted her. He had started to—he had started to feel something, even. That had been so, so stupid of him.

He had even started to—

Love her.

Shit, shit, shit.

He called her phone, which went to voicemail immediately.

"Call me back now," Jack said into his phone, his own tone sounding more harried, frantic, than it had in years. "Ava, what the fuck? Where are you?"

He slung his bag over his shoulder and walked out the door. He'd rent a car, or a motorcycle, or something. He'd—

The front desk attendant was sprinting out the door, waving their arms. "That's my car!" they were yelling. "Hey, *stop*, that's my car!"

Fucking Ava.

Jack slipped out the door, adjusting his mask a little higher over his fake beard.

In the distance, sirens were wailing.

Had they caught her already?

A second later, reality slammed into Jack.

No. No, the cops were not going after Ava.

He broke into a run, finding a park at the end of the block and ducking into the tree cover. The cops were coming for *him*, because Ava Cavalcante hadn't just run off on him.

She'd sold him out.

Chapter Thirty

Ava stole Bucko's shitty little Corolla, which was missing a hubcap on each side—not the best ride to take her to Cale's private mansion, but she was going to have to figure that part out later.

She'd stolen Jack's map of the mansion, and most of his other shit, too, come to think of it. The invite she'd scored would get her into the mansion, and hopefully the black wig she'd brought with her and the makeup she was wearing would be enough to get by. At least until she could draw Jack's gun and put an end to all this.

The road curved abruptly, signs warning that it was a dead end, a private road.

Cale Jacobson's.

When she had first started researching Cale, she was still living in the little house in Iowa that felt haunted by Ari. It had been two days after the small funeral, and one day after Ava had blown things up with any remaining friends she and Ari used to hang out with. Ava had been sitting on the love seat when she'd found Ari's hoodie, a soft, worn gray pullover she'd worn the day before she'd gone to the hospital and never come home.

And something in Ava had changed.

Not the days in the hospital, not the day she lost Ari forever, not even the day of the funeral.

That day, clinging to Ari's sweatshirt and sobbing.

After that, there had been nothing left but the revenge. Because if Ava Cavalcante had nothing else, at least she'd have that.

Tears blurred her vision, and she took the next turn too fast. She'd let herself get distracted.

Stupid, stupid, *stupid* of her to let herself start caring. That hadn't ended well for her, not ever. Fuck Jack for tricking her, and fuck Ava for not seeing every red flag and running for her life.

She slowed the car as the turns through the forest tightened, the road narrowing.

Few people took this road—rich people with drivers who drove them here, maybe. Staff who worked at Cale's mansion, certainly. But most of Cale's guests would be flying in on their private planes and landing at the airstrip north of his home, where they'd be driven to the mansion for the gala. It was meant to support some nonprofit educating people about the environment, but—in Ava's opinion, at least—it was nothing more than tax write-offs and a chance at some good PR.

The trees that lined the highway were tall, moss clinging to the trunks. Ava took one hand off the wheel and swiped at her eyes.

She had called the cops when she left, told them that Ava Cavalcante and her accomplice were hiding out at the hostel. Told them his name was Jack O'Sullivan. Even if it wasn't true—that stung, too, not knowing if she even knew Jack's real name—it would at least slow him down.

And—

Oh, fuck.

The road had straightened out here, and she could see a vehicle behind her. A motorcycle, its rider wearing a tuxedo and a black helmet.

Ava stomped on the gas. She had no idea how Jack had conjured up a whole new motorcycle out of thin air, but she did know one thing: He was not going to ruin this for her. He'd ruined everything from the beginning—dragged her off Cale that day at the café, stopped her from finishing it then and there. She should have seen it then. She should have *known* better.

Fuck Jack for delaying this for her. Fuck him for making her think he cared, even a little, fuck him for making her feel *safe*. It would have been better not to feel safe at all if it was just going to be taken away from her in the end.

It was *always* going to be taken away from her.

And fuck Ava, most of all, for ever thinking otherwise. Her phone buzzed as she pressed the gas pedal down as hard as it would go.

Jack.

There were two numbers saved in Ava's phone now. One more than she should have had.

She sent the call to voicemail. She'd block him, but she wasn't sure she could figure out how to do that without careening off the road as she did.

Then, as always, she went back to the last voicemail Ari had left her in the before days. The phone connected to the car's speakers.

Hey, baby, Ari's voice filled the car.

Ava could listen to it only so often, because just the sound of Ari's voice left her sinking so heavily into her grief it would sometimes take hours or days or weeks to pull herself back out.

I know things are tough right now. Thank you for being brave for me. I ordered Indian food for us to eat tonight, and I thought we could watch our favorite. Maybe the episode where Dean flirts with that girl and Sam says—

Ari's voice faded off into a rustle and the sound of a door opening. Ava swiped at the tears on her face, her hand shaking.

Supernatural had been *Ari's* favorite, not Ava's, but Ava would never have told her that. Or maybe it was Ava's favorite, too, but only because she had loved her wife more than anything in this world.

Sorry, baby. I'm back. We'll keep trying with the insurance, okay? It'll be okay. I promise.

And that was it.

They'd never had their *Supernatural* marathon, and Ari's takeout had molded in the fridge, because that night she'd flatlined.

Now the motorcycle was gaining on Ava.

She had the car, though. She could run him off the road. She could—

She couldn't do much, because she couldn't currently stop fucking *crying*.

The motorcycle roared over the yellow line, swerving and then accelerating until it was keeping pace parallel to Ava.

Jack turned his head to look at her—she couldn't see his face, but she knew him, would know him anywhere.

And then he pulled a gun from his waistband and leveled it at her.

Chapter Thirty-One

Jack should have put an end to this a long time ago. He'd known that, hadn't he?

But he'd been tricked by those fire-bright hazel eyes, just as thoroughly as he'd been tricked by his client. Carson.

Ava swerved the car, nearly running Jack off the road, but he had expected that. He slowed the motorcycle, gun still in his hand—and then fired.

There was an ear-shattering *pop* and then a hiss as the bullet went through one of her tires, and then she spun uncontrollably.

His stomach sank, despite himself.

If it were anyone else, he would have shot through the window, and he would not have missed. But he couldn't, not even now. Not even when she'd let him spill his guts about Jay and then turned around and set the cops on him and left him behind.

Her car spun slowly off the road and down into the grassy ditch, coming to rest at the base of the trees.

Jack slowed the motorcycle, too, glancing up to make sure there were no security drones visible overhead. A man approaching Cale Jacobson's home with a gun drawn was unlikely to be received well.

Ava staggered out of the car, gasping for breath and reaching for her bag—and probably his gun, still stowed inside. "You *fucker*," she snarled. "I'm going to fucking kill you."

Jack held the gun out, advanced calmly. "We're going together, Ava," he said coldly.

She stepped forward, her jaw set. Her hands were the only thing that betrayed her—they were trembling.

"Do it, then," she said.

When Jack didn't move his finger to the trigger, she laughed.

"Why?" she demanded. "Why wait?"

He didn't have an answer for her.

"You sold me out," Jack said. He hated how vulnerable he *still* sounded. He wanted to know *why*, almost as much as he wanted to be above begging for answers.

Ava laughed again, the sound so hard and sharp he barely recognized it. She opened her mouth to respond, but the sound of another vehicle approaching stopped them both.

Jack shoved his gun back into its holster beneath his suit jacket. "Follow my lead," he hissed.

"Literally never again," Ava told him. "Go fuck yourself, O'Sullivan."

A black SUV with tinted windows approached, slowing to a stop. Inside were four armed men—a security team, likely from the gate up ahead, who had heard the *pop* of Jack's gun.

A few men stepped out, the driver remaining inside.

The first security guard surveyed them both. "Can we help you folks?"

"Just had a tire blowout," Ava told them. "I'm so sorry, it's *totally* on me. I thought the 'low pressure' light was more of a . . . worry-about-in-six-months thing, you know? Not a *now* problem."

Over the last few weeks together, Jack had learned to read her tones, her expressions, her moods, fairly well—but there was nothing he could divine from her now. Just still waters, running deeper than he'd ever realized.

Just like that day in the fucking café.

She was good at this. Better than he was.

"We're just—" Jack began.

"What are you doing all the way out here? The road ends just up ahead," the security guard told him. The men with him were standing with hands resting on their guns, the warning clear.

Jack opened his mouth to come up with a lie, but once again Ava Cavalcante was the faster liar.

"We're on the guest list," she said. "For Mr. Jacobson's party?"

Well, fuck.

Jack was going to have to shoot his way out for sure now. Fucking *Ava*.

The security guard looked as if he were more likely to believe Ava if she said the sky was green, but he tilted his head, considering her before asking: "Name?"

"Ms. Jacobson invited us," Ava continued. Her tone was bright, but with a hard note running beneath. "Clara? This is AJ Reed, my husband. He saved Cale Jacobson's life a few weeks back."

That day stood out so clearly.

Rain on the café windows. Red dress, scraped knuckles, sadness in her eyes. There one minute, gone the next.

He'd fallen for it all.

The security guard stepped back, spoke into the piece he wore, words unintelligible. When he turned back to them, there was surprise on his face. "Welcome, Mr. Reed," he said. "And your name, Ms.—"

"O'Sullivan," Ava said smoothly. "I kept my name when we got married. I'm a modern woman."

Nobody ever knew what to make of Ava, least of all this security guard, but he somehow—miraculously—stepped back. For a moment Jack had worried the guard would recognize her—but the wig, the makeup, the dress and blazer, all of it was impeccably done.

"We'll have a tow get your car," the security guard told her. "Do you want to ride in the back with us, Mrs. O'Sullivan?"

Hearing his name attached to her this way was making Jack lose his shit, just a little. Anger and longing wrapped together so tightly he couldn't untangle any of it.

"I'll take the motorcycle," she said airily. "My husband is probably tired of riding anyway."

"We'll go together," Jack said, fixing her with a look.

She masked the shiver at his tone, but he saw it anyway.

"If you kill me while I'm driving," Jack whispered in her ear as she mounted the motorcycle behind him, "we'll both die, and you still won't get to kill Cale."

He almost called her *Boss,* the old nickname rising to the surface. He caught it just in time as he handed her the second helmet.

"I'll kill you *after*," Ava said, shoving it onto her head. "Don't worry, O'Sullivan. You don't get to get off *this* easily."

<>

The mansion rose out of the trees, long windows on each floor, and a pristine garden rising to the left of the building, wrapping around toward the back, where Jack knew there would be a pool, tennis courts, and, beyond that, a driving range. They were early for the gala by a few hours, but security escorted them to the front entrance.

Jack had to ditch his gun, and Ava had to ditch hers, somehow, before they entered. More security milled around the entrance, and he had no idea what Ava had done to get them on this list—how she had found Clara's number. How she had scored this invite.

Ava had held on to him rigidly the whole way here, her arms tight around his middle.

It was a far cry from just yesterday, when she had reached for *him*, when she melted into his touch.

Jack parked the motorcycle, offering his key to the valet who approached them. He reached out instinctively for Ava, and she took his hand as she dismounted.

Their eyes locked, and then she yanked her hand away.

"Would you wait just in here, please?" a security guard asked them.

The entryway was sleekly modern, a line of gold sculptures extending down the hallway.

Jack sat down on a bench, easing his gun out of his jacket before depositing it into a potted plant.

"What did you *do*?" he hissed at Ava.

"You had Clara Jacobson's card in your wallet," she answered. She'd sat down next to him but was looking straight ahead, refusing to make eye contact. "And I remembered that you met them, that first day. So I called and said I was your assistant, and could we have an invite to their party, for you and your wife?"

Jack stared at her, dumbfounded. "That was incredibly fucking risky," he hissed. "What the fuck?"

"Well, it *worked*," Ava said. "We're here, aren't we?"

Her auburn hair was tucked beneath a black wig. Her makeup was striking. She hadn't been recognized, not yet.

But *Ava* was striking, and heads turned wherever she went, so it was only a matter of time, probably moments, before someone recognized her despite the perfunctory disguise.

"We could have just gone together," Jack said acidly. "We had a *plan*. I included you at every step, I did everything you wanted, I—"

I told you everything.

And you left me behind.

Ava's eyes met him. "Everything?" she asked.

The click of heels on marble interrupted them.

Clara was coming down the hall in their direction.

She was wearing a business skirt that went to her knees, and a blazer that had probably been personally tailored to her. She held her phone in one manicured hand and was walking toward them in her high heels with *purpose*.

"Mr. Reed," she said as she approached. "I was so delighted to hear from you. This must be—"

Her eyes widened as she reached them.

Ava was on her feet, her smile polite but deadly. "Yes," she said. "Yes, you know who I am. I'm here to see your brother, actually. No, don't call for them."

Clara's eyes had flicked to the security guards, but at Ava's command, she froze.

Still, there were at least half a dozen guards near the door, and Ava would be dead before she reached Cale. This was a stupid fucking idea.

"I—"

"You'd be dead before you screamed," Ava said conversationally. She lifted the lapel of the black blazer she wore over her dress, revealing the gun—Jack's gun—she carried. "And at this point, I don't care which Jacobson sibling I take. Let's take a walk together, somewhere quiet. Just you and I."

Clara's eyes flicked to Jack, as if expecting him to *help*, and then understanding settled in her expression. He had been only tangentially connected to Ava that first day when he'd dragged her off Cale. It had been easy to play himself off as an unrelated stranger who had done a good deed.

"Ava," he said.

"Just you and I," Ava said. "Or I'll kill you right here, Clara."

She would, and Jack hoped for all their sakes that Clara knew it. Because Ava Cavalcante didn't care whether the only shot she fired was her last. She didn't care about any of that, just like she'd never cared about Jack.

"Of—of course," Clara said. She smiled, the expression only a little wobbly, at a few staff members who walked by them, unaware. "This way, then."

Jack stood, shrugging off his shock.

"Stay," Ava told him.

"Ava—" Jack tried one last time.

"Why does it matter?" Ava's gaze settled on him, those hazel eyes he could never look away from. "You already got paid for killing me, didn't you? What do you care if I finish this first?"

And then Ava was walking away with Clara, who kept nervously looking around her—though she dismissed a security guard who looked at them with a wave of her hand.

Jack was royally fucked, but the realization had finally, *finally* caught up with him.

Ava hadn't betrayed him for no reason, after all. And now she was about to take on the Jacobson family. Alone.

Chapter Thirty-Two

Ava and Clara walked up a long, curving flight of stairs together. Clara had tried, twice, to talk to Ava, but Ava was past all that. She'd needed at least one Jacobson—she had one. She could use Clara to bring Cale to her, she could kill him, and all this would be done.

Any moment her luck would run out. And when it did, when Clara decided to raise the alarm, Ava could at least kill *her* before she died.

When they reached a quiet hallway on the third floor, Clara slowed her pace. "Ava," she said. "It is Ava, right? We can talk."

Ava drew her gun, leveled it at Clara. "Let's do that," she said. "On the roof."

This was Jack's gun, the one he'd made for this hit.

He had emptied this magazine into another man just for touching Ava.

That thought froze her in place, if only briefly.

Clara made a small, scared squeak, but to her credit, despite her wide eyes, just raised her hands slowly.

"Text Cale," Ava said as she spun Clara around, pressed the gun into her back, and prodded her to start walking. "Tell him he needs to meet you on the rooftop ASAP."

"We can talk about this," Clara repeated breathlessly. "Whatever you want, we can get it for you. There must be something you want."

Clara was good. A skilled negotiator, good at people, able to handle any conflict. When she and her siblings had inherited their father's empire, she had been the one to keep it all afloat during the transition.

Ava knew this, and she wouldn't be tricked by whatever deal Clara might try to offer.

"You don't have anything I want, Clara," Ava told her, jabbing the gun hard into the other woman's back. "Now walk, and don't make any trouble, unless you want me to use some of the bullets I'm saving for your brother on *you*."

Clara walked, her heels still tapping a pattern on the floor. They turned left past another elevator.

"Swipe your badge," Ava told her as they reached the door leading up to the rooftop. "Slowly."

"I'm sure we can resolve this," Clara said, though she sounded more breathless than she had a moment ago. Shakier, too. "Ava, let's just take a minute and—"

Ava slid her finger over the trigger. "I have a rule," she said. "To keep my finger off the trigger until I intend to fire. Do you know what I am doing right now, Clara?"

Clara sucked in a sharp breath, peeking over her shoulder at the weapon in Ava's unshaking hand. Then she swiped her badge before handing it slowly back to Ava.

"Good," Ava said. "When we get to the roof, you'll send your brother a text. Maybe both of your brothers. We'll have a whole family reunion."

"None of this is necessary," Clara persisted as they climbed the stairs. "Ava, I don't know what it is you need, or what it is you blame us for, but I promise. We can resolve this together without any further violence."

"Was it not clear to you?" Ava asked. Her own voice was thick with tears. "When you denied treatment my wife needed to live? When you delayed the appeal until it was too late for her?"

Of course this family had assumed her gripe was about something like insider trading. Of course they had no idea about the lives they'd ruined, of what their policies and pursuit of profit had *meant*.

Clara pushed open the door to the rooftop, the wind greeting them with a roar.

There were two helicopters on the landing pads, neither running. Between the landing pads, there was a stretch of rooftop garden that included a few trees and well-maintained flowers, nodding in the wind.

Ava shoved the wig off with one hand. Her natural hair sprang free, cascading over her shoulders. "Hand me your phone, Clara."

"What do you want, Ava?" Clara asked. She held her phone out to Ava, slowly. "We'll give it to you, whatever it is."

Ava wanted so much.

Ari, next to her on the love seat.

Her old life, gardens and softball and evenings working library book clubs.

Jack, too. His broad hand at the small of her back, a promise he was there, that he would keep her safe. That he *cared*.

"I want you to pay for what you did to my family," Ava told her. The gun in her hand was shaking now. She had rehearsed this in her mind so many times—the look on Cale's face, the gun in her steady hand, the moment sating her rage, if only for now.

Ava took the phone in her other hand. "Get on your knees," Ava told her. "Lace your fingers together on your head. And stay still."

Clara did as she was told, her eyes darting back and forth between the helicopters and Ava's gun.

Ava scrolled through Clara's contacts until she found Cale, who she texted—

Meet on roof ASAP.

His response was quick—

Why? Some guests landed early, and you know how they get. There's also been a security issue, so where the fuck are you? I thought you were handling all that.

Get here anyway, Ava texted back. This is more urgent.

She hesitated, almost telling him to bring his brother, to take all members of this cursed fucking family out in one go, but—but it was going to be hard enough to pull this trigger once, no matter what she had been telling herself.

"Are you going to kill us?" Clara was kneeling on the concrete beside the rooftop garden, her tight skirt straining, the position looking increasingly painful. "All of us?"

"That's not your business," Ava said. "Sit there." She gestured toward the rock wall.

"Are you worried about my comfort?" Clara scoffed as she pushed herself to her feet. "Minutes before you're going to kill me?"

Before Ava could answer, the door swung open, and Cale stepped onto the roof.

"You better make this quick," he was saying as he stepped through, his voice hard as the concrete beneath Ava's feet. "Because I swear to god, if I have to apologize to Gary or Gilbert or whoever the fuck downstairs—oh, *shit*."

His tirade cut off when he took in Ava in her little red dress, come back to haunt him.

As if out of instinct, his hand went to his jaw.

He had probably had the best doctors on the planet available to him, but there was still the smallest red mark on his face, and that gave Ava a little jolt of satisfaction.

"Join your sister," Ava told him coldly. "And toss your phone here first. No fucking funny business, Cale, because last time I only had my fists. This time I have a gun."

"I—I can see that." Cale's eyes flicked between Ava and Clara, who nodded at him slowly.

"Do what she says," Clara said. "Cale, do it now. She's not playing."

"No," Ava said. "I'm not."

Cale crossed the space slowly, tossing his phone down on the ground with a clatter, and skirting around Ava by a wide berth.

"Why are you here?" he asked. "Why are you coming after me? I don't even know you. I don't know why you hate me so much."

"Because you deserve it," Ava said. "And you shouldn't be asking me why I'm here. You should be asking why *you're* here."

Her heart was thundering in her chest, louder than the roar of the wind. Despite herself, despite everything, she wished Jack was beside her—well, the version of Jack she had *thought* existed. The one who held doors and brought cinnamon buns and kept his hand at the small of her back and did unthinkable things to her in dressing rooms and on gun ranges and in motel showers.

She didn't want to do this alone—but maybe she had always been destined to be alone, even before Ari. She *had* been alone before Ari, and Ari had changed everything. Twice. Once when she came into Ava's life and once when she left it.

"Why—why are we here?" Cale asked, his eyes darting to his sister again. "Are you going to hurt us? Do you have a grudge against all of us? Do I need to get Carson up here, too?"

He looked almost hopeful as he glanced at his sister again.

Ava's stomach twisted. By the look on Clara's face, she felt the same.

"Your sister had to be threatened with a gun a few times to get *you* to come up here," Ava said sharply. "And you're just volunteering your brother?"

One thing was certain: She'd picked the right Jacobson sibling.

Cale's face paled dramatically. "I—that's not—"

"Shut *up*," Clara told him.

"So no, it's not about all of you. It's about *you*, Cale," Ava said. "About the policies *you* introduced. About the coverage *you* denied."

Of course, in so many, many ways it was about this entire family, this entire company, this entire industry. And in another way, it was only about Ava and Ari and Cale.

But Ava only had so much time before Jack found his own way up here. No matter what she did, no matter how she slowed him down, he always seemed to fucking find a *way*.

"Oh," Cale said. "Ah, fuck. Why am *I* here?"

"You," Ava told him, "are here to confess."

Chapter Thirty-Three

This was all Jack's fault. *All* of it.

If he'd only been honest with Ava, if he'd only told her what was happening, it would never have come to this. And she'd trusted him, hadn't she?

Jack eased his gun back out of the potted plant—that had been a Hail Mary attempt to escape detection, anyway—and stood, confidently making his way down the hall. He was dressed as if he belonged here. He was on the guest list.

And people walking with a purpose were less often stopped.

One security guard glanced his way, and a member of the waitstaff team stopped to ask whether he needed a drink.

"I actually need to find Mr. Jacobson," Jack told him. "Carson?"

He didn't know where Ava had taken Clara, couldn't waste time on guessing. But if he could find Carson, he could get some answers that would lead him there.

The waitstaff pointed him up the stairs, where Carson was supposedly with a few investors who'd flown in early. Maybe the investors were part of this, maybe not.

When Jack reached the third floor, he turned sharply right, stalking toward the wing where the waitstaff had told him he'd find Carson, to a home office with wraparound glass windows that overlooked the grounds. He'd studied this building, every inch of it—he could walk these halls in his sleep.

But no matter how prepared he was, the calm he usually had when carrying out a hit was nowhere to be found. Gone was any reserve or patience or care. Gone was any thought of escaping when this was done. Gone was any chance of subtlety or silence.

Ava was here.

And Jack wasn't leaving without her.

He walked into the meeting room with every ounce of confidence the billionaires in front of him had. Carson was near the window, talking to an older investor, a white man with graying hair and a tan line where he'd taken off his wedding ring.

Near them was a table of food—hors d'oeuvres that looked like they cost more than most people would spend on groceries in a month.

Jack pulled his gun from his pocket and fired.

Just once.

Carson stared back at Jack across the dead body of his investor, his mouth hanging open.

"What the fuck? You can't," Carson said. "No, you *can't.* Security—where's security?"

"Move," Jack said. There was no cost Jack would not pay to get Ava back—and if she didn't want him, wouldn't hear his explanation, he could at least try to save her life. He knew it was cold, calculated. Knew what it made him, that he didn't care about the life he'd just taken.

There was nothing but *Ava.*

"I—where?" Carson asked. "Oh god. Is this about Cale?"

"Yes," Jack said icily.

This man had *hired* him, for fuck's sake. He'd hired Jack to kill his own brother, and now he had the audacity to play dumb about it all.

"Listen, if you're here because of the investigation—"

Jack gestured his gun at the dead investor on the floor beside them. "Do you think that's why I'm here?" he asked. "Where the fuck is Cale?"

If he found Cale, he'd find Ava, everything else be damned.

Jack was going to jail for this—or getting killed for it, more likely—but if he could get to Ava, if he could get her *safe*, it would all be worth it.

"He—he just left," Carson said. "He had to go up to the rooftop for something. He was pissed about it, but—but he had to go."

A braver man would have said he didn't know where his brother was, but Carson looked like he was all but pissing himself.

"Please, *please*," Carson begged. "I don't know anything, I didn't *do* anything—"

Jack crossed the space between them with two long strides, and Carson shut up with a little terrified noise. "*Move*," Jack said.

"Where are we going?" Carson asked shakily. "Please. Wait—I *know* you."

Recognition flooded the other man's face. Jack's beard could only go so far—he'd met Carson face-to-face before, and he'd known then that it would make this job harder.

Jack usually didn't do this with jobs—talk to the mark he was going to kill, give them time to beg or wonder or even know something was about to happen. It wasn't that he clung to any compunctions that there was a morality to his work, that anything he did was justified. He was long past caring about that. But it seemed both easier and kinder for them to never know they were at the end of their life, even if they deserved it.

"I'm the person who's going to fucking kill you if you don't take me to your brother," Jack told Carson. "And you're going to give me some answers."

He didn't particularly care that *he* had been lied to about this job. He assumed, when he met most clients, that anyone willing to hire someone to commit a murder on their behalf would also have no issue lying to him about it, or making sure he took the fall for it.

What he *was* furious about, though, was that they'd included Ava at all.

"Why Ava Cavalcante?" Jack asked, jamming the gun between the man's shoulder blades with one hand and grabbing the man's shoulder with the other, steering him from behind toward the staircase. "Why is she involved?"

"Who?" Carson asked. "Who the fuck? That crazy bitch who—"

Jack spun him around, halfway up the stairs as they were, and smashed the butt of the handgun against the man's nose. "Don't talk that way about my *wife*," he snarled.

The words stopped him in his tracks. For a moment Jack and Carson stared at each other, both of them wide-eyed and horrified, though for vastly different reasons.

Ava wasn't Jack's wife. Ava wasn't his *anything*—she'd made that clear enough when she'd called the cops on him and run off alone to finish the job. He couldn't blame her.

Carson reached a hand to his nose, which was pouring blood on his fancy tailored suit. "I didn't know she had a husband," he said in confusion. "She was harassing my brother."

"Don't play dumb with me, Jacobson," Jack said roughly, spinning Carson around again and shoving him forward up the stairs. "I know you hired me to kill your brother. And I know you wanted me to kill Ava, too, because you think she knows something about the investigation into your family's less-than-legal business practices."

Carson opened his mouth and shut it again. "You're—you're him," he said finally. "You're the man they've been looking for."

"Open the door."

Carson opened it and stepped through.

The wind roared in to meet them, the sun still strong up here even as it started to sink toward the forest to the west.

Clara and Cale were seated on a rock wall along the rooftop garden, and there, Jack's gun in her hand, wearing that tantalizing little red dress he'd picked out for her, was Ava.

Chapter Thirty-Four

Jack had caught up with her. *Again.*

She'd known he would, hadn't she? She'd known he would that night she ran off with his rental car, too. He was never more than one step behind her, and now he had Carson with him, who was bleeding and crying a little bit and shaking, and Jack's eyes burned when they met her gaze.

"Ava," he said. "I can explain."

"Jack," she said bitterly. "No the fuck you can't."

"I *can*," he said. "And you're right to be angry with me, you are. But first, I can help you. With them."

"Why?" she snapped. "So you can kill me after? Who hired you to do that? Who wanted me out of the way, Jack?"

Jack shoved Carson forward. "He did," he said. There was a hard look to him, a set in his jaw that said there was no way Carson was walking away from this.

Jack had worn that look on his face when Ava had been kidnapped. He had worn that look when he was standing over Devin's body, gun still outstretched in his hand.

"He wanted his brother dead," Jack told her. "And he hired me to do that. And then you brought them some spectacularly bad press, so he asked me to get rid of you, too. That's why—"

"Shut up," Ava told him. "Shut *up*."

She couldn't hear this, couldn't let him back in. Couldn't get her hopes up, *again*. Not when he'd done this to her.

The three Jacobson siblings were watching them with expressions that varied from keen interest (Clara) to horror (Carson). Cale was crying quietly, twisting his hands together.

He had scooted farther down the rock wall, as far from Carson as he could.

"Did you?" he asked his brother finally. "Did you hire this man to *kill* me?"

"Take off your beard," Ava told Jack irritably.

If he was going to be such an asshole, if he was going to be such a *liar*, he could at least still be worth looking at.

"Really?" Jack stared at her. "Right *now*?"

"Well, you got up here, didn't you? What do you need your disguise for at this point?" She'd taken off her disguise, flung that stupid wig into the wind because she wanted Cale Jacobson to know that an unemployed ex-librarian from Iowa was the reason he was going to stop breathing today.

Jack looked as if he couldn't quite believe she cared about something like this right now, of all times, but Ava was going to die soon, or at the very least go to prison for the rest of her life. So she might as well enjoy the little things. Like Jack's stupid face.

"Cale was just about to confess," she said, lifting the phone Cale had discarded. She held it up to him, using his face ID to get into the phone. "Weren't you, Cale?"

"I was," Cale said, his eyes darting to his brother again. "But, uh, wouldn't it be better if *he* confessed? Since he's been—you know, plotting my *death*?"

"I don't care about that," Ava said. "I'm literally pointing a gun at you. It's what *you* did that I want to talk about."

She opened his social media account, something on a video-based app where he had a blue check mark next to his name. He had a verified account with about thirty thousand people following—following him just because he was wealthy, for fuck's sake. She started a Live, holding up the phone in one hand and the gun in the other.

"Tell everyone what you did, Cale."

Cale began to tremble.

Jack stepped toward Ava, so she swung the gun and pointed it at him.

"Ava," he said.

"Cale, *talk*," Ava said.

Social media would take this video down, but with as many followers as he had, *someone* out there was probably screen-recording—or they'd start as soon as they realized what they were seeing.

Someone was always watching, always recording, always seeing. Jack had taught her that much.

"I'm—I'm Cale Jacobson," Cale said into the camera.

"Cale," Clara said warningly.

Ava turned the gun back toward Clara, who promptly shut up.

"I'm the CEO of Jacobson Health," Cale said. "And I—I'm guilty. I—I did do it. I know there have been rumors swirling since the investigation started, but I did it. I made deals I shouldn't have, with information I had, and I'm sorry—"

"Not *that*, you dumbass." Ava cut him off. "I don't give a fuck about the insider trading. Do you think any of us do? I want you to talk about the people you've hurt. The people you've *killed*."

Cale stared at her, open-mouthed. "I—I don't know what you mean."

He *should*. He should know that he'd hurt people. He should know that when his company refused to pay for the care people needed, he was killing them. He was ripping apart families.

He had ripped apart Ava's whole world.

For a moment she was on the love seat again, clinging to Ari's hoodie. She was standing on her porch alone, reading the approval letter from the insurance company the day of Ari's funeral. A tear slipped down her face, and she swiped it away with the back of her gun hand.

Jack winced—probably at her absolutely rampant disregard for gun safety—and she settled the barrel in the direction of Cale again.

"Ava, please," Jack said again. "We can still go. We can still get out of this."

"I'm sorry," Cale babbled. "I don't know who I hurt. I don't know what you mean."

"You *should*," Ava snarled. "You should know that a denial is as good as a death sentence. But you don't know that, so I have to teach you. You killed my wife. And now I'm going to kill you, Cale Jacobson."

The app glitched, the Live ending abruptly. Enough people had reported it, probably.

"Ava, we need to *go*," Jack said.

"I'll triple your payment." Carson stood, hands up, advancing slowly toward Jack. "Kill her, and kill Cale, and I'll triple your payment."

"Carson." Cale's eyes widened, another tear trickling down his pale face. *"Why?"*

"Because he wants your job," Ava said, but Jack hadn't responded to Carson's offer, and Ava was suddenly aware of just how little she could do to stop Jack if he decided that now was the time to kill her. "Or some other stupid reason. Cale, stand up."

"Do we have a deal?" Carson's face was also deathly pale, but he was advancing, oh so slowly, toward Jack.

Jack hadn't moved. His face was an unreadable mask, not a speck of emotion visible. "We have a deal," he said, and Ava's heart cracked in two for the second time. "But I want half of that payment now, and I want that helicopter to take me out of this country."

Carson nodded, moving slowly to pick up his phone.

"Jack," Ava snarled. "You fucking liar. You *asshole*. You—"

Every word out of his fucking mouth was a lie.

Carson had his phone, had his bank app open, was showing Jack.

She could kill Carson, but in that time, Jack would snatch her gun. It would only take seconds—she'd seen him in action enough times to know how good he was. And if she wanted Cale dead, that wouldn't work.

He was ruining *everything*.

She wanted to put both hands on his chest and shove him hard, prove again to herself how immovable he was. She wanted him to grab her hands and stop her and use that low, gravelly voice of his to tell her things would be all right. She wanted *this* version of him not to be true.

And that was when Clara slammed into her, taking Ava to the ground.

They scrambled for the gun, rolling over each other across the hard concrete, Clara's hands clawing at Ava's, and the gun went off, a bang louder than anything Ava had ever heard, and then—and then—

The gun was knocked across the floor and Cale picked it up, leveled it at his brother, and fired. Just once.

Carson crumpled to the rooftop and lay there, eyes open, staring at the sky.

Cale dropped the gun with a clatter, his eyes wide.

Ava and Clara were still on the ground, frozen at the sight.

Jack stood above them, his gun still in his hand, his face a mask.

"Ava," he said. "Get up."

Clara rolled away, snatching the gun off the ground and leveling it at Jack. "No," she said. "Get it *done*."

Jack startled, something shifting in his face, as if things, at last, made sense.

"You," he said softly. "Not Carson. *You*." Almost to himself, he murmured, "*A generous sentiment*. I knew you sounded familiar."

Cale's eyes widened, and then his gaze fell on Carson's body, his open, staring eyes. "*No*," he said. "It—I thought it was Carson? Wasn't it Carson? *Wasn't it Carson?*"

"You're an idiot," Clara told him coldly. Her eyes were fixed on Jack.

Clara, *Clara* was the dangerous one and Ava hadn't seen it.

Cale was trembling now. "Why was he making deals? Why was he—"

"Shut *up*," Clara said. "Our brother was trying to save his own skin. Something you've never been smart enough to do."

"But I didn't *do* anything," Cale insisted shakily.

And Ava had heard enough.

She staggered to her feet. She had no gun, no hope, no plan. No future, either. It was time to end this, for Ari, for herself, for everyone Cale and his family had hurt. She charged at Cale, her body slamming into him, carrying him backward toward the edge of the building.

He opened his mouth to scream *no*, and then he hit the railing and went over it, Ava toppling with him.

Chapter Thirty-Five

Jack dropped his gun and dove, following Ava, one hand clinging to the rail of the building, one hand reaching—reaching—

And then his hand closed over her wrist, and she was there in his grip—he had her, *he had her*.

For one long horrible moment Cale was still falling, mouth open, arms reaching up toward them.

Then there was a crash below, Cale's body making impact on the concrete.

Ava's scream was piercing.

Jack hauled her up until she could reach the railing, which she scrambled over, red dress and all, and then he pulled himself back up, too.

Clara had a gun in each hand, staring them down. "That was impressive," she said. "It's a shame you won't be leaving this rooftop."

"You have what you wanted," Jack said, stepping in front of Ava. Let the first bullet find him, at least. Let her have a chance to run. "Cale did this. Cale shot one of the investors—maybe he knew something about the insider trading—and then killed Carson and then himself. You have everything you wanted. Cale out of the way, the company yours. All of it."

"You cannot *imagine* the amount of goddamn incompetence I have put up with from both of them over the years," Clara said coldly. "But you must know, Jack. That is your real name, isn't it? You must know that you were never going to walk away from this. Did you know that the first three people I spoke with wouldn't touch a target like Cale with a ten-foot pole?"

"Figures," Ava said shakily, but her head was held high. "He was a gross piece of shit. Much like you."

Oh, Ava.

She was going to be the death of him.

"You were stupid enough to take this job." Clara ignored Ava's bait. "So that means you were never going to walk away from this. And little miss Ava here was always going to be a problem."

"We won't be a problem," Jack said. "We'll just get on the helicopter and leave."

"Why?" Clara asked. "Why *her*? You work alone. I know you do. Nobody ever finds you, and nobody even knows you're behind the hits you've done, that they're connected at all. So why did you let her *get* to you?"

She sounded genuinely curious, as if she could not fathom feeling anything for anyone that would stop her from reaching her goals.

Jack took the smallest step forward he could, and then another, closing the space between them inch by inch. "Because she's as bright as the fucking sun," he said. "Because she's determined and fierce and funny and because she's better than I ever was. Because she deserved the life you stole from her, and she deserves a life after this."

Clara scoffed. "I can push a button and have security swarm us up here," she said. "Why do you think they stood down earlier? Why do you think there were so few barriers between you and my brother? I let you get as far as I wanted, and now—you go no farther."

"Oh, *fuck* you," Ava said. "That's a load of shit. You didn't plan all of this. You're not some genius mastermind because you're *rich*. You didn't even start this company. All you had to do"—she stalked forward, her shoulder slamming Jack's as she passed him—"was get lucky. You were born into your wealth. You didn't earn this, you're not smarter than anyone else for having it, and you were stupid enough"—she jammed a finger against Clara's chest, ignoring the gun still in Clara's hand—"to get stuck on the rooftop, holding the gun that killed Carson."

Clara's gaze flickered. "I can make that go away," she said. "I can make *you* go away."

Ava moved so fast Jack barely registered what happened.

He had taught her this, though, back in the motel—

She grabbed the gun by the barrel, twisting as she ducked out of the way. The gun fired, the shot going wide, and then Ava peeled the gun out of Clara's hands and sent it flying. It arced over the edge of the roof and dropped, following Cale to the ground below.

And then Ava had Clara by the wrist, her other arm hooking Clara's waist and—

"Was that a hip throw?" Jack asked her as Clara hit the pavement with a thump. He pulled his remaining gun—it had been strapped to his back beneath his suit jacket.

"Maybe," Ava snapped. "Help me get her up and into that helicopter."

Clara protested immediately. "You won't get away with this," she said. "You *won't*."

"Oh, I think we will," Ava said. She looked at Jack. "Why did you save me? Tell me right now, and no more bullshit. No more lies."

"I'm sorry I didn't tell you earlier," Jack said. He took Clara's arm, pinned it behind her to hold her there, and talked over her yells and flails. "I thought I could keep you safe, that I could keep the client happy until we killed Cale together, and then I'd just get you safely away. But I never even considered doing it, Ava. That's the truth. The whole truth. I got the text asking me back when we were burning the SUV, and even then I couldn't imagine doing it because I—I love you, Ava."

Was it the wind on the roof that robbed him of breath, or was it the words he was saying? Or was it the truth in those words, the truth that took his breath away? That after all this time, Jack O'Sullivan was still capable of the kind of love that left him trembling?

He hadn't felt this way, not since that little fifth-story apartment building with sunlight streaming in. Not since he'd been clinging to Jay's hand, hoping the world would turn out right.

"Oh, for fuck's sake," Clara said. "*Now* is the time for this? Let me go, and I might still let you live. Your whole situationship is—"

Ava's fist landed hard on Clara's nose, blood spurting immediately. "Would you shut the *fuck* up?" Ava said, withdrawing her fist, which was bloody at the knuckles.

Jack would need to stop and get her some antibiotic ointment, and bandages. Maybe he could find some of the kind they made for kids with special prints on it. Ideally strawberries.

Ava turned to him, her fist still raised, blood dripping down her knuckles. "Well, I love you, too, you dumbass," she snapped at him. "Now, can we get out of here? And if you ever agree to kill me again—"

"You'll probably sabotage me, steal a car, and send the cops after me. I know." Jack leaned in and kissed her, one blinding moment with his lips on hers, and then he drew back and started dragging Clara toward one of the helicopters.

"So you *do* know how to drive a helicopter?" Ava asked. "Or—do you call it driving? Flying? Piloting? Whatever."

Clara was still bleeding profusely, but she struggled in Jack's grip. "You're going to add a kidnapping charge to all the murder charges?" she said. "You won't get away with this. They'll find the bodies, and come after the helicopter, and—"

"Oh, we only have to get to your private landing strip," Jack said. "Which is—what, Ava? About a ten-minute flight from here?"

The private airstrip, where private jets would be landing over the next few hours for the gala, was a few miles down the road—shorter by helicopter.

Ava wrinkled her nose at him as she stalked across the rooftop toward the helicopter. "I mean? You're the map nerd. How am I supposed to know how long a helicopter flight would be? Why don't we just send Clara to join Cale and then get out of here?"

"No," Clara said, struggling against Jack's hold again. "No, you wouldn't."

"You ordered a hit on me," Ava said, turning to look at Clara as they reached the helicopter. There was a fierce spark in her eyes, something that was almost a smile but not quite. "He'd empty his clip into you if I asked him to."

Jack's heartbeat accelerated, his pulse pounding as he looked at Ava, bloody knuckled in her red dress. She was right: He'd do anything she asked him to.

Anything.

"I'm going to tie her up," Jack told Ava. "You watch her while I fly. Don't take your eyes off her."

"Damn," Ava said, taking Jack's offered hand as she clambered into the helicopter. "That's a shame. I wanted to do . . . other things while we were in the air."

Clara looked horrified. "In *my* helicopter?"

"Would you rather we throw you out of it when we get high enough?" Ava asked her.

Jack pulled a coil of rope from the helicopter, probably one used for lifting or lowering cargo—he'd seen these even in commercial fliers—and bound Clara's wrists and then her ankles. "Stay put," he said. "She's meaner than me."

He looked at Ava as he climbed into the pilot's seat. "Can you trust me? It's going to be loud in a minute, and we won't be able to talk—and I don't think I really have time to explain—but I have a plan."

Ava's hesitation was long, the moment taut between them like a cord about to snap. Finally, she nodded, settling in beside Clara.

"I trust you," she said.

And Jack opened the throttle.

Chapter Thirty-Six

Ava would be lying if she'd said she wasn't disappointed that they had to bring Clara with them. Whatever Jack was planning, they needed her to get out of this mess—but Ava really would have liked a chance at joining the Mile High Club, and she had a feeling that if she'd asked nicely enough, Jack would have obliged.

Of course, their circumstances were dire and all that. But if Ava gave herself a chance to feel the bone-deep exhaustion, the relief and anger and grief and love all rolling toward her like a wave, she'd be pulled under. So as always, it was better to focus on the horniness of it all.

They lifted off the roof just moments before half a dozen men came pouring onto the rooftop, guns drawn. They wore no badges or identification, probably Clara's security team—maybe the same people who had kidnapped Ava, actually. Had some of those men been standing guard while Devin backhanded her, tied her to a chair, asked her how she liked pain?

Ava shivered at the thought.

She kept her eyes fixed on Clara, as Jack had requested, as he maneuvered the helicopter away from the mansion. In some other moment Ava would have loved the wind in her hair and the ground growing smaller below, but this one required all her focus.

Jack had estimated the flight correctly—in about ten minutes, they were past the pool, tennis courts, and driving range, flying over trees until a long airstrip appeared, carved out of the forest. Jack landed the helicopter with a few bumps, but Ava held on to Clara until they had landed.

Jack helped her down, and they crossed the landing strip together toward a large private jet, Jack half carrying Clara, who was protesting and yelling the whole way.

When they reached it, Jack loosened the ties on Clara's ankles and let her walk. He hung on to the rope attached to her wrists with one hand and then drew his gun with the other.

"Are we stealing a plane next?" Ava asked in a stage whisper. It was kind of hot, but at this rate they were both going to be in prison for the next ten lifetimes.

"Trust me," Jack said. "I have a hunch."

Jack O'Sullivan, meticulous planner and cold-blooded killer, was doing all this on a *hunch*. It shouldn't be comforting. Or heartwarming.

But it was somehow both of those things, maybe because Ava was down *bad* for a man she had thought was plotting to kill her only this afternoon.

"I'm going to kill both of you," Clara spat. "You aren't going to get away with this. Wherever you are, I can reach you. I will send people after you. I will *kill* you."

The plane was empty, leather-bound couches that hugged the curves of the aircraft stretching out on each side, and beyond that an opulent bathroom was visible.

"This plane is fueled and ready to fly south," Jack said to Clara. "Yes? So get your pilot here, without raising suspicions, and have him get us in the air. Or I'll shoot you and fly this plane myself."

Ava stared at him, open-mouthed. He couldn't possibly *also* know how to fly a private jet. Actually, she was fairly certain he didn't really know how to fly a helicopter, either, and had used wikiHow and his infuriating ability to be good at everything the first time he tried it. Or something. She was going to get to the bottom of it later.

Clara looked like she was considering calling his bluff, but Jack leveled his gun at her head.

"You threatened my—" His eyes flicked to Ava, clearly biting back whatever he had been about to call her. "You threatened Ava. And she's right. I'd empty this magazine into you in an instant. Do you understand me?"

"You're a monster," Clara said.

"Yes," Jack said. "But I belong to *her*."

Ava's throat constricted. She must be monstrous, too, to hear that and feel nothing but elation and *love* pounding in her chest.

"Fine," Clara said. "But then I need some kind of guarantee that I'm going to survive this."

"What you need is to listen," Jack told her. "You're going to tell your pilot to fly to Tahiti, leave the plane for half an hour, and then fly back to the US. I know you pay them well enough not to ask any questions. You won't be on board—you'll be safe and sound, right here—and your pilot doesn't even have to see us."

Clara's mouth opened and then shut. "I'll go down for this crime," she said. "My prints are on the gun that killed my brother. I left a homicide scene. I flew away after my other brother got thrown from the roof. Nobody's going to believe me."

Jack shrugged. "That's not my problem."

"You have an army of lawyers that can take care of that," Ava added. "Cry to them about it."

In the end, Clara made the call.

The pilot had been on standby—Jack's hunch had been good, that Clara kept both a pilot and a plane ready for her. Like Jack had predicted, the pilot asked no questions, not when it was Clara Jacobson giving the orders.

They were in the air soon after, the pilot shut in his cockpit as Clara had instructed.

Ava sank down onto the couch, something that probably cost more money than she had ever seen in her life. "Did we do it?" she asked in disbelief. "Jack, did we *do* it?"

Jack laughed, a sound that filled her with warmth she had thought she would never feel again, and then he scooped her off the couch and into his arms.

"My Ava," he said as the forest, the West Coast, the United States entirely, grew small below them. "*We* did it."

Epilogue

Six months later

Their escape may have been the least meticulous job Jack had ever carried out, but he had landed in Tahiti with his accounts full of money and the woman he loved most in the world on his arm, still wearing her little red dress. Well, it may have been a little torn from their shared . . . enthusiasm.

But that could hardly be considered his fault.

Now Ava was asleep beside him in their little beach condo, a place they paid for in cash, which he'd emptied from all his US-based accounts before they had the chance to be frozen.

After all the chaos of Clara being arrested at her airstrip and her fingerprints on the gun that killed her brother, it had taken law enforcement a while to catch up. But they had, eventually, after Clara and her army of lawyers had given them enough footage of Jack and Ava in the mansion, footage that had gone as viral as Ava with her fist raised above Cale.

By then, Ava and Jack were settled in Tahiti. Jack had grown the beard he'd promised, and Ava had cut her hair a little shorter. He'd gotten a job driving a boat with a local tourism company, and Ava was waiting tables at a little restaurant by the water. Back in the United States, the media was obsessed with the couple who had taken down an empire—the woman in the red dress and the man who protected her.

"Jack." She sounded sleepy. Peaceful. He'd seen that here—that peace—more than he'd ever seen it before.

"Ava," he responded.

"I like this game," Ava said, rubbing her eyes and smiling up at him. "I should get dressed. My shift starts in about an hour."

"Well, then," Jack said, rolling over and pinning her beneath him, his hands wrapped around her wrists. "I'd say I have an hour, don't I, Boss?"

She made a noise of protest but pressed against him eagerly, opening her mouth just slightly. "Green," she said. "But I'm going to complain."

"Oh, I don't think you'll be complaining soon," Jack said confidently.

In the six months they'd been here, he'd made it his focus to study just what his Ava liked best. They'd tried . . . well, everything.

"Maybe I'll complain the whole time," Ava said. "You don't know—"

Her words ended in a moan of pleasure as Jack's fingers found their place between her legs.

"That's right," Jack said softly. "That's my Ava."

<>

If Ava was a little bit late for her shift and was walking stiffly, well, that just meant he'd given Ava the kind of time she'd wanted.

As he watched her go, dressed in a pair of short jean shorts and a loose flowing shirt, he didn't miss the long, lonely years of working his contracts.

Murder may still be a meticulous business—but the love he shared with Ava was anything but.

Acknowledgments

I owe thanks to so many people, but first and foremost, always, is my wife, Arynn. Thank you for making me a deadline menu, listening to me angst about whether or not to keep that unhinged seven-thousand-word scene, and being better than the best love interest I could ever dream up. It's all for you, baby.

Claire Friedman: I don't know how I would do this without you. There's so much I could say (probably should say!), but I'm going to go with this: You're a baller. I'm so fucking grateful to have you in my corner.

Lauren Plude: Thank you for your enthusiasm for my characters, for brainstorming calls that have gotten me unstuck many times, and for letting me run with my wildest, most fun ideas.

Amy Pierpont: Thank you for the detailed notes, understanding my characters at such a deep level, and working so hard on this project.

To the whole team at Montlake: I have been in the best hands, from the editorial side (thank you, copyeditors, for knowing the difference between *lie* and *lay*—a feat I will never accomplish) to the publishing, marketing, and author-relations folks. You are all a dream to work with.

Grace: If you need a sign to go book a plane ticket, well, now it's in a published book, so it's probably time to go on an adventure. Anyway, now that I'm done abusing the power I have here, thank you for listening to every book idea, reading the late-night messages, and always showing up. Mo dheirfiúr, I'm grateful.

Paul: You are a gift, and every time I write somebody truly good into my novels (a rarity), they're at least a little bit like you.

Daniel: I appreciate your bravery and your willingness to always ask questions and understand. Your openness and drive to travel and learn inspire me, and I think the world would be better if we were all a little more like you.

Sam: I'm so grateful for all the book events you show up to (and life events), the way you always go the extra mile to take care of your people, and how goddamn funny you are. If you're reading this right now, it's probably time to go pinch Paul.

Thank you to the countless other friends, family, and writing community who have supported my career and me. I love you all more than words can say.